A Wedding to Remember

by

Iona Morrison

A Blue Cove Mystery

A Wedding to Remember

Cover Art by *Lisa Dawn MacDonald*

The Wild Rose Press, Inc.
PO Box 708
Adams Basin, NY 14410-0708
Visit us at www.thewildrosepress.com

Publishing History
First Edition, 2025
Trade Paperback ISBN 978-1-5092-6104-8
Digital ISBN 978-1-5092-6105-5

A Blue Cove Mystery
Published in the United States of America

Dedication

I dedicate this book to all the wonderful doctors and nurses who work in the hospital every day. I was privileged to see their skill and dedication up close and personal as they worked to save my husband's life and many others. Their kindness saw us through some hard times. A lot of what they do may go unnoticed but will never be forgotten by those who have experienced it.

A special thank you to family and friends for all your support. It helped more than you'll ever know. And also, to my Editor Dianne Rich who checked on us many times and was a great source of encouragement.

Chapter 1

Jessie's attention was captured by a single brilliant red leaf as it danced across the sidewalk in front of her store, pushed on its way by the blustery wind. "Where are you off to, my little friend?" she mused. She followed its progress until one huge gust sent the leaf twirling up into the air and propelled it on an otherworldly adventure. Flittering across the street, she saw it skip across the grass to join with the gold and orange of all the others that had fallen to the ground. She sighed. Autumn was beautiful for such a short period of time.

She should get to work, but she couldn't force herself to move. The feather duster still lay on the book table where she had placed it earlier. She glanced once again at the church across the street and the cemetery next door. Only a few short weeks remained until her wedding. A celebration with all their friends and families that she was looking forward to with some reservation.

Matt was more attentive than ever and could hardly contain his excitement when he talked about their special day. Although she was excited too, there was a nagging feeling in the pit of her stomach. As she stood there, she saw several cars turn into the church parking lot including Reba's, her special friend and mentor. There must be some women's meeting this morning.

Jessie continued to watch as other cars pulled into the lot.

On her first day in town, that picturesque church across the street had altered her life forever. "All thanks to you, sweet Gina," Jessie whispered as the memories flooded her mind. As she had driven by the church that afternoon, a young woman in a pretty floral dress had waved at her and acted as if she had been waiting for her to come. Later while on a tour of the building, Jessie was shocked to see the young woman's picture hanging in the narthex and was told how she had died. Gina was the first ghost she had ever seen, at least as far as she could recall.

Gina was the young associate pastor at the church, and it was the secretary who found her body outside near the tree on her way into work one morning. The older woman promptly quit her job and moved away from Blue Cove after the traumatic event, which opened up the secretarial position for Jessie.

There were many ghosts since Gina, but she wasn't keeping count. Gina's story would always remain special to her and so would Gina's family. She had checked on them several times since her murder had been solved. Her kids were gradually getting over the loss of their parents with lots of support.

More than once, Jessie had wandered over to the cemetery to have a chat with her when something stumped her about a case. Would her ghost show up at the wedding? Without Gina, she wouldn't have met Matt and there'd be no wedding. Jessie smiled. In some strange way, her ghost had brought her and Matt together.

It was almost time to open, but she still couldn't

get herself to move. The trees continued to sway from the squall, shaking their leaves with each new burst of air. All over the cemetery, leaves tumbled to the ground and swirled among the graves. It wouldn't be long before all their branches would be stripped bare, their glorious colors would be gone, and snow would cover their bare limbs. Life always seemed to change a lot like the seasons. Hers was about to go through a major one. Gone was the little girl of yesterday to maybe someday having one of her own. Was she ready? Would she ever be? The activity in the cemetery had more than leaves moving around, which kept her from getting any work done.

If she were reading the situation right, her fast-approaching wedding would have several guests that neither she nor Matt accounted for. And she wasn't talking about a long-lost family member, or then again maybe she was. There were so many skeletons in her closet they fairly tripped over one another trying to get out. They often showed up unannounced and in the strangest fashion. Like Johanna Murphy, her look-alike ancestor from Ireland. Jessie had a sixth sense the next few weeks wouldn't be as uneventful as she longed for them to be.

As their big day approached, she went from ecstatic one minute to wanting to run the next. Not from Matt of course, but from all the strange things that randomly happened that could mess up her life with her soon-to-be husband. *Husband*, now there was an exciting but scary word. At least, her cousin, Peyton, and best friend, Katie, helped keep her grounded the last few weeks and way too busy to overthink everything like she usually did. They were a blast when it came to wedding plans and shopping. Their trips to the city had been too numerous to count. Between wedding dress alterations, bridesmaids' dresses, and of course, all the items that Katie said were absolutely necessary for any bride, Jessie's head was spinning, and Matt was complaining he never got to see her alone. Thankfully, the plans were finished except for a few minor details. Her cousin, Madison, still had to have her final fitting on her dress.

Maybe that was her problem. With the wedding details almost done, she finally had time to think, and for her that could be dangerous. Jessie sighed again. She should be deliriously happy, but why did she feel the opposite? True, when it came to her and special events, there always seemed to be a big question mark. The unexpected was sure to show up, but she couldn't help but wonder in what form and when. She had a lousy track record. Oh well, no use worrying over what might or might not happen. Either way, theirs would be a wedding to remember.

Jessie reached for the feather duster and got to work. In all the crazy things that had taken place in her store, no one had ever cleaned for her. She dusted the counter another time for good measure. Her ghosts were not cleaners like the ones who occasionally visited Joe's it seemed, but they sure liked to toss books and mess up the place. She smiled to herself. Jessie could still see the day she snatched a book midair before it hit Peyton.

"You, chime baby, live an enchanting life." Jessie ran the feather duster over the book table as she passed by. The term was new to her. She had learned its meaning while on her recent trip to Ireland. The very same trip that convinced her it was time to set a date for her wedding. The belief long held by her ancestral line was that a baby born in the chime hours could see spirits that others could not see and were endowed with special gifts. She would never regret finding out about the gift passed down to her from her ancestors even though at times it had been a tad bit inconvenient. She was learning to embrace this part of her life, as was Peyton.

"Hi, Molly." Jessie opened the doors to Joe's coffee shop and waved at her friend. Molly's baby was due around Thanksgiving a few weeks after the wedding.

"Hi. I'll be over in a few." She patted her cute rotund baby bump. "I have something new for you to try."

"I'm happy to be your test subject. You haven't disappointed me yet." Jessie turned on her computer on her way to unlock the front door.

She turned the sign around to Open and got ready to start her day. Molly's surprise baby shower was coming up in a couple of days. Molly already had a gender reveal party with balloons at Joe's a few weeks earlier because the customers kept asking if the baby was a boy or girl.

One morning, Joe's had several bouquets of blue balloons filled with blue confetti. A big banner confirmed that she was having a boy. Since hearing the news, her wonderful customers had scattered to buy little boy clothes and toys. Jessie heard many of them talking about what they bought. There should be enough gifts to keep the tiny fella in clothes until he was a toddler. Jessie could see Molly as the mother of a boy. She would do great because she wasn't easily intimidated and seemed to have lots of energy, which she would need. After hearing the tales of Matt and his brothers and learning more all the time, Jessie was convinced it took a special kind of woman to raise three boys. Thankfully, Molly would start with only one.

With Peyton back to work at the school, Jessie spent her mornings working alone in the store until her cousin arrived after school. They were back to winter hours, and the store closed at five. Audrey still came in for a couple hours several days a week. She promised to work when Jessie went on her honeymoon. Matt kept the destination guarded and top secret. Katie swore up and down she had no idea where he was taking her. Which was true because if Katie knew, there was no way she could ever keep the location a secret. Jessie had tried every which way to tug the info out of Matt, but no amount of flirting budged him. The man was a rock when it came to holding firm.

The bottom line, her last few weeks as a single woman had been uneventful as far as the otherworldly was concerned, but the temperature of anger around the globe, Blue Cove included, hadn't cooled even a little since returning from Ireland. She didn't want to give voice to her concerns, but they permeated her thoughts all the time. Which probably meant her wedding would have more than a few distractions. All this quiet time was almost too good to be true.

Her ringing phone interrupted her wayward thoughts, thankfully. "Idle Time Books, this is Jessie. May I help you?" There was a pause with heavy breathing on the other end. She flipped on her small recorder to tape the conversation as the pause continued. When no one spoke, she hung up the phone, but it quickly rang again. She answered, and that's when the man's sing-song voice responded with a monotone cadence.

"To answer your question, love, no you can't, dear. But maybe with my help you'll live to see another day. That is, if you call off the wedding to the cop that everyone in this town is talking about. I'll be in touch." A maniacal laughter punctuated the end of the call.

"Well, darn. Here we go again." The gauntlet had been thrown, and all she had to do was to figure out by whom. She sent Matt a text. —*When you get a chance call me.*—

Jessie was grateful for the customer who walked through the door a few minutes later. Talking about books and helping the woman find the titles she had heard about from friends as must reads was exactly the tension reliever she needed. Her sense of relief grew even more when Matt walked in the door at noon and gave her one of his grins. The knot in her stomach went away and her body started to relax.

"I got this message from someone who wanted me to call. I decided to come and see the beautiful lady in person." He pulled her into his arms, looked around the store, and leaned in to kiss her. "What did you want, sweetheart?" he asked when he let her take a breath.

"I thought you might want to hear this conversation." She stepped out of his arms and handed him her small recorder. "I hope you can hear it clearly enough. They called on the business phone."

"Damn, sweetheart." He shook his head frowning. "I thought we were going to have smooth sailing until the wedding. Any ideas who he is?" Matt's hand fisted at his side.

"Not a clue." She pursed her lips. "You're the one who said ours would be a wedding to remember. I guess we'll find out soon enough if that's in a good way or not."

"Maybe on some level both those statements could be true. I mean the fact I am marrying you is good no matter who shows up or what we have to fight along the way. There's no way our wedding won't be amazing." He put his fingers to her lips. "That's my final word on the subject. We've waited too long and gone through too much to let anyone or anything ruin our special day." He pushed her hair away from her face. "Agree?"

"Of course. I'll try not to worry, but I can't guarantee I won't slip once in a while." She gazed into his incredible dark blue eyes and handsome face, which made it hard for her to hold a thought in her head.

"With that said, considering the times we are living in and the animosity everywhere, it wouldn't be smart to sleepwalk through the next few weeks. Keep that recorder handy, and if he calls again, keep the guy talking. Maybe we'll be able to trace the number that he's calling from." He kissed her goodbye, and she walked with him to the door. "I've been meaning to ask you—is your ghost still in residence?"

"Yes. I find his grumpy presence reassuring." She chuckled. "I know how that must make me sound, but I can live with it."

"And that's one of the many reasons I love you. Knowing you the way I do, the longer he remains on the premises the more his demeanor will change. He won't be able to help himself." He kissed her again. "Who can resist you? I couldn't."

"And before you ask, only a few of the artifacts are still upstairs, and I'm not sure why. But at this point, I don't think my warrior ghost would let us move them, which makes renovations upstairs impossible for now. You were thinking they would be safer somewhere else; I did at first, too. But I'm convinced he'll take care of them."

"You know me so well, a sure sign we're meant to be together." He grinned at her. "When you say some are still there, what are you talking about?" Matt asked.

"All but the chest is gone and the jeweled dagger. The chest may be waiting for the scrolls or who knows what because it is locked. All the other artifacts may be locked inside, but I don't have a clue. I only know about the dagger because it rests on top of the lid. And, of course, my pendant is still with me. I guess we'll learn soon enough what and why anything still remains."

"I would feel better if I didn't have to worry about a robbery in your store, but like you said, he'll guard them better than we can. I need to get back to work. See you later." He lifted her chin. "If you have plans tonight, cancel them. We are going to dinner." He walked out the door.

Ever her charming man who couldn't help telling her what to do. She waved when his car pulled away. As hard as she tried not to worry, as the day progressed, she was failing in that department. The caller had bothered her on so many levels. She didn't want to admit her feelings to Matt, but she knew he could sense her emotions. She glanced at the stairs. The fact that the warrior, as she liked to think of him, remained in her store meant he was still needed, which didn't bode well for the near future. But she knew she could count on him if she had to.

****

The frown on Matt's face became more pronounced as he drove away from her store. As far as he was concerned, the sooner the wedding was over and they were out of town the better. He wanted Jessie to have the perfect day. She deserved it. What she didn't need was another ghost, murder, or threat to mess up the next few weeks. Hell, he couldn't stop another catastrophe even if he wanted to. She seemed to attract the strange and the unusual by her mere presence in town.

He parked in his marked space at the station but didn't get out of the car right away. The tape Jessie had him listen to bothered him. He wanted to believe it was a prank, but the call seemed legit to him. He needed to keep his head in the game. The last turn off Main Street had toppled his open briefcase, and several files had slipped to the floor. He could have prevented it if he hadn't been so distracted.

He bent to the side and leaned down to reach for the files and loose papers while castigating himself. Without warning, the passenger window exploded, raining glass down around him. Matt stayed as low as he could press himself. The shot had come somewhere from the park. He called Kenny asking for back up. The next bullet went through the passenger door and tore a huge hole in the seat near where he had been leaning. He waited, his shoulders tense. "Matt, you're a sitting duck."

When he heard Kip and Dylan, he slowly turned to open the driver side door and eased out of the car. He flattened himself on the ground while they gave him cover. He watched under the car for any movement. The sound of his heart thumped in his ears as he drew his gun from its holster.

Dylan barked orders, and he could hear their footsteps as they took off in several directions. Where was the shooter? When the next bullet hit the back side window, he heard one of the officers yell.

"He's in the park," Kip shouted and took off running.

Matt got to his knees, reached for his vest inside the car on the seat. How it remained undamaged he would never know. He went in the direction the others had gone. After searching the area to no avail, Matt returned to his damaged car.

"Are you okay?" Dylan asked. "I hope you're better than your car."

"I'm fine. I would be a hell of a lot better if people would stop shooting at me." Matt walked around his car. "Looks like the work of a high-powered long gun." He opened the station door for Dylan. "The others are still searching for evidence in the park. Jessie got a disturbing call earlier and now it makes more sense." Matt told him about the message from the caller.

"Looks like you both need protection." Dylan reached for his coffee cup. "I need this to steady my nerves." He laughed.

"It's been over the top in town lately. If anyone needs me, I'll be in my office. I have some thinking to do. Tell Kip to come in and report when he returns."

Matt went into his office and turned his chair to watch some of his team working through the park. How did the shooter get away? Matt was baffled. Two months without any trouble but the petty stuff, and now here they were again. He needed to rethink his life. This job was getting too damn dangerous.

Chapter 2

Matt picked up his phone to call Jessie and then put it back down. Could someone be tracking his phone? He pushed the button for the front desk. "Kenny, get Jessie on the phone," Matt told him. "Keep trying until you get her." She needed to hear this from him and no one else. He started opening the mail on his desk.

"Okay, boss." Kenny hung up. "She's on line two," Kenny told him a few minutes later.

"Thanks." Matt pushed line two. "Hey, sweetheart."

"What's up? Are you all right? Your voice sounds strained," she said.

"Remember when you told me caring is a two-way street? I wanted to tell you myself and not have you hear the gossip later." He explained what had just happened to him.

"Oh, Matt. Are you sure you're okay?" she asked. "No wonder you sounded odd."

"I'm tired of being shot at. You could say I'm shaken, but yeah, I'm fine." Matt clicked his pen on and off. "I guess that call wasn't a prank, and we may have a problem getting through the next few weeks until our wedding."

"Do you have any idea who would want to shoot you?" she asked.

"Now there's the million-dollar question. We both

might need to think about the answer for a while. We've made some powerful enemies this past year and a half." He picked up an envelope with no return address. "We'll talk later at dinner."

Matt reached for the letter opener but hesitated before he opened the envelope. As strange as it sounded to him, something felt wrong about what he held in his hand. Jessie was rubbing off on him, but maybe that was a good thing.

Matt went into the supply room and took a pair of gloves and an evidence bag. "Precaution only," he said to himself. It was better to be safe than sorry. But his gut instinct told him that the envelope and its contents would be in the bag.

****

Jessie stood at the counter after Matt's call. She was thankful Matt told her but concerned that the caller had something to do with what happened to Matt. Who shot at him? Was it random, a prank, or someone angry with him? Jessie glanced at the ghost. "At least I understand why you are still here. I may need you yet again." An idea formulated in her mind as the words had left her mouth.

"Hey, cous. How was your morning?" Peyton asked when she walked in the door. "Get the tea ready. I saw Reba headed this way when I got out of my car."

"Stands to reason she'd be coming at this exact moment. Why don't you give Molly a heads-up. She told me she was going to bring me a new creation to taste. Grab a few lemon bars for Reba." Jessie reached in her purse for money.

"This is one is on me. Next time you can pay." Peyton waved her off. "Don't worry. I won't forget

Reba's favorites. I'll be back in a few with tea and lemon bars and maybe a surprise or two. Tell Reba to get comfy." Peyton walked into Joe's.

Jessie met Reba at the door and held it open for her. "Peyton said to get comfy. She's getting your tea."

"Bless the dear girl. I can always use a cup of tea." Reba went to the table in the middle of the store and placed her jacket on the back of the nearby chair. "I see our friend is still standing guard." Reba sat crossing her legs at her ankles.

"I'm happy he's still here. A few of the artifacts are still up there, and he keeps them safe." Jessie sat beside Reba.

"You too, I think." Reba patted her hand.

"What makes you think that?"

"Think what?" Peyton asked when she placed the tray with tea and goodies on it on the table in front of them.

"Reba mentioned that the warrior was still here to keep me safe." Jessie reached for one of the mugs of tea.

"And you wanted to know why, and so do I." Peyton handed Jessie a wonderful looking treat. "Molly's attempt at a profiterole, and I'm sure it's a winner."

Jessie took a bite. "Oh my, yes, this is delicious. It takes me back to the small sidewalk café in Paris. Reba, you must taste this bit of heaven." Jessie cut off a piece of the sweet treat and placed it on Reba's napkin.

"My, how lovely." Reba licked her lips where a touch of the chocolate ganache remained.

"Okay, we are fortified with tea and sweet treats. Lay it on us, Reba." Jessie gave Molly a thumbs-up when she caught her looking.

"I'm glad you like them," Molly said when she dropped in for a minute. "When you talked about the profiteroles, I knew I had to try and make some."

"Wrap two in a box. I want Matt to have one. I will pick them up before I leave."

"You can add two in a box for me, sweet girl. Lawrence will love them." Reba handed her a twenty-dollar bill. "Keep the change for the tip jar. You all work hard over there."

"Okay, your reprieve is over, Ms. Reba. Let's hear it," Peyton told her. "Quick, before someone comes in and we get interrupted." She leaned forward in the chair toward Reba as she said it.

"Simply put, girls, like I told you before, there would be trouble for a while. It wouldn't be solved in one case or two. These are tough days for the world, and your odd guest is needed to keep both of you girls safe. And unless I'm off track, I think Matt will need him, too. The old and new will collide with the past and the present and stir up trouble. Getting you two married is one of our grumpy friend's tasks. The men you girls marry must love you as you are. Matt is that man for you, Jessie, and he must be protected, too."

"That's nice to know because someone shot at him when he pulled into the station earlier." Jessie told them what happened. "His car will need some major repairs."

"My goodness, I had no idea that it would happen this quickly. Well now, that makes his presence all the more important." Reba took a bite of her lemon bar. "It's time to put our heads together and try to figure what the old and new is that you'll be contending with."

"You two will have to start without me," Jessie

said as she jumped up to help a customer. "In case you need to leave before I get back to you, this weekend, I have my final fitting on my wedding gown. My mom can't make this fitting, and I would love for you to come with us to the city. That's if Lawrence can let you go for a Saturday." She leaned close to tell Reba.

"Oh my, I would be honored." Reba dabbed her eyes with the napkin.

"I'll take care of this customer," Peyton said and patted Reba's hand.

"Thank you, dear girl. You two girls are the daughters I would have loved to have had. We can talk on our way to the city." Reba's eyes grew misty again.

Jessie shook her head. "We can't talk then because Katie is coming, and our conversation can only be lighthearted and fun. Katie won't tolerate anything else. Our continued friendship is built on no talk of ghosts or anything strange."

"That's fine. We will still find ways to talk without offending your dear friend. Speaking of friends, has anyone seen any sign of our dear friends and sisters Mila and Elida. I'm sure they'll show up in one form or another to your celebration. Their help might be needed for this wedding to go off without a hitch."

"I haven't seen them," Peyton said as she walked past where they sat to greet another customer.

"Nor have I, but that doesn't mean they aren't around somewhere." Jessie took comfort speaking her thoughts aloud.

****

"Well, sister, I had no idea when Celeste sent us back that we would find Johanna and her protector in the area. Nor that we would be in action this quick."

Mila flittered around the stairs where the warrior stood guard. "In our line of work, you never know who you'll run into and where."

"I can only imagine all the folks visible and those unseen guests who will show up for this special event. The door might be left open to those who want to be there in spirit. This girl has helped a lot of them over the past many months. Matt needs our presence, too, even if he doesn't know it. I'm still trying to figure out how I want to show up for the wedding. I'd like to be one of the guests and party too." Elida did a two-step, twirling as she hummed. "I do so love a good party."

"We'll have to see if Celeste gives us permission to attend as guests. We don't have to make the decision right now. For now, our orders are to remain incognito, but it might be fun to take them by surprise." Mila flittered her wings. "At least, we'll get to see New York with them this Saturday. It's been a long time since I've been to the city. I bet there have been many changes since our last visit many years ago." Mila landed on the warrior's shoulder and smiled when he swatted at her with his hand. "Still a grumpy old pain in the backside, I see. Age hasn't changed you much in that regard." Mila pointed her tiny finger at his face.

"Maybe we'll get some fresh ideas in the city. You know me—I like to be a guy, and you like pretty dresses. Maybe this time we can go as sisters." Elida fluttered her wings, spreading gold dust on the irritable curmudgeon. "There now, that should improve your disposition a wee bit."

"For now, our job is to get these two safely to their wedding and as you see from this morning's activity we might be kept busy chasing bullets." Mila frowned and landed on the beam above the guardian ghost's head. "We'll sweeten this one before our time here is done." She swirled her wand around his form, and still he refused to grace them with even a tiny smile. "Although, our magic hasn't worked on him yet over all the years." She tapped her small fingers against her forehead. "Celeste always says, magic finds a way, especially when you're dealing with people who believe. I'm not sure if those words apply to this one, though." She tapped him on the head with her wand for good measure.

Chapter 3

When the tow truck arrived, Matt was cleaning his belongings out of his patrol car. "She's ready for you, Lenny." Matt closed the door with his laptop case in his hand. He had scratched his head in thought more than once as he noticed bullet hole details.

"We'll take good care of your cruiser, Chief," Lenny told him. "From the looks of it, you were in quite a war. I have no idea how long the repairs will take, but it shouldn't be too long. You'll get priority. I'm sure you have another ride, being the chief and all." Lenny hooked Matt's car up to the tow truck.

"I'll be fine. Let me know when I can pick her up." He walked with Lenny to his truck.

"Will do." Lenny drove away towing Matt's car.

Several things Matt had taken note of when going through the car convinced him of the fact that he shouldn't be alive at the moment. The bullet hole locations were proof positive that he had been beyond lucky. He couldn't imagine, much less explain, how he had managed not being hit. Words failed him. Of course, Jessie would say it was magic or meant to be. At this point, he was grateful to be standing upright whatever the reason. Even bent over, the bullet that went through the door had him dead to rights, but it took an odd turn and buried itself in the seat. Damn. He raked his hand through his hair. He shouldn't be standing upright.

"I guess you're wondering about the same thing I was when I checked out the damage to the car." Dylan saw the look on Matt's face. "I had the same expression you have now. How's it possible you didn't get hit?"

"Damned if I know." Matt shook his head.

"Katie would say you were lucky. Me, I'd say it's damn near impossible." Dylan reached for some of Matt's belongings to help him carry them inside.

"Jessie would say it was magic, and I would go along with her to keep the peace." He stepped inside the door Kenny held open. "You know I'm leaning her way more every time I have one of these close encounters that make no earthly sense to me."

"I've been around you both the past year and a half, and I still don't get it. Another report that will have some unexplainable facts and details left out."

"Which would be okay, but the suspect is still on the loose and could strike again at some point." Matt placed his laptop on his desk. "What I need now is a cup of strong coffee." He walked into the hall. "I'll admit seeing my car shook me."

"Yeah, well, it did me too. It's a good thing Jessie didn't see it. Your car looked a bit like her cottage did after the shooter finished there. The difference is that you two weren't in the space. You were in that car, my friend, and I'm glad to see you made it out alive."

"Me too. I've waited a long time for Jessie to agree to marry me, and I damn well want to make it to the wedding."

"I think we need to see if you have any suspects you put away over the years who were recently paroled." Dylan walked with him to the coffee station.

"Sounds like a good place to start. I'll have Gary check the recent records from prison." Matt stirred cream into his coffee.

"How are the wedding plans coming along?" Dylan asked.

"Fine as far as I know. All the details I've left to Jessie and the ladies. I got fitted for my tux, and I'll show up. My part is done. I've got the honeymoon planned, and I'm ready to get away with her."

"I know that feeling. The wedding was a blur, our honeymoon was blissful, and marriage is one big learning curve. But I love going home to Katie every night. I wouldn't trade it for the world." Dylan smiled.

"That's good to know." Matt sipped his coffee. "I'm ready to learn if it means going home to Jessie when the day is done. As it is, I come up with every excuse I can find to see her during the day." Matt topped off his cup. "I'd better try to get some work done. I'm not sure what to think about this morning. Something feels off to me."

"I can understand why." Dylan filled his cup before he followed Matt down the hallway.

Matt walked into his office and sat in his chair. A simple action, one he had repeated several times daily for the past year. But the hair standing up on his neck wasn't normal. Before he could analyze his thoughts, he felt a hard shove in his back, which sent him sprawling down onto the floor in a strange awkward position right before his office window shattered from the force of another bullet.

"Matt, are you okay?" Dylan crawled in the door.

"Yeah. Besides wanting to know who is shooting at me I would like to know who shoved me in the back, knocking me to the floor right before the bullet ripped through the window. I'm not that easy to knock down, or maybe it was simply a gut reaction on my part. Let's keep that part between us for now, Dylan. At least, until I can figure out what the hell just happened."

Dylan nodded. "Who'd believe me anyway?"

"Matt," Kenny called in, "they're chasing the guy. Kip saw where he was hiding when he shot the last time. I've sent backup and called for glass repair. A bulletproof glass might be needed. Your window may have to be boarded up until the glass can be made. We'll know soon enough as soon as they come to take measurements."

"That's the least of my problems. According to this note—" Matt held up the bag containing the note. "—someone doesn't want me to marry Jessie."

Dylan read the cryptic note. "Damn, that's short and to the point."

"My thought, exactly. It doesn't change anything for me. As long as I'm breathing, I'm going to marry her. It doesn't matter if I'm threatened that I'll die unless I call it off."

"I thought that would be your position. I wonder who wrote this." Dylan placed the note back in the bag. "Seems to me whoever it is has already tried to make good on his word."

"Looks that way." Matt followed Dylan low to the ground out his office door.

The rest of the afternoon was uneventful. His window was measured and fitted with new glass, a thicker premium glass, which the company had in stock and the guy gave the city a deal on. Matt didn't think they needed to order bulletproof glass, an added expense that the department's budget couldn't handle this year along with his car's repair.

He knew he needed to tell Jessie about the second attempt on his life. It seemed to all center around her, and he knew she would have a theory. The suspect had got away, which meant he probably wouldn't give up. Kip pursued him by foot and then car. He made a getaway out of their district, but it didn't mean the guy was gone for good. Kip called the plate number in for other authorities to be on the lookout for.

Someone didn't want him to marry Jessie, and he wanted to know why. There had to be more to it than a jealous man from her past or an angry person in town. The way the note was worded, the person felt like somehow their union would be his demise, which made no sense at all. Yep, he needed to talk to Jessie and let her read the note. She would get it.

He glanced at the clock. He didn't have long before he picked her up for dinner. Hopefully, he'd get a few answers to some of his questions.

"Hey, Matt." Kip poked his head in the door. "Our suspect's car has been found abandoned near Hanover. Jaxon is talking to the authorities about what they've found. There's no sign of the suspect but there's always fingerprints, or shell casings if we're lucky. I'll keep you updated."

"Thanks, Kip. Any break would be great."

****

Jessie spent the afternoon in thought as she worked, or at least as she tried to work. Back at winter hours, the days were shorter, and she was happy to close at five. By closing time, she had worked out a lot of ideas in her mind, if not her orders of new books.

24

Matt might be interested in some of her theories. He seemed to take her ideas in stride. It probably helped his ability to accept each new one that all the craziness came in doses over the past year and a half and weren't dumped on him all at once. It also helped that he fell in love with her while they both fought the idea.

She hadn't started out with ghosts in her store throwing books, or she might have gone back to New York the first chance she got. Thankfully, a lot of normal filled in around the strange happenings in her life. Going to dinner with the man of her dreams and chilling with her friends along with customers, books, and of course, her cottage by the sea, her home since moving to the cove, to name a few. The normal that helped her to navigate the often-strange times.

Matt's house and soon to be hers, too, was beautiful, especially when she could put her small touches here and there. But nothing would be as cozy as her cottage with its view of the cove. The biggest plus for her was walking out the front door and running to the marina. She loved the view, which seemed new each time she ran the path. She turned the sign to Closed, locked the front door, and waved goodnight to her fierce protector standing guard. "One of these days you're going to smile at me. You won't be able to help yourself." Jessie smiled at him and winked.

Chapter 4

Jessie opened the door to her cottage and was hit with a wave of nostalgia. She would only be in this room a few more weeks. Already her belongings were making their way into boxes, including a book manuscript she had started and never finished. The articles giving voices to victims were starting to pile up. She couldn't imagine never having shared their stories. She had learned lots through the process. She picked up a series of articles on top of the box ready to be taped shut, the ones she had written on the Native American women who were found and the many others who still remained lost and forgotten. She couldn't be prouder of the work she had done on each of their stories.

One of the highlights of her life was to meet the families of the girls she had seen in her unusual travels and learn about the dreams that they each had that would never be realized. To bring their stories alive to readers was a great honor. Testifying at Sonny Webster's trial, their killer, was another high moment too. Webster would be in prison for the rest of his life for what he did to those girls, and rightfully so. Their families were grateful. In her heart Jessie knew Sonny was only one of many people responsible for the many missing Native American women. Making people take notice and care was a whole other issue. She would continue to try.

In September, she had found herself bouncing over a dirt road to arrive no worse for wear to a trading post at Low Mountain to meet the one girl who managed to get away from her attacker. As the girl described her escape, Jessie relived running through the darkness with her, grasping at sagebrush as she stumbled and fell down the rocky ledge to the wash below. All the while she could hear Webster's angry, cursing voice calling out as his truck drove down the road. Her bravery in the face of a serial killer still filled Jessie with awe.

Besides her trip to Ireland, meeting these families meant more to her than words could say. How many other victims were out there with stories still waiting to be told? Jessie fingered the envelope on her desk with the notice that her series on the Native American girls was up for an award. Maybe this recognition would bring even more attention to the issue. She crossed her fingers and placed the articles in the box.

Jessie glanced at the clock. Matt would be there in a few minutes. She brushed her hair, put on her lip gloss, and checked her reflection in the mirror. "You had no idea what your life would be like when you first moved here, did you, girl?" She shook her head. "Now look at you." She chuckled. "You're still the same old me but with a new twist." She flipped her hair over her shoulder and went to get her coat.

"Today was a day for dawdling, but no more," she admonished herself. "You have too much to get done and little time to do it in." She rushed to the door when Matt knocked.

"Hi, sweetheart." He leaned close pulling her into in arms. He rested his face against her neck. "You smell good." He took a deep breath.

"I should hope so." She laughed.

"I missed you." He pulled back. "I know, I saw you earlier at the store, but I can't seem to get enough of you these days. I relax every time I'm with you." He held her coat for her to slip into. "We need to talk."

"I thought we would. Where are we going for dinner?" she asked.

"To the first place I ever saw you. Patterson's, of course. You were there with Katie, and you took my breath away."

"But not your ability to talk." She laughed. "You told this New York girl I'd be heading back to the city because I'd get bored in your small town. I can honestly say I haven't been bored yet. I do have to go the city to find a moment of peace though."

After they ordered dinner, Matt reached for her hand across the table. Jessie sighed inwardly at his touch. Moments like this made up for all the crazy ones. His touch made all the butterflies in her stomach start to dance. Would it always be like this? She sure hoped the magic would remain between them.

"You're quiet. What's on your mind?" Matt rubbed his thumb across the top of her hand.

"That's a loaded question." She chuckled. "I've done more thinking today than I've done in a while."

"I hope some of those thoughts were about me." He turned her hand over in his and brushed his fingers over her palm.

"You're doing that on purpose." She tried to pull her hand away, but he held tight.

"Who, me?" He grinned. "Am I bothering you?" Matt asked kissing each of her fingers.

"You're incorrigible. You know I can't think

straight when you do things like that."

"Nice to know." He smiled and let go her hand as the waiter approached the table. "I guess you won't have much thinking in your future."

"Don't forget to save room for some of Patterson's famous chocolate cake," the waiter said after he placed their meals on the table.

"Of course," Jessie assured him. "I can always make room for his chocolate cake."

"What kept my girl's mind occupied today?" Matt picked up his fork.

"You mean other than a strange phone call and you being shot at?" She raised her eyebrows.

"Shot at twice. You haven't heard about the second time yet." Matt ate a bite of his steak and filled her in on the details of his afternoon. "All this leaves me wondering who wants me dead."

"At least, I understand why my mind traveled the strange paths that it did today." She took a sip of her water.

"Care to enlighten me?" His brows rose.

"I've had two main areas of thought all day. I'll tell you about one now, and the second we can talk about later because it will make more sense." She wiped her lips with her napkin.

"I'm listening."

"I'm not one to go in search of the strange. Truth be told, I wrote lots of articles over the past few years but never found myself involved in the stories. Yes, I've always been a bit touchy when it came to the way women were treated in the workplace, but I can't say I thought much about the people in the stories after I finished them."

"Are you saying something has changed?" Matt asked.

"This past year has changed everything. I have no idea if I traveled through time in reality, or simply saw visions of things that happened. I'm not sure that matters. All I know is that from Gina to Johanna Murphy, their stories have impacted my life. I found new friends among their family members, and learned how many women are statistics that are forgotten. Telling their stories has given my life purpose, and for that I will always be grateful."

"Purpose?"

"You know, meaning. The reason for all this." Jessie waved her hand in a circular gesture. "I've been pretty selfish most of my life."

"Aren't we all in some regard?" he asked.

"Yes, but the past eighteen months introduced me to a whole new world. One I'd never taken the time to look at much less think about." She glanced down at her hands in her lap. "I'm sad to admit most of my thoughts over the years have been centered around what I could get out of life. But lately I've been confronted with the idea about what can I give to make the world better."

"And what is your conclusion? I think you've made my world a whole lot better." He waggled his eyes at her.

"I'm being serious." She slapped his hand playfully. "I'm here to tell their stories. Those who no longer have a voice. It's not about ghosts as much as about their lives cut short. It's about families who have to pick up the pieces after losing those they love. And at the end of the day, presenting repeatedly the question—

is this the kind of people we want to be?"

"Well now, that makes me seem small minded. Most of the time I'm thinking about you and our wedding in a few weeks." He thanked the waiter that cleared the table and told him to bring two pieces of cake and two coffees, one a decaf.

"Never fear, I think about our wedding too." She fluttered her lashes. "Several times a day in fact."

"That's good to know because ours has been a strange courtship built around murders and solving them. We both need a world where love exists. It's what keeps me going. Today wasn't one of my better days."

"I can imagine." She covered his hand with hers.

"Do you have any theories about who might want me dead, and better yet, why I'm still alive?"

"I have a thought or two on the subject," she told him.

"I thought you might. Before we talk more, we're going to enjoy our dessert like a normal couple in love. Tell me about any new wedding plans."

Jessie filled him in on all the plans and showed him a photo of the final wedding cake design. "On Saturday, Grams and Reba are going with us for the final fitting on my wedding gown. I can't wait for them to tell me what they think. The dress is everything I imagined." She took a bite of the decadent chocolate cake and closed her eyes. She sighed. No one made it any better than Joe Patterson.

****

"Sister, I was hoping she would tell him more about his potential shooter. He kept us busy today."

"At least now we can understand why Celeste

wanted us here early." Mila swirled around the young couple gazing lovingly into each other's eyes. "Ah, young love is glorious." She smiled.

"I got such a rush trying to outmaneuver the bullets and keep them from hitting that handsome young man." Elida dashed back and forth across the restaurant as fast as her wings would take her. "They make a dashing couple, don't they?"

"Yes. Between incidents today I checked in on Sally and Destiny, and things are going quite swimmingly with them. We can be proud of our work, sister."

"On that subject we agree. Do you think it will be safe for both of us to go to the city on Saturday or should one of us stay behind to watch over him?"

"Good question. I'll check in with Celeste on those new-fangled instruments she gave us to use. She likes us to keep up with the times, and I might be a tad slower than some of the others at grasping technology. I'm determined, though."

"If she says one of us should stay, I'd be happy to keep watch over him. I do like the sense of action that comes with keeping him safe. You know how restless I can get when I have nothing to do." Elida landed on Matt's shoulder and left a touch of gold dust as she did. "Here's to a touch of starry-eyed love."

"I will keep that in mind when I talk to Celeste. She always knows what's best. For now, we need to continue to pay attention to their conversation. Jessie has an idea, and I bet it's close to what Celeste told us." Mila landed on Jessie's shoulder next to her sister and tuned her ears in to listen.

Chapter 5

Jessie and Matt walked out of the restaurant. "That was nice." He squeezed her hand in his. "I admit I was pessimistic after the day I had, but now I think we're going to make it to our wedding in one piece. You do that for me." He opened the car door but kissed her before he let her get in.

"Hmm, that was nice." She touched his face as she slipped into the passenger's seat sighing to herself. In her heart Jessie knew she had nothing to do with his assurance. Magic was in the air even if she couldn't see where it was coming from.

"You mentioned you had something else to tell me later. Does now constitute later?" He glanced at her as he put the key in the ignition.

"You know how I like my classic, but there are times when I wish had one of those keyless cars that you can start while you're nice and warm inside." She buttoned her coat and stuffed her hands in the pockets. "You can tell that fall is here with the cool crisp mornings and chilly temps when the sun goes down. It's my favorite time of year."

"Are you ignoring my question?" He looked at her when he stopped at the light on Main Street.

"Not at all. I'm gathering my thoughts and holding a conversation about a valid observation while I do. I think a car that can start without a key and parallel parks itself would be a win for me is all I'm saying." Jessie smiled to herself when she heard him exhale.

"When you deflect like this, I know you are trying to make a subject more palatable for me. As soon as we get inside, lay it on me. I need to know what I'm up against." He parked the car and went around to open her door. He waited for an answer. Once inside her cottage he asked her again. "What are we looking at?"

"I did tell you that the second part would make more sense to you if you heard the first part. Because I've learned, with the help of Reba, my own ancestors, and you, especially you, to be who I am and to accept the purpose of my life. I know at times I can get too serious, and I try to lighten things up for you. I still like to have fun." She squeezed his arm.

"I know you do, but it doesn't seem we've had many chances to have fun. I promise to try and remedy that, but now is not the time." He helped her slip out of her coat.

"I know, but I can't forget the time you flew me to San Diego so I could see the sunset over the Pacific." She framed his face with her hands and kissed him. "You're full of surprises, and a true romantic guy. I wouldn't have guessed that about you when we first met."

"What? I'm quite charming." He gave her a lopsided grin.

"Knock it off. I'm attempting to be adoring." She fluttered her lashes. "Besides being too handsome for your own good—and mine," she said under her breath, "you've come to mean everything to me. It may have taken me a while to come to terms with and accept this strange new part of my life, but you've helped me.

During the arduous process of this past year and a half, I've also figured out I can't do life alone. I don't want to. As Johanna had Patrick, who made her stronger, I have you. Someone obviously knows that from our last cases and will stop at nothing to keep us apart."

"I don't like the sound of that. I was hoping for smooth sailing over the next couple of weeks." Matt sat on the couch beside her and pulled her into his side. "Damn." He frowned.

She glanced at him. "What?"

"You tell me," he answered.

"I'm not worried this time. I mean there might be a few hurdles to get over, but I think we have more than a few friends looking out for us. Consider your day. From what I've heard about how badly your car was damaged, I'm sure I'm right or you'd be gone already." She pried his clenched fingers open to hold his hand. "I'm right, aren't I?'"

He nodded. "Where'd you get the information about the car?" He scrunched his face.

"This is a small town and news travels fast." She laughed. "Which is why I'm always amazed that there isn't more gossip about me. Maybe there is and I'm simply too dense to know it or refuse to hear what folks are saying."

"I haven't heard anything either, and if it were out there, I would. The only ones who talk about you and your ghosts are my team." Matt chuckled.

"You mean the same ones who were placing bets on whether we would ever get together?" she asked.

"The same ones." He laced his fingers through hers. "Who among your friends are here to help us, and would I know them if I saw them?"

"Not unless they choose to show themselves somehow. Right now, I haven't seen them, but I know they are somewhere nearby."

"That's good enough for me." He reached for the remote and turned on the TV. He placed his arm around her shoulder, and she rested her head against his chest. The peace she had sensed earlier at Patterson's remained with them sitting here. She had a good idea who her unseen friends were, and she was grateful to have any help they could give.

****

"Sister, did you hear what she said?" Elida asked.

"I did. She called us her friends, and she knows we are here to help. I hope Celeste will allow us to show ourselves at the wedding." Mila tapped her small finger to her forehead. "The most important thing she said was that the same spirit we fought in the time of Johanna is what we are dealing with now. He's had centuries to continue the fight and even won a few rounds but lost the war against too many generations to count."

"Now that we have an idea of who we are dealing with, all we need is a good plan." Elida landed on Matt's shoulder.

"Celeste wrote down some important details for us and instructed me to research page four-thousand four in the Intermediary Manual for more answers. She reminded me we wrote the pages on how we dealt with him before." Mila smiled and swirled around the heads of the young couple sitting on the couch, moving her tiny wand back and forth and twirling it as she went. Gold dust settle around their heads as she blew misty kisses of peace and goodwill their way.

"I love our job, sister. They are happy and I like to

think we played a role in their happiness."

"We have. No doubt about it." Mila sighed as she watched the couple share a kiss.

The two sisters settled down to watch over their charges. Mila knew the days ahead wouldn't be easy and they would have to be on their toes. She glanced at her dainty slippers. But they were up to the task. Elida had saved Matt several times today with a wee bit of her magic. They would do all they could to make this special occasion a wedding Blue Cove would never forget and one that would fulfill all of Jessie's deepest desires for her big day.

Chapter 6

Matt walked the familiar path back to his car. How many times had he walked back and forth over this path the past year and a half? Enough to have left a footprint or two along the way. "Damn, what was that?" He swatted at whatever buzzed by his head.

One thing he wouldn't miss was leaving her each night. His mind filled with images of Jessie being with him each night. Holding her in his arms, watching her sleep, and kissing her anytime he wanted. With her permission, of course. She had trained him well. He smiled to himself. His hand reached out to grab whatever had made another pass by his head. Too close for comfort since he had no idea what it was.

Their conversation tonight left him wondering if there was more to come. When it came to life in Blue Cove the past year, there would probably be more trouble before he could say "I do." Jessie seemed to think help had come in the form of some old friends. She didn't use the word fairy, and he was grateful for that. He loved Jessie, but life with her had stretched every logical thought in his brain.

Although, he knew something, or some*one*, kept him from dying today and even he couldn't deny the fact. Matt reached in his pocket for his phone.

"Hey, this is Matt," he answered.

"Chief, I thought I should let you know the suspect

has not been found yet. Be careful," Kip told him. "The local FBI in the area where the car was found is working with the police department searching for evidence. It's true what they say—that law enforcement frowns at crimes against one of their own. You're priority one for them. They promised to contact us soon."

"Thanks, Kip. I'm on my way home where I plan to stay until morning. I suggest you call it a day too." Matt got in his car and turned over the engine.

"Whoever you are, thanks for saving me today." Matt glanced over his shoulder as he backed out of the parking space. "I hope you'll hang around for a while. I might still need you." Matt shook his head. Now he was talking to someone he couldn't see. Ah, hell.

****

Jessie stood at the door and watched Matt leave. Who had shot at him? In her heart she knew why but not who. The poor man had more trouble than one person could handle since she had come into his life. She was happy he still wanted to marry her and could only hope he wouldn't change his mind in the next couple of weeks.

She smiled when Matt swatted at the air. Mila or Elida must have gotten too close or maybe they purposely let him know something was nearby. "Keep him safe, dear friends," she said closing the door.

"Hey, girlfriend," Katie's cheery voice said when Jessie answered her phone. "I hope you're ready for our New York adventure."

"I am. Why are you calling this late? Usually by now you're cozied up with that handsome hubby of yours."

"He is handsome but he's also working. You've got to talk to Matt about that. A new wife shouldn't have to worry about her husband working late."

"What can I say? It's the nature of their job." Jessie set the alarm code. "Reba is coming with us too. My mom can't make it this time, but Reba and Grams can."

"Sadie I don't mind, but you have to admit Reba is a little strange. I know, I know, you like her. I'll tolerate her because it's your special day. But she'd better not talk about weird stuff. You know how I feel about that."

"I do, and she won't. Don't worry. Let's talk about the book we're reading." Jessie picked up the book from her nightstand and turned to the page where they had left off last time. She needed to keep Katie on a safe topic.

"I know what you're doing, Jessica Lynn, and I'll let you win this time. Besides, I can't wait to see you in your dress. Maybe once you're married, Matt will stop you from getting into all this crazy stuff."

Katie warmed up to the subject of Matt controlling her. Jessie blocked out half of what she said. They never did get to the book. Katie would always be her friend but somedays the girl could drive her nuts. Thank heavens that her cousin Peyton understood this part of her life. Jessie could tell Peyton all the odd details, and she understood and vice versa.

"Katie, you should go. Dylan will be there soon." Jessie interrupted her before she could start into another one of her rants.

"You're right. We can talk over the chapter another day. Bye." The line went silent.

Jessie took a deep breath. Oh, blessed silence. Her

friend could get worked up over nothing. She smiled when she thought about the many times Jessie found herself in trouble siding against her friend when Katie warmed up to a subject she considered a just cause. More than once, Jessie had found herself on the wrong side of an argument and went down in flames standing with Katie's somewhat faulty reasoning. Their friendship had endured many twists and turns over the years, although her new life had threatened more than once to break it. She had to tread lightly these days and keep the conversations on safe ground. Katie would come around eventually. At least, she hoped she would.

Jessie went through her bedtime routine. Plumping the pillows behind her, she stretched her legs out. She pulled up her covers and sent Matt her nightly goodnight text. She sighed at his romantic return message. He was a keeper, no doubt about it. Was it possible to love him more than she did at the moment? The answer was a definite yes, according to the wise words of Grams.

Jessie shut off the light and turned over onto her side unaware of the tiny creature flittering around her. Tired, she yawned, but she was too hyped to sleep, or so she thought. As the gold dust swirled around the pillows, her eyes closed, and her body relaxed. Dainty fingers tapped three times on her forehead followed by a gentle kiss.

"Sweet dreams, my darling girl," Mila whispered in her ear. She landed on the pillow beside her head.

****

She found herself sitting on a familiar rock in the forest. The mist rose from the ground, and the thick canopy of trees let the sunlight filter to where she sat in an almost ethereal manner. Light danced around her in delicate patterns, while a gentle wind swished the vegetation near her feet back and forth. Jessie was mesmerized by the beauty and the life around her. At peace in the enchanting place, she waited.

Time didn't disappoint. Her friends, along with too many others to count, fluttered their tiny wings as they moved among the dancing lights weaving in and out of the lacy designs spreading their golden dust as they played tag. Their laughter filled the air with merriment. Jessie found herself caught up in the sheer joy of the moment. Mila landed on one shoulder and Elida on the other.

"Watch, my dear, and learn," Mila whispered in her ear. "Life is not without purpose no matter how short or long it is."

"Every human story is important whether for good or ill," Elida chimed in her other ear. "You have made a difference in the lives of those who stand before you."

"Open your eyes, my dear." Mila laid her tiny hands over Jessie's eyes and quickly removed them.

Standing in front of her were those who were familiar and some she had never seen before.

Mila touched her shoulder "Even if you don't know some of these folks, they know who you are. You see, dear, every life impacts many besides their own. Listen; you are about to hear their stories and appreciation." Mila waved her wand and all the movement around them stopped.

They flew from all the places where they had been hiding and encircled all that were present. Where there had been laughter a holy hush now descended, and all eyes turned to follow the progress of a young woman in a flowered dress as she approached Jessie from the back of the crowd.

"I have been waiting for you to come. There was no one to help me. I'm sorry if my actions scared you, but your endeavors on my behalf gave closure to my parents and kept my children from a father who was a murderer. Because of you I can rest in peace," Gina told her.

It was right that Gina led the group because she was the first one to appear to Jessie. After Gina came Abigail leading a group of children. Each one told her how grateful they were to be safe at home. Abigail recalled how in her desperation she had tried to reach anyone who could hear her thoughts and somehow Jessie had. Tears ran down Jessie's cheeks as each one stopped to hug her.

"If not for you we would be living in slavery some other country and not in our homes with our family." Abigail whispered in her ear, "I will never forget you," before she turned to follow the others back among the group. Jessie remained transfixed as she was privileged to hear how her tiny actions or articles had given voice to those who stood before her. For as long as she lived, Jessie believed she would remember this moment with humility and awe.

Jessie glanced at the clock when she opened her eyes, rubbing them. How long she had sat among all her new friends she had no idea. Whether real or only a dream their words reinforced what she had told Matt earlier. Purpose was important to her, and Matt was a big part of how she went about helping others. He had the intuition to figure out how to solve an issue. She simply followed her heart when one of these folks tugged on it.

Chapter 7

"Good morning." Jessie turned her brightest smile on her stern friend still standing guard. She went about her opening routine and couldn't wait to tell Molly how much Matt liked the profiteroles, her latest yummy creation. She opened the doors into the coffee shop.

"Molly, Matt loved them," she said to her friend and gave her a thumbs up. Molly was super busy behind the counter. The coffee shop and cafe seemed to get busier each day. Molly served more than coffee and the word *cafe* seemed to describe her business better. And why not? Molly served some of the best food in town. Buying this property beside Joe's was one of the smartest business decisions Jessie made when she moved to town. Even her dad, a bit of a skeptic, admitted she had made a sound choice. Especially after he saw her latest profit margin on the spreadsheets from the accountant that she showed him the last time he was in town. Truthfully, she hadn't been sure if a bookstore would be profitable, but she always wanted to own one. Maybe she had let her desire rule her business sense, but hey, it had worked out well.

Ever since her first visit to the school library, she loved the world of books. All the stories and words opened new realms for her. Her childhood memories were filled with reading by flashlight under her covers long after her mother turned off the light. A practice that continued into her college years where fiction was often replaced with ideas. Authors with their great thoughts took up residence in her mind and gave her many pleasurable hours of mulling over and debating concepts. One of those ideas birthed in college made her a bit of an activist for women, which seem to fit in with who she was right now.

"Reading was one way for me to be a lifelong learner since staying in college for years wasn't financially feasible," she said, glancing at her somewhat less grumpy friend.

She couldn't think of a happier place to work than right here among these wonderful books and of course, her customers. Jessie unlocked the front door and turned the Open sign around. What a joy it was to come to work every day. Add to the books the never-ending stream of unusual visitors, and this was the perfect place for her to be.

"I wonder what this day will bring," Jessie mused as she smiled at the two ladies who walked in from the coffee shop. "If you need help finding anything, let me know."

"We thought we might sit here in your lovely store and enjoy our coffee," the younger of the two women said. "My best friend—" She pointed at the woman next to her. "—is in town for a short visit and I want to enjoy every minute of it."

"You're welcome to sit in any one of the cozy spots. They're perfect for a nice conversation. I'm here if you need me." Jessie went to help another customer who walked in the front door.

The fact that her morning was uneventful with only a few customers gave her plenty of time in between to consider her dream or whatever it was. One thing she knew for sure was her fairy friends had their hands in the past few days. It made facing the days up to her wedding and what was happening with Matt a lot easier to handle. She could only hope he wouldn't have any more close calls.

When Reba and another lady arrived, her day got a bit more interesting. "Hi, Reba." Jessie waved as she glanced at the woman beside her friend.

"This is my sister, Barbara, who is here for a quick visit. I couldn't wait to have her meet you. She's a bit eccentric like we are."

"It's nice to meet you, Barbara." Jessie extended her hand. "How long are you in town for?"

"Call me Babs. All my friends do, and I'm sure we are going to be great friends." She smiled at Jessie. "Regretfully, I'm here only for the day. My sister has told me about you, and I knew I had to come to the cove with the express purpose of meeting you and to see my sister." She took Jessie's hand in hers. "I can see what you mean, sister. There is a strong connection with this one. She has a loving heart."

"I told you." Reba smiled at Barbara.

"Something recently happened to you that has impacted you greatly. I can't wait to hear all about it." Babs squeezed Jessie's hand slightly.

Jessie told them about her night. "At least, I think it was dream, but it seemed real, and the details were vivid. All I know is that I won't be the same."

"How blessed you were to have such an event. So much love goes unspoken and unheard. But you were privileged to hear those kind words while still living. Let them take bloom in your heart. I have a feeling you deserve them." Babs turned to Reba. "Let's get some of those tasty treats you've been telling me about and we can spend the afternoon catching up. Of course, you need to tell me the story about the unusual presence I can sense here."

For Jessie, the afternoon flew by. Reba was prim and proper, while Babs seemed a tad more liberated and eclectic. A whole lot more, to be truthful. Those two were as different as night and day except for their gifts. They played off each other. Jessie enjoyed her day and found herself laughing quite often. From talking about Matt, the wedding, and of course her store's newest occupant, the whole conversation had been enlightening and fun.

****

"I enjoy moments like this, Elida. I'm reminded of the good times we have with our friends as I listened to these ladies speculate and laugh all afternoon. I think these three are fun. We've never had the chance to work with Babs, but something tells me she would be a hoot." Mila fluttered her wings and stretched out on one of the books, resting her hands under her chin.

"I was thinking the same thing, sister." Elida sat beside her sister with her little shoes hanging over the edge of a book. "I've been wondering if I'll I be staying behind to watch over Matt when you go to the city. What did Celeste say?"

"Yes, she wants you to stay here, and she will send Basil to help you." Mila saw Elida's face turn red and wrinkles appear on her forehead.

She jumped up and fluttered high, spinning in circles until she reached the ceiling, then plopped down beside Mila once more. "I don't need help and especially not from him." Elida tapped her tiny fingers to her forehead, frown lines becoming more prominent. "He's such a prankster. Basil doesn't have a serious bone in his body. He has tormented me on more than one occasion. Let him try any funny business, and I will give him what for." She doubled up her tiny fist.

Mila turned her face away from Elida to stifle her chuckle. "Well, that's why he's coming. Not to torment you, of course, but Celeste thinks you can help him. The experience will be good for him. He has to grow in his skills like we had to." Mila smiled to herself because Celeste thought he could help Elida to lighten up a bit too. Truth be told, Elida could be a bit feisty herself.

"I guess if Celeste thinks I can help him then I'm willing to try." Elida smoothed her pretty blue dress down over her legs.

"Our esteemed leader always knows what is best in any situation. You're perfect for the job. Who knows, sister, maybe you'll even have fun." Mila pushed herself up to a sitting position.

"I doubt that." Elida turned to glance at Mila. "Did Celeste happen to tell you whether we can attend the wedding as guests or must we remain incognito?"

"She said she will give our idea some thought and let us know before the wedding. She thought our plan had merit. I believe she is leaning in favor of the idea," Mila said. "We must be off. There is much for us to do."

"One more question if you please, sister."

"Yes," Mila responded.

"Are you looking forward to seeing New York again?" Elida asked.

"I can hardly wait."

"Then be sure to record all the changes on that newfangled thing you carry, so you can show me all the changes. It's been a long time since our last visit."

"Of course, sister." She gave Elida a high five and flew off to her next destination.

Chapter 8

Matt had texted Jessie several times with no response. Knowing Jessie, she'd misplaced her phone and hadn't paid attention to it all afternoon. She would get back to him when she found his text.

Kip knocked on his open door. "Got a minute?"

"Sure. What's on your mind?" Matt pointed at the chair in front of his desk.

Kip sat. "Jaxon called and told me they pulled some prints from the suspect's car and confiscated a cache of weapons and ammo from the trunk. Whoever the guy is, he came armed, which makes you wonder if there is a deeper plot here that we don't know about yet." Kip leaned forward in the chair. "Jaxon promised to let me know when they have more info."

"I'm still trying to figure out why me. I'm nothing in the grand scheme of things. A larger plot I can maybe understand, but I have no idea how I would figure into it." Matt took his glasses off and rubbed his temples. "Did you make it to the tux rental place yet?"

"I did. I looked snazzy in it if I do say so myself." Kip chuckled. "I'm not fond of the whole dress-up thing, but for Jessie I'd do almost anything. She's all right in my book."

"I'm with you there. Hey, you never know what good-looking woman you might meet at a wedding. Peyton's sister is a looker." Matt grinned. "Weddings have been known to bring couples together."

"I guess one can hope." Kip shook his head.

"Hope, what?" Dylan asked when he walked through the door.

"That there'll be some pretty women my age at Matt's wedding. I could use a bit of fun at this point." Kip glanced at Dylan.

"What happened to you and the girl who worked at the inn?" Dylan asked.

"Let's just say it didn't work out. She walked a bit on the wild side, and I cramped her style. After this past year I'm ready to settle down more. I don't like to party every night. I'm too tired."

Matt laughed. "You're younger than me and you already feel that way. I must be keeping you too busy."

"Peyton's sister will be in the wedding. Who knows what might happen?" Dylan clapped Kip on the back. "I never met a girl at a wedding, but you might be different. Don't lose hope." Dylan stood. "Speaking of a woman, I have a special one waiting for me. She'll be happy I don't have to work late tonight. She thinks you work me too hard." Dylan laughed. "I wouldn't be surprised if she walked in your office one day to have a chat with you about the subject. In case she does, I want you to know I didn't put her up to it. Katie has a mind of her own."

"So I've heard." Matt grinned at his friend.

"Once a thought takes hold of her, she won't let it go. No amount of talking will stop her." He waved on his way out the door. "See you guys tomorrow."

"Maybe I can wait a while to get married. I'm not sure I want to tangle with another person when I get home from work. She sounds like a handful." Kip shook his head.

"I haven't heard Dylan complaining. I think he's happy and finds his wife fascinating." Matt reached for his glasses and slipped them on. "Discovery is part of the mystery of love."

"I guess you're about to find out." Kip stood. "I'll let you know or have Jaxon call you if they find out anything more on our suspect."

"Wait and I'll walk out with you." Matt gathered up his papers and put them in the folder on his desk. He grabbed his phone and slipped on his jacket. He walked out of the station with Kip to his car.

Once in the car, he read the text from Jessie and called her. "Dinner at your place sounds perfect, sweetheart."

"Sorry I took my time getting back to you. I spent the afternoon chatting with Reba and her sister, Barbara."

"I didn't know Reba had a sister. You'll have to tell me all about your visit when I get there."

"Reba might have mentioned her in passing, but I don't remember if she did. I had a fun afternoon with them. We never talked about her, but from now on I'll be asking about her. See you soon."

"I'll be there in ten, and I'm bringing my appetite with me." He pulled onto the street and headed toward Main. The best part of his day was seeing Jessie.

****

Jessie placed the glasses on the table after filling them with ice. She lit the candles, and dinner was ready for her hunky cop. With a bit of help from Molly's dessert brownies, Matt's favorite, and her oven baked chicken, she would make sure her hungry guy was taken care of. He could use some special pampering after the last couple of days.

Jessie rushed to open the door when he knocked. "I hope your day was better today than yesterday."

"At least no one shot at me." He pulled her into his arms and hugged her. "This makes the day perfect." He pushed the door closed behind him with his foot right before he kissed her.

"You're getting pretty good at multitasking. I like your style, Mr. Parker." She took his arm and tugged him toward the kitchen. "Dinner will get cold."

He stopped her forward motion to lock the door. "Now we can eat." He followed her into the kitchen. "You went to a lot of trouble. This is nice." He gestured at the candles.

Jessie couldn't help but notice how tired he looked. She kept the conversation light during dinner and talked about meeting Reba's sister. "Babs, as she likes to be called, is the opposite of Reba in some ways, but when it comes to insight, she is a carbon copy." Jessie smiled at Matt's raised eyebrow expression.

"Another case of two in the same family is what you're telling me. How is that possible since I never even heard of one until I met you?" He cut a piece of chicken and took a bite. "This is great, by the way."

"I'm glad you like it." She took a sip of her iced tea. "Matt, when she took my hand, she knew that I was like them. We had such a fun afternoon laughing. They know what's happening around them, but they also know how to have a good time. My big takeaway from the afternoon I got from them is our wedding will be quite the event. I must agree." She stood and kissed his cheek before she brought him his brownie. "Would you like coffee with your dessert?"

"I shouldn't. I had a lot of coffee today, but I'll take a cup of decaf if you have it." He shook his head. "I can't believe I even said that." He grinned at her. "But yes, I mean it."

"You know I have it." She poured the hot coffee into his cup. "I always like coffee with my sweet treats. Reba is always about the tea."

"Do you mind if I eat this in the living room?" he asked.

"No, I was going to suggest that. The chairs are more comfortable, and you look tired. Why don't you go ahead while I put away the food and clean up. Watch your scores." She carried his coffee in and placed the cup on the coffee table.

"I can help," Matt told her.

"Not tonight. It'll only take me a few minutes." She handed him the remote and returned to the kitchen.

Jessie could hear the sportscaster talking about some great play or another. She put the food away, placed the dishes in the sink to do later, and took her brownie and glass of milk into the living room to sit beside Matt.

The TV was on, but Matt was out. Sound asleep, his feet on the coffee table with his head leaning awkwardly to the side. He looked uncomfortable. The first thing Jessie did was slip his glasses off his face and lift the open folder from his lap. Matt didn't move. How could she move him into a more comfortable position without waking him? She started by slipping his shoes off his feet, not noticing the small figure that rested on his shoulder. Lifting his legs, she moved them from the table to the couch. Wow, he stilled hadn't stirred. He must be really tired. How was that even possible? Jessie tugged on his legs pulling him carefully until he was flat on the couch. She reached for a pillow and placed it under his head. Covering him with a throw, she turned off the TV and the lamp. She kissed his cheek and went to finish the dishes. He wasn't going anywhere soon.

****

Mila smiled to herself. "Magic, dear. A little gold dust here and a misty kiss or two blown his way and he went out like a rock. He needs the rest, and sleep is a part of my plan for him tonight."

Mila waited for Jessie to go to her room for the night and she set her plan into action. "Young man, it's time for you to have an understanding of what you're about to get yourself into." Mila tapped his forehead three times. "She'll need your strength and your understanding." Mila waited and knew the moment when his illumination took place.

Chapter 9

"What the hell." Matt sat up rubbing his eyes. He'd fallen asleep, which rarely happened when Jessie was near. Where was she anyway? He rested his head in his hands. Something had knocked him out—at least he felt that way.

"Good morning, sleepy head." Jessie walked in from the kitchen carrying a cup of coffee and placed it on the coffee table in front of him. "I don't remember you going out that fast before. You didn't stir when I took off your glasses, moved you around, or even kissed you goodnight."

"It's the strangest thing. If I didn't know better, I would swear I had taken a sleeping pill. I still feel a bit groggy."

"Hmm. Something about this seems familiar. You didn't dream, did you?" she asked.

"Not really, but there was a voice speaking at the edge of my mind. I hope I can remember what was said because I feel it's important." Matt took a sip of coffee. "Where are my shoes anyway?"

She picked up his shoes and handed them to him. "Do you want something to eat? I can put a bagel in the toaster."

"I need to swing by my house before work." He reached for the file before he stood. "Why did you ask if I had a dream?"

"The way you went out last night made me think you might have had a bit of help, and I don't mean a sleeping pill either." Jessie stood beside him.

"What do you mean?" he asked.

"I'll let you know once you recall what you heard if anything. It's only a theory and not important at the moment." She gave him a quick kiss. "Don't forget I'll be going to the city tomorrow for the final fitting on my dress. I hope you miss me."

He pulled her into his arms and kissed her like he had wanted to ever since she walked in the room looking gorgeous. A man could get used to the sight of her every morning. He pulled back and then kissed her again. "I'll miss you." He hugged her tight. "Tonight, I owe you dinner. It's the least I can do after falling asleep on you last night. I didn't even help you clean the kitchen. Sorry, sweetheart."

"Not a problem. I'd be happy to have dinner with you. You'll have to work hard to make it up to me. Your morning kiss earned you a few brownie points. Let's see what else you have in you."

"I'm sure I can come up with something to please you." He kissed her again.

"I'm sure you can." She gave him a playful push. "You'd better hurry or you'll be late."

"You can detain me anytime, beautiful lady." He opened the door and turned to kiss her one more time. "I'll see you later."

Matt hadn't been entirely truthful with Jessie. He had a lot of disjointed images and words that went with those images in his mind. He had to do some thinking before he tried to explain to Jessie what he saw. One takeaway for him, Jessie would need his support as much as he needed hers. And he was the right man for the job. Hell, he knew that without being told. He'd defy anyone who said he wasn't. Since they were about to be married, he needed to be upfront with her as soon as he figured everything out.

****

Jessie watched Matt until he drove away. How she loved that man. His swagger was part of his charm. She reached for her coat, shoved her phone into her purse, and headed for the door. She didn't have the heart to tell Matt that her tiny friend was the reason for him falling asleep early last night. He went out and stayed there. She wondered if it was Mila or Elida who had a good reason. Hopefully, Matt would remember what he heard. Jessie locked the door behind her. It gave her a sense of peace to know that her friends were nearby. They would do all they could to keep them safe. Matt would soon come to appreciate their kind of magic, but he would do some grumbling first.

Jessie laughed when she thought about maneuvering Matt as he slept. He wasn't easy to move. Dead weight came to mind. She had tried hard to take care not to wake him, but nothing would have awakened him. All of her concern had been lost on him.

The route from the cottage to her store was the same one she drove each day for the past year and a half. It seemed strange to think of approaching her shop from another direction. She would miss honking at Katie each morning as she passed the inn and all the special points of interest she passed on her way into town. Among the places she would miss seeing change with the seasons was the garden and her favorite point that overlooked the cove. Who would live in her cottage when she moved out? "You'll find out soon enough," she said.

She had mostly good memories attached to her time living in the cottage, but there were a few memories she would like to bury and not to think of again. Never would still be too soon. She turned her radio up playing one of her favorite tunes. "I actually love my life." She tapped her finger on the steering wheel and sang along. And made short work of the drive into town with her one unseen passenger rocking in the back seat to the beat.

After her morning routine, Jessie unlocked the front door and waved at Molly. The message light on her phone was blinking. This was one message she wished she hadn't listened to. She knew the voice and the way he delivered the message.

"Give up your dream on your wedding or you'll be a widow as soon as you're a bride."

Jessie listened to the recording several times. Something seemed familiar about the voice, but what? Every time the voice came over the speaker, her guardian ghost became agitated and flew around the room. Did he recognize the man's voice too?

"Hey, cous," Peyton said as she walked through the door.

"Aren't you working today?" Jessie asked.

"No, we are on a small break until Tuesday. I think it worked perfectly for our trip to the city tomorrow. Aren't you excited?" Peyton placed her purse on the counter.

"I'm getting there. I'm a bit nervous after listening to this message though." She played the recorder for Peyton to hear.

"Dang, that's not very nice. What a jerk." Peyton frowned. "Will it ever stop? I mean, how often will we be in the middle of all this crazy stuff? It makes me worried for Jaxon, as you must be for Matt."

"This is our life, Peyton. And you'd better get used to it. You'll be here while I'm on my honeymoon, so I'm thinking you'll have your hands full." Jessie shrugged.

"I know you're right. At least you've had the last eighteen months for you and Matt to get used to working through so many cases together. Jaxon and I have had a few, and I don't mind being on the sidelines although I know from the scrolls and the gift I have I can't stay out of the game all together."

"Of course, you can't. We've made it through together, and that's the way it will always be as long as we both are alive." Jessie placed Peyton's purse behind the counter and told her about Reba's sister Barbara. "We had so much fun together. I wish you could have been there. She might meet us in the city tomorrow. I hope she does. I want you to meet her."

"Put me to work," Peyton told her. "I'm yours for the day. And you have to let Matt listen to that message."

"Don't worry. I will. That's one thing the past year and a half has taught me. Matt needs to know what I sense or what I know."

"Something we both need to remember." Peyton gave her a skeptical look.

"What? I mean it. Like you tell Jaxon everything?" Jessie shook her head.

"You're right. Let's make a pact to do better." Peyton held up her little finger. "Pinky swear."

"I can live with that." Jessie connected her finger with Peyton's. "Looks like it's time to get to work." Jessie went to greet the two customers who walked in the front door.

"You're about to get real busy," one of the ladies told her. "There's a busload more to follow. We're here on a New England autumn tour. It's a gorgeous time to be here."

"One of the nicest," Jessie told her.

"My friend and I were saying the church across the street would be a perfect place for a wedding."

"Well, my cousin here is getting married right over there in a couple of weeks." Peyton squeezed Jessie's shoulder.

"Perfect. Congratulations. I hope you don't mind if we get coffee and come back and look around."

"Please do." Jessie smiled at them as they walked into Joe's.

Boy, was she thankful that Peyton was there. The woman wasn't kidding when she said she was about to get busy. Days like today reinforced the idea she had made a great business decision. There was a sparkle in the air; it literally crackled with excitement, and at the moment she didn't care what the man said. There was no way he would make her a widow right after becoming a bride.

Chapter 10

Matt's morning had flown by. Until now, he had been too busy to take a break. He glanced at the clock. It was almost two. No wonder he was hungry. Jaxon had called him earlier and told him they were closing in on a possible suspect. They had a man under surveillance. Matt admitted he was relieved that they might have a suspect. The last few days had left him shaken. Falling asleep at Jessie's and his dream didn't help either. Dreams were Jessie's department, and he wanted to keep it that way. He liked things the way they were. No ghosts, no premonitions, and absolutely no dreams. Still, it was like someone turned the light on his mind and he understood what life with her meant.

He was smart enough to know there were things that he couldn't always explain. Didn't even want to try. He doubted that even Jess understood half of what she had seen or heard the past year. The one thing he did understand—as much as he wanted to walk away from his job when it got hard, he couldn't. Like a preacher feels called to a church, he was where he was supposed to be, helping people the way he knew how to do best, and so was she. Matt headed out the door to a patrol vehicle. His car was almost done.

What could he tell her about what happened last night? He could tell her the truth—he was where he was meant to be. And he could promise to always be there for her as long as he was alive. The rest of the dream seemed nonsensical to his logical brain. "Jess will understand," he uttered as he pulled out of the station. Joe's and, of course, the bookstore. It was automatic to his way of thinking.

He arrived at the perfect moment. A car pulled out of the spot in front of her store, and he parked his cruiser in the exact spot.

She was busy with a customer when he popped in and waved. "I'll catch you before I leave," he mouthed as he strolled past her to the open doors into the coffee shop.

Matt ordered and sat at a table where he could see Jessie at work. He smiled as she talked with one of her customers. Her joyful laughter was like music to his ears.

****

Jessie knew he was watching her. She was happy to have him close. His continuous glances her way made her feel special. Her guy was a charmer. But how charming would he be when he heard the message on her phone?

"Are you going to tell Matt about your recent message?" Peyton leaned against the counter next to Jessie.

"Of course. I've learned my lessons well." She smiled. "He has a way of finding out anyway."

"I love the way he looks at you with his heart on his sleeve." Peyton placed her hand over heart.

"Oh yeah, those heated glances make this girl go weak in the knees and tell him anything he wants to know." Jessie laughed and glanced his way. "That's the look I'm talking about," Jessie whispered to Peyton.

Peyton glanced at Matt and waved. "He knows we're talking about him."

"Sure he does, but he has no idea what we're saying." Jessie turned her back to him. "My guess is he'll be in here soon to find out."

"Unless I miss my guess, he's on his way now," Peyton voiced. "Steel yourself, cousin. He has an odd gleam in his eyes. I think he means to kiss you." Peyton sighed.

Matt pulled Jessie back into the circle of his arms. "What were you two talking about?"

"This and that." She leaned her head back and glanced up at him.

"Would you care to elaborate?" he asked.

"Not particularly. You know—girl talk." She pulled out of his arms. "Nothing that would interest you."

"Humor me." Matt gave her a lopsided grin.

She gazed in his eyes. How she loved his smile. "I have something you need to listen to." She played the recording for him to hear.

"Damn. I was thinking our sick friend would have given up by now, but no such luck."

"I guess not." Jessie framed his face with his hand. "We are destined to ride the roller coaster to our wedding. Why should we expect anything else at this point? Our time of knowing each other has been nothing if not unconventional, and should we say interesting?" She kissed him.

"I'm not sure I would choose the word interesting, but definitely the past year hasn't been boring." He kissed her back, hugging her tight. "Our life together is sure to be noteworthy." He rested his chin on the top of her head. "Have I mentioned that I'm looking forward to sharing our life together and coming home to you at the end of the day?"

"I won't be the little lady waiting for my hunky cop to come home from work. I'm a businesswoman, lady activist, but being together at the end of the day sounds nice." She sighed. "I hope you know what you're getting into." She laughed, her chin edging up. "This past several months has thoroughly warned you, I'm sure."

"How can I forget? I will always think of you as my warrior." He let her go when the bell at the front door rang. "I'll pick you up at your house after work. I need to get back." He headed toward the door. "Good afternoon, ladies." He tipped his head at the two women who walked past him.

Jessie smiled to herself as her eyes followed him. How she loved the man. Now if they could only reach their wedding without anything else major happening, she would be one happy person. What were the odds of that happening? Quite high, if her two friends were present. They still hadn't shown themselves openly, but in her heart she knew they were nearby, or she would have lost Matt already. "Thank you for keeping him safe," she whispered.

****

"Did you hear that, sister?" Elida asked. "She knows we kept Matt safe, and she thanked us." Elida did a merry jig on the top of one of the books. "They're both such sweet girls. I'm not sure if we have received many thanks over the years for what we have done."

Mila smiled. "That's because most people aren't aware we are at work. Remember, we can help, but they must believe it's their idea. One of the main rules in the Intermediary Manual. I'm not sure why Celeste has allowed us to reveal ourselves to some people and not others, but I'm sure she has good reasons."

"Still, don't you think it was lovely to hear her say thank you? I find it exhilarating to chase down the bullets and redirect them away from their target, and it's nice to have someone notice that I did a good job." Elida plopped herself down on the edge of the book with a dreamy expression on her face. "I hope we can go to the wedding like other guests. I can see myself dancing at her wedding and having a good time."

"We'll see what Celeste has to say, but it will be fun either way, I'm sure." Mila sat beside her sister. "Now we must plan our course of action. I'm going to the city tomorrow, and you will have to fill your assistant in on the details without me."

Elida frowned. "Why did you go and ruin a perfectly happy moment reminding me of him? Where is Basil anyway?" Elida shook her head. "He'd better behave himself. That's all I have to say, or Celeste will hear from me."

"He'll be here before you know it, and you must be nice, sister. You're supposed to be helping him."

"Like I believe that." She waved with her hand. "He's beyond my help."

"Elida, you shouldn't say that. No one is beyond help, not even our little mischievous Basil. His heart is in the right place. It's his antics that get in the way sometimes."

"I'll try, Mila. You know I will, but my heart isn't in it."

"Of course you will. Basil wants to grow as much

as the both of us do. Basil will behave, and you'll be a good teacher." Mila took her sister's hand. "Tell me how you are going to keep Basil from making of mess of the job and help him see how serious it is."

The sisters chatted until they came up with a great plan. One that they ran by Celeste, talking to her on the new-fangled contraption she had given them. She loved all their ideas and told them Basil would be there soon. She had given him a strong talk and warning before she sent him on his way.

Privately Celeste had told Mila this was Basil's last chance to get it right or he be stripped of his powers and sent back to fairy boot camp, which would be humiliating for him. Mila promised to help Elida any way she could. But Celeste said this job was important for Elida as well as Basil. Mila knew Celeste was up to something. But what?

Out of the corner of her eye, Mila saw the little hooligan fly into view. His spiky red hair and freckles across his nose made him look every bit the part he played. The bright red shoes on his too large feet for his size didn't help his image either. Was it possible he wasn't as infuriating as he wanted people to think he was?

A thought raced through Mila's mind that she wanted to believe. It was possible he was acting out a part for others, while deep inside he wanted to be taken seriously. She had a lot to think about. He had a tough image to live up to—his grandfather was one of the legends written about in their manual. It must be tough for him. Basil could be protecting himself from the sense of failure. She needed to talk to Elida when he wasn't around.

"Hi, Basil." Mila waved at him while Elida frowned. "Welcome to Blue Cove. You've got a lot to prove on this job, and I would suggest you be on your best behavior. Elida isn't as patient as I would be," she said when he flew up behind Elida and tugged her hair.

"If I had my way, you'd be starting over in boot camp." Elida slapped his hand away from her hair. She doubled up her fist at her side. "Would you please be still?"

"So here I am. What do you have for me to do? I'm ready to give you girls the help you need." He flexed his tiny muscle as he twirled and floated above their heads.

"As I see it, you need our help more than we need yours. Listen up, Basil, you are here in the nick of time to plan. Celeste said she made it clear to you that you're on probation and this job is important for your future."

"Ah shucks. No one likes to have any fun or adventure." He forcefully blew out his small pouty lips as he plopped down beside them. "Lay it on me, sisters."

With that Elida gave him what for, while Mila shook her head. It would take more strength than she had to keep those two from fighting, but she would try. "Stop! Our mission is too serious for you two to be at each other's throats. Elida, you are aware of how grave this is. I think the two of you will find enough adventure keeping our humans safe."

"Did you say adventure?" His pointy ears perked up. "Sign me up right now." Basil snapped his fingers.

"You're already signed up." Elida poked her tiny finger in his chest. "Now sit down and listen." She began to tell him their assignment.

"Chasing bullets, keeping the human from getting hit, and dealing with bad guys sounds right up my alley. Wait until the others hear about this gig I got." Basil slapped Elida's tiny hand in a high five.

"Listen, you, this isn't a lark. This is serious. His life depends on it." She rubbed her stinging hand on her dress.

"I know you might not believe me, but I can do this." Basil frowned. "I'm really not a bad sort. I get bored easily and at times have too much energy, but I'm no one's dummy."

"We couldn't agree more. Celeste believes in you and so do we. Right, Elida." Mila pinched her sister's hand and mouthed the word *Behave*.

"Yes, I suppose we do." Elida pursed her lips.

"Then it's settled. I'll show you, my doubting friend, I can do whatever you say and not mess up." Basil tugged on Elida's hair once and did it again for good measure.

"We'll see. You can start by not pulling my hair." She huffed and flew off to follow Matt.

Mila wouldn't let him follow. "You would do well not to test her, Basil. My sister is good at what she does. She's like you in many ways but has learned to channel her energy in the right ways. You can learn from her. Let her have time to work through the idea of you being her partner. She'll see the rightness of Celeste's plan, but you have to do your part too." Mila spent the rest of the afternoon showing Basil the ins and outs of their mission and all about their friends Matt and Jessie.

Chapter 11

Matt drove away from her store with reassurance, but still had no idea why. Jessie didn't seem worried. He took his cue from her when it came to cases. Of course, that didn't mean that it couldn't all change at any minute, but he would enjoy the peace of the moment. Matt pulled into the station parking lot and saw Dylan getting out of his car. "How's it going?"

"Good. I had lunch with my wife. She's excited about her trip to the city with the ladies tomorrow." Dylan closed the car door after grabbing a file. "Kenny told me you should have your car back at the beginning of next week. I'm anxious to see how they repaired it. I don't know how the repairs were possible."

"I hear you. The car was messed up. Lots of body work was needed. If I would've had time I could have done it. I rebuilt Jessie's after it got shot up. My little brother Jason helped. He flirted with Katie and Jessie the whole time. Truth is, he'd flirt with anything in a skirt. A lot like your brother-in-law Liam used to be."

"I remember you two working on that car while you recovered from a gunshot wound. That, plus who can forget that honey of a truck you restored? You're good at restoration, and Jason will grow up some day, but he's not husband material yet." Dylan chuckled.

"It's up to us to keep our womenfolk safe from him." Matt laughed. "And others. I've seen how the guys look at Jessie when we're out together."

"You and me both." He clapped Matt on the back. "On a more serious note, have you heard anything else about the shooter?"

"Only what Jaxon shared with me this morning." Matt explained the earlier conversation he had with Jaxon Kincaid as they walked into the station. "I'm hopeful we'll have some answers soon."

"I'm with you there," Dylan said, following Matt down the hall to his office.

Matt worked on the shift schedules and assignments for the next week. Every time he went through the roster, he was reminded again of what a great group of people he worked with. They were a big part of his life, and he couldn't be prouder to serve with each of them.

His promotion hadn't been easy for anyone at first, seeing he was the one who had to shoot Chief Anderson. Anderson was his mentor and had strayed to the wrong side of the law, but everyone in the department had loved him. It would have been hard for Matt to shoot him too, had he not seen the chief ready to kill Jessie. That one moment changed everything, and he took aim and fired. The whole sordid event seemed like years ago, but it was only a little over a year. And now here he was chief of police, doing time rosters and assignments on a Friday afternoon. Who would have believed it possible? Not him for sure.

He was grateful that the department lined up behind him with their full support when the town council made him the new chief. If there was resentment, he never knew about it. A guy couldn't ask for more than that. He needed to get the rosters done for when he was on his honeymoon too. Keeping the location a surprise from Jessie hadn't been easy, but he had managed so far. He was more than ready to get away with the love of his life. All he had to do was make it through the wedding alive.

****

Jessie closed the store and rushed home to get ready for dinner with Matt. She'd be lying if she said she wasn't excited about her trip to the city. She couldn't wait to see what Grams and Reba thought when they saw her in the dress. She remembered how she lit up when she had tried the gorgeous dress on. Before that she had tried on several gowns, but this one was perfect. It was like someone had designed the dress with her in mind. Too bad you only wear the dress one time. It seemed such a waste. She ran the brush through her hair and applied her favorite lip gloss. She smiled at her image in the mirror. "I hope Matt knows what he's getting into. I come with a lot of girl stuff and strange baggage."

Her guy, a bachelor for a few years and one of three boys, had no idea about all the paraphernalia that came along with a girl invading his domain. "I wonder how you'll handle my invasion, Mr. Parker." She went to answer the door when he knocked. She might miss this most of all. The anticipation of him waiting on the other side of the door. His eyes always told her what he was thinking. She found that moment quite romantic.

"Hey, you." He pulled her into his arms and kissed her. He gently pushed her hair off her face and framed her face with his hands. "How's my favorite girl?"

"Oh, please." She glanced up at him. "At this point, I'd better be your only girl." She smiled at him. She slipped her arms into the jacket he held for her.

He grinned and took hold of her hand. "There's no one but you, sweetheart, except for maybe my mother. At least, she would like to think she is."

"I can live with that. After all, a son who is good to his mama can't be all bad." She strolled out the door he held open.

"No shop talk tonight." He rested his hand on her back when he caught up to her after locking the door. "I want to hear all things wedding tonight from you."

"Sounds good, but I warn you, you might get bored. Do you really care about the ribbon color on the small bags with rose petals in them? Those are the crucial details that Katie has informed me are of the utmost importance when it comes to wedding details." She laughed. "I can see your eyes glazing over, and we haven't even begun. Maybe the details of the honeymoon would be more to your liking."

"No, you don't. Mum's the word for me. I want my plans to be a surprise. Don't worry, I'll find a safe topic of conversation."

"I can count on you." Jessie latched her seatbelt. "Where are we headed?"

"Some place quiet where we can talk."

Jessie loved the place he chose but as soon as she was seated, she wanted to stand up and run. They were seated by a window with a beautiful view of the ocean, but something wasn't kosher. The prickles began at her neck and scurried down her back in waves of chills. *What is going on?* Her mind raced through possible scenarios. She searched the restaurant and didn't see anyone who seemed out of place. She twisted several curls around her fingers.

"What's up, Jess? You only twist your hair when you're bothered." He pulled her hand toward him and placed his on top of hers. "Something I haven't seen you do for a while."

"Something is wrong, Matt." She took a deep breath. "It doesn't make sense. I can't see anything, but I can sense it."

"What do you want to do?" Matt asked her.

"I'm not sure. I think we should leave." She placed the menu on the table.

"Let's go." He stood and moved to where she stood. The familiar sound shattered the quiet atmosphere of the dining room, sending people screaming and running in all directions. "Damn, sweetheart, how did you know? And how did he miss me?"

"If you hadn't moved toward me at that exact moment, I hate to think what would have happened." She shuddered.

They stayed low and crawled toward the front of the restaurant. Matt showed his badge and took his gun from the holster. "Keep her safe," he told the host, who was on the phone talking.

He nodded. "Police are on their way. Be careful."

****

Matt waited for backup to arrive and went out to meet them. He showed them his badge and explained where he thought the shooter might be. They searched the grounds, but no suspect was found. Matt's frustration level rose when each officer returned saying they found no one. Damn, he couldn't even have a meal out with his girlfriend without having to worry. How he had escaped being shot was a mystery to consider, but not at the moment. He went back inside with two of the officers. He answered a few more questions and showed them where they were sitting.

"Man, you were lucky," the officer told him, shaking his head.

"Don't I know it." Matt handed him his card, answered a few more of his questions, and went to find Jessie.

"Are you okay?" Jessie asked when he placed his arm on her shoulder. "Did they find anyone?"

"No, which makes me wonder." Matt frowned and pulled out his phone.

"Hey, Jaxon, did your man lose track of the suspect?" Matt told him what had happened.

"I don't think so. At least, no one informed me. I'll make some calls and get back to you. I don't see how he could slip out with the guys watching all points of entry to the house, but anything is possible."

"I'm wondering if you even have the right guy. Has anyone questioned him? Maybe it's time to have a chat with him," Matt told him.

"I'll check with Tom Maxwell and pay the guy a visit myself. As soon as I know, I'll get back to you. Stay safe."

"Stay safe, ha. That's laughable. How am I supposed to do that?" he muttered under his breath.

"Did you say something?" Jessie brushed some dirt off his sleeve.

"Nothing important." Matt reached for her hand to hold.

"Matt, do you see what I mean about someone looking out for you?" She tightened her hand around his. "That bullet could have taken either of us out, but something slowed the trajectory or changed it at the last moment."

"What kind of something are you talking about?" Matt glanced at her.

"I would say more like who helped, but I might be guessing at the moment. Still, you've had three close encounters. Even you have to admit it is more than luck." Jessie walked through the door he held open.

"Let's go to my place. I'll order takeout." He unlocked the car. "I know it's more than luck, but I'm not ready to define what yet," he told her as she slipped into the passenger seat. "I do thank whatever has been working to keep me alive. I'm willing to go that far. What I want to know is who is shooting at me and why." He called in an order for pizza before he started the car.

"I'm sorry our night was ruined, but I'm glad we can share the rest of it together." She smiled. "Alive and in one piece is good any day. Besides, pizza sounds good."

"Jess, I want you to understand, I don't discount what you tell me. I'm simply not ready to acknowledge the reality or see what you see myself. When you say you believe someone is helping to keep me safe, I find assurance in your words because I trust you. I will support you and defend your ability. But I'm not in any way like you in this area, and I don't want to be."

Jessie glanced at him. "Patrick, Johanna's husband, didn't have the gift she had. He simply loved and supported her. They were a good team, like we are. His love and trust freed her to be who she was meant to be. I don't want you to be anyone but who you are, and your love and support lets me be me. To me that's a winning combination."

"With that out of the way, I confess I have seen a few things I don't understand. When Anderson was about to kill you, I saw a spirit floating around you before I shot him. That was a shock to me. I've also had a couple of dreams. Their meanings are still elusive to me. I'm good with not seeing anything else. I want to be honest with you."

"I'm fine with you the way you are."

"Good to know because what you see is what you get. I'm a simple man."

Jessie laughed. "There's nothing simple about you, my hunky cop."

"I'm hungry." Matt pulled into his driveway. "Pizza should be here soon." He opened the car door for her. He placed his hand on her back. "I like the idea of you living here soon."

Chapter 12

Elida and Basil flew out of the car when Matt opened the door. Elida landed on Jessie's shoulder. Another mission success, but she didn't have time to get satisfied. This guy meant business, and she needed to stay alert. "Come on, Basil. We go where he goes."

"Wow, that was amazing." Basil couldn't stop flying back and forth in front of Elida. "Did you see how I rode that slug until right before it hit the glass. I moved it off its target. I saved him." Up he flew and back down again, buzzing around her head.

"Would you please be still? You're making me dizzy." She swatted at him as he passed by doing a backstroke. "Are you ever serious?" Elida asked him.

"Do you ever have any fun at all? I thought that was a jolly good adventure. The best one I've had in years. Will there be more?" he asked.

"We hope not but must be prepared in case there are. Our job is to keep him safe." Elida frowned. No wonder Mila got exasperated with her. She could see her actions in his. "Yikes," she muttered under her breath.

"And we will. I know I shouldn't, but I kind of hope we do." He brushed past her doing a breaststroke.

"Basil, take this seriously, please, and be still. We don't want to draw attention to ourselves yet." Elida turned her face away to hide her smile.

She could relate to his youthful enthusiasm. The thrill of the chase, sometimes riding a bullet and tilting it at the end, sending the round off its mark was downright exhilarating. Outrunning the shot just because you could. She still had the magical ability after all these years. Not that she was older than Basil because they were the same age. He seemed younger because he didn't take the job seriously. Of course, Mila didn't get nearly as excited as she did, but the exhilaration seemed to delight Basil.

Maybe Celeste was smarter than she was given credit. Although Mila thought the sun rose and set in her, Elida had never gone that far in her admiration for their leader. She might need to rethink her position. Basil was turning out to be a pleasant surprise. She wouldn't tell her sister yet until she was sure. Mila would do that whole I told you so routine and get all smug. For now, she would remain mum about Basil. His spiky red hair and freckles were kind of endearing in some odd way.

"Elida, I think you're pretty awesome for a girl." He giggled and tugged her long hair. "Any girl fairy who can chase a bullet down is all right in my book."

Elida shook her head. Endearing wasn't the word she would use for him at the moment. What a pest. This wasn't going to be easy. She blew out a deep gasp and followed Matt and Jessie into the house, ready to defend them if needed. Basil followed and never left her side. The entire evening, he kept watching her. When Mila showed up, she laughed until Elida wanted to hit her. Basil's worshipful glances nauseated her.

****

Another strange night for the record books. Jessie

stretched out in her bed and shut off the light. Matt had been quiet and preoccupied. She couldn't blame him. Three near misses were enough to shake even the strongest man. She had an idea why, and even who, but not what human form this one had taken.

She appreciated Matt's honesty. His support meant everything. Along with his kisses, what more could a girl ask for? He was a gem. Jessie heard her phone buzz.

"Hey, cous, are you awake?" Peyton asked.

"I just got into bed. It will take me a while to get to sleep." Jessie chuckled. "I have too much on my mind."

"Jaxon told me what happened tonight. How are you doing?" Peyton asked.

"You mean other than our dates beginning or ending with one of us being shot at? I'm okay, but we're both tired of it."

"I can imagine. Jaxon said the guy they thought was the suspect wasn't involved at all. He said Matt wasn't surprised, but he wasn't happy about it."

"I bet. He mentioned Jaxon was going to question the guy. Matt must have suspected something. Tonight proved the perpetrator was still out there." Jessie adjusted the pillow behind her back when she sat up. "Three extremely close calls that missed their mark have me wondering if we might have a little help from some unseen friends. At least, I hope we do. Otherwise, how many close encounters can someone have before their luck runs out?"

"I'm sure I wouldn't want to test the idea of close encounters with great outcomes too often. I want to believe we have extra help in this case though. Maybe that's another reason our grumpy ghost is still standing guard at the store."

"Could be. With us, stranger things have happened." Jessie curled her legs up.

"Are you ready for your dress fitting tomorrow?" Peyton asked.

"I am. I fell in love with the dress the first time I tried it on, but sometimes it's hard to remember what it looks like. I need the refresher tomorrow." Jessie laughed. "I'll see you bright and early."

"Sounds good. At least, I remember your dress, and it's perfect. The lace is exquisite, and so is the princess scalloped neckline."

"I always said I didn't want a strapless dress because I didn't want to fuss with pulling the top up all the time, and the mermaid style wasn't for me. I love the A-line and mild flare of the dress. No tiny spaghetti straps either. I can't wait for Grams to see it."

"Besides, the back is as gorgeous as the front. I think Grams will like the simple elegance of the headpiece you chose. I can't wait to see the whole look together tomorrow. You'll make a beautiful bride, cousin," Peyton told her.

"And so will you when your time comes." Jessie could visualize Peyton, who would make a stunning bride.

"I'm in no hurry. For now, I'm happy to wear the bridesmaid dress in a perfect shade of soft dolphin green. I love everything about the dress from its sheath style to its square neckline."

"It's fun to talk about this with you. Matt doesn't care about the details."

"I don't think any guy does. They have other particulars on their mind." Peyton laughed. "See you tomorrow."

Jessie wanted to talk to Matt and get the skinny on what Jaxon told him. Was it too late to call? Jessie glanced at the clock and sent him a text. She was ready to give up fifteen minutes later. She could talk to him in the morning on her way to the city. Placing her phone in silent mode, she snuggled beneath her covers. The vibrating sound against the nightstand put her plan to sleep on hold. She pushed up into a semi-sitting position and grabbed her phone, checking the caller ID.

"Hey, Matt. I had given up hearing from you until tomorrow." Jessie pushed her hair out of her face.

"Sorry, I just saw your text. I wanted to call and tell you to have a great time tomorrow, anyway. Jaxon kept me on the phone longer than usual."

"Peyton told me the man they had under surveillance checked out and wasn't involved. Now what?" Jessie asked.

"That's what we were talking about. The guy had reported his gun and car stolen earlier in the day. So that's why his fingerprints were everywhere. Stands to reason that the suspect wouldn't be that careless. All my guys couldn't find any sign of him in the park. Jaxon is going to help with Maxwell's approval. We're thinking we could try to set a trap. I'm the bait, of course. Whoever it is out there hunting me seems hellbent on killing me."

"Not if I can help it." Jessie frowned. "If I didn't have an appointment tomorrow, I wouldn't go."

"Yes, you need to go. I prefer not to have to worry about keeping us both safe at the same time."

"Don't take any chances. Although I think you'll be okay, I don't want to bet any money on it."

"I'm not going to risk my safety, but I'm not willing to go down without a fight either. Especially with the wedding this close. I only wish I knew who the enemy is."

"Promise you'll check in with me tomorrow and let me know you're okay. I'll be concerned until I hear from you."

"I don't have to work tomorrow, and I plan on staying close to home. I should be okay. I'll text you throughout the day. But hey, don't worry. Jaxon is going to hang with me and plot. We're going to work on something special for the house. And before you ask, no, I won't tell you what. Have a great tomorrow with the ladies," he said. "I love you, Jess. Get some sleep."

"I love you too."

"My magical friends, if you can hear me, please keep him safe for me, and while you're at it, keep me safe for him too. This is bigger than both of us, and it may take him time to understand. I know he'll get it eventually, and I will too," she whispered into the dark room.

"Yes, you will," came the quiet reply from the corner.

Chapter 13

Jessie shoved her phone into her purse on the way out the door, which seemed to be a common practice for her. "Good morning, cous, and thanks for holding the door." Jessie had already set the alarm and double-checked to make sure the door was locked. She couldn't be too careful at the moment.

"Grams and Reba are in the car and Katie is raring to go. She has already stopped for coffee and treats from Joe's. New York City, here we come." Peyton laughed.

"I hope she stops once in a while at a rest stop. Once my friend sets her mind on getting somewhere fast, there is no stopping her." Jessie smiled as they walked the path to the waiting car.

"Do you want the front or back seat?" Peyton asked.

"I want to sit in the back. It will be up to you, Peyton, to keep Katie occupied." Jessie opened the back door and got in the car. She latched her seat belt. "Good morning," she said as she reached for the coffee Peyton had in her hand. "Katie, thanks for getting this."

"Of course, but I have no idea why you even bother to drink the stuff. It's mostly milk." Katie giggled.

"Aww, but it's my drink of choice, and you know exactly how I like to drink it, my friend."

"This is going to be such a fun day. I've been

looking forward to hanging out with you gals all week. Dylan laughed at me every time I mentioned our trip to the city. Guys don't understand our need for socializing with our friends. He did, however, give me some money to spend on myself and tell me to have a good time." Katie glanced in the rearview mirror at Jessie.

"Sounds to me like you've got a good man," Reba told her. "Lawrence is thoughtful like that."

"Are you excited, dear?" Grams patted her hand. "I know I am. Reba and I can't wait to see your dress." Sadie took a bite of the scone Peyton gave her, brushing the crumbs into her napkin.

"You'll love the dress, Grams." Peyton handed everyone an extra napkin. "I can't wait for you to see Jessie in it."

"I'm sure she'll be a beautiful bride." Sadie swiped at the tears filling her eyes. "I'm happy to be here to see her big day. You girls mean everything to me."

"We love you too," Jessie told her as she patted Sadie's hand.

Once they were settled, Katie drove past the inn and waved at Dylan getting into his car. She turned onto the road that led to the highway out of town. Happy chatter filled the car, and no one seemed to notice the tiny hands that occasionally grabbed a few of the extra yummy crumbs from the napkins in the back seat.

****

Mila watched the ladies with a smile on her face. The scene reminded her of the good times among her special friends at home when they got together in the common area after being away on assignments.

She wondered how Elida was faring with Basil. If

Elida was honest, Mila thought to herself, she liked Basil more than her sister was willing to acknowledge. Opening your heart to another fairy was risky. How well she knew. Her guy had gone rogue and turned to the dark side. Basil could go either way. Maybe Elida could help him. But as Mila knew all too well, not even love was enough to keep Aelfric on the straight and narrow. For a while, she was angry at him, but equally she mourned his loss. The lesson had been hard to for her to accept. Celeste with her wisdom had guided her through the pain until she understood she couldn't help everyone, nor make humans believe even when they saw the magic for themselves. All she could ever do was her best. Thankfully, this car was filled with believers except for Katie, which made her dance for joy, flying around them, settling a sprinkling of golden sparkles all around the women. She hoped to remedy Katie's doubt a smidge soon.

She placed another yummy morsel in her mouth. Mila brushed the crumbs from her lap. This mission was an important one. Keeping these precious humans safe was of utmost importance. She needed to be alert to any challenges against her charge. New York City awaited their arrival, and she couldn't wait to see how the city had changed, but she was also aware of the possible danger that might hide there.

To this point, the violence had been toward Matt, but that might not mean that Jessie was safe. Her little pointed ears perked up, and she began to listen in on their conversation.

****

"Hey, are you ready to get to work?" Matt asked when Jaxon pulled into his driveway.

"Sure am. I also have some information for you. What do you want to do first, talk or work?" Jaxon followed Matt into the garage.

"How about we talk and work?" Matt laughed. "I want to get this done. It's not often I get to surprise Jessie."

"Sounds good to me. What do you want me to do?" Jaxon took off his jacket and rolled up his shirt sleeves.

"All these trim pieces need to be painted, and the ones over there need the finish brushed on them." Matt pointed at the table.

"Why ivory? Everything you usually do is stained wood." Jaxon reached for the paint brush.

"Ecru, according to Peyton." He chuckled. "She is serious when it comes to design, and I wanted to fix up a nice office space for Jessie, and with all the wood in the house I wanted to soften the space for her."

"Sounds reasonable. I take it this is a desk for her." Jaxon filled his brush with paint, careful to remove all the drips.

"Yes. I picked up a great desk chair that matches the color of her eyes. I created a nice reading nook in the space, too, complete with a wingback chair and ottoman. I took my cue from some of the new pieces that Peyton put together in her cottage after the shooting. Jessie seemed to really like the new look. And I had Peyton approve my ideas."

"She has a good eye for interior design. She has helped at my place. I want to have an open house soon. With the great built-ins that you made and her furnishings, it's coming together nicely."

"With our small talk out of the way, tell me what's going on." Matt leaned his hip against the worktable.

"Do you remember a case you worked on with the FBI that put one William Barber in prison?"

"How could I forget? He had stolen weapons from his Army base and had great plans on how to use them. I worked the case with Hathaway, Corey, and Sanders." Matt put on his safety glasses.

"Barber was paroled a couple of months ago but never showed up for any of his meetings with the parole officer. He came on our radar a few days ago after Sanders was shot and is fighting for his life in the hospital." Jaxon dipped his brush in the paint can.

"Damn. Sanders is a good man. He has a couple of kids, doesn't he?" Matt asked.

"Yes, and he was shot while playing basketball with his son at their house."

"What does that have to do with me? Sanders was the lead on the case." Matt pulled off his safety glasses.

"The thing is, we interviewed some of the people Barber hung with in prison, and they said he was blaming all of you for the loss of his family. While he was serving time, his wife divorced him and took the kids. He figured he might ruin your lives for destroying his."

"The hell you say. He was the one who stole the weapons. He has no one to blame but himself." Matt slammed his hand on the table.

"We know that, but he doesn't want to acknowledge his wrong in the situation. Here's the other problem. Corey was recently shot at too. He's okay, with only damaged windows in the house, but his kid was near him watching the TV when it happened. Maxwell is betting there could be a connection to your shooting." Jaxon balanced the brush on the rim of the can to let the excess paint drip off. "Here's a recent picture of him. We have no idea if he's working with anyone or alone."

"I'll make sure the guys see this. He hasn't changed much." Matt shook his head.

"There's a bench warrant for his arrest if and when we find him." Jaxon painted another piece of the trim on the table.

"It almost seems too convenient if you ask me." Matt frowned. "Still, it's a damn shame about Sanders."

"Well, for now he is our only lead," Jaxon said.

"I guess that's better than nothing." Matt turned on his electric sander and got to work smoothing out the desk piece in front of him.

Matt's work in the FBI had led him into some tough situations. That was one of the reasons he had quit and moved back to Blue Cove. His job on the force had been a piece of cake until Jessie and the past year. At least with her, they were able to stay one step ahead of the madness.

But Sanders and Corey were good family men. They didn't deserve it, and neither did their families. He didn't want to have to worry about his job coming back to hurt those whom he loved later on. Matt shook his head. He had to stop his wayward mind, but he hoped Hathaway would come through unscathed.

"You want to grab some lunch?" Matt asked. "We can finish these after we eat."

"Sounds good. You've got a lot done." Jaxon placed his brush in the cleaning solution with another one. "You've been miles away."

"Working with my hands is the best therapy I know." Matt closed the garage door down and went into the house followed by Jaxon.

Chapter 14

Jessie stood with her back to the mirror as the attendant slipped the silky material over her head and began to fasten the tiny buttons on the dress. "Can I turn around yet?" Jessie asked.

"In a few minutes. I'm almost done. I want you to get the full effect. I have one more thing to do. No peeking now." She began tugging and twisting Jessie's hair. "Okay, sweetie, turn around."

Peyton and Katie stood beside her as she took in her appearance. "I loved the dress when I tried it on, but I didn't realize at the time how perfect it was." Jessie smiled as she slipped her hands over the lace that covered the silk. The scooped-neck fitted bodice looked phenomenal from the front and back. She turned to the side to view the flare of the dress and the court train in the back. She hadn't wanted a dress too frilly or extreme, yet she wanted elegant. Mission accomplished. She stole another glance in the mirror.

"Jess, you look beautiful. I couldn't imagine any other dress on you. Wait until Reba and Sadie see you." Katie got teary eyed. "I love your hair like that."

"I agree. No veil is the right choice. You're gorgeous, cousin." Peyton took her hand. "I'm going out to prepare them for your reveal. Madison should be here soon if she isn't already." Peyton opened the dressing room door. "I'll come and get you when they are ready."

Jessie waited for Peyton and followed her out when she came for her. She stood on the small platform and turned in time to see the expressions sweep across Sadie's and Reba's faces. Their tears made her cry.

"My dear girl, you're beautiful. That dress was made for you." Reba dabbed at her eyes.

"I have no words." Grams reached for the tissue that Reba handed her. "I'm glad I lived to see this day." She wiped her eyes.

"Grams, it wouldn't be the same without you. I'm glad you are here to share this special moment with me. As soon as I get out of this dress, it's your turn to find yours. This time it's my gift to you." Jessie patted her grandmother's hand. "I won't take no for an answer." Jessie turned to the saleslady. "Maybe you can pick out a few dresses for her to try on in the same soft green palette as my wedding colors.

"I'd be happy to help." The shop clerk smiled. "Jenny, put her in dressing room two. I'll bring in several dresses for her to try on."

"Jessie, dear, before you take off the dress, my sister wanted to see you, and she just walked in the door." Reba held onto her hand. "Babs, doesn't she look stunning?"

"Oh my, yes, she does." She stood near her sister and leaned close to Jessie. "I've been thinking about you. I know you are one of a long line of amazing women and you have a special purpose for this time. Don't ever lose sight of who you are."

"I'll try not to." Jessie turned to follow the lady to remove her dress.

"I won't let her," the tiny voice spoke unheard by

all present. "She will be reminded many times in her life."

"Before I forget, Peyton. Sally wants us to pick up her dress too," Jessie called over her shoulder before she went in the room and closed the door.

They spent of the rest of the time finding a dress for Sadie. They finally settled on a pretty soft agave-green dress that made her eyes appear bluer than normal. If only the guy who danced with her in the pub in Dublin could see her now. Jessie smiled and hugged her grandmother's shoulders.

"I was thinking if your friend in Dublin could see you now he'd be on the next plane to dance with you at my wedding." Jessie smiled at her.

"I might need to confess to you girls. I've been keeping a secret from you. That night he asked for my email, and I gave it to him. We have been writing ever since. I don't expect anything to come of it, but it's nice to chat with him once in a while. He made me feel special."

"Can you let us in on his name?" Peyton asked.

"Grams, you're a stinker. If it makes a difference, I think it's great. And yes, please tell us his name." Jessie hugged her grandmother.

"His name is Ronan Fitzpatrick. The name has a nice ring to it doesn't it?"

"Yes," both girls answered at the same time.

"Is anyone ready for lunch?" Katie asked once their purchases were made. "I made reservations at a tearoom."

"It sounds lovely to me, dear girl." Reba reached for a couple of the bags to carry to the car.

With their dresses zipped into the protective bags

and safely tucked into the trunk of the car, they went to lunch. Babs and Madison joined the group. Jessie glanced around the table at her family, new friends, and of course, her best friend and sighed with the contentment washing over her. She couldn't have asked for a better day. Her text from Matt telling her his day with Jaxon was a good one and he was safe, along with a few more personal and loving words, made this special moment perfect.

"I thought we would take in the art museum while we are in the city. There's a special Renaissance exhibit that I thought might be nice to see. Does that sound good to everyone before we head home?" Katie asked.

"It sounds perfect to me. I want to stop by and see Neil Dempsey, my old boss, and I will meet you all at the museum." Jessie slipped in the back seat. "You know where to let me off at, and the museum is a quick two block walk from there. I want to make sure he got his invitation to the wedding and extend a personal invite. He's always been so good to me."

"You got it." Katie stopped in front of the office building to let her out. "See you in a few. Don't be too long. I want to leave the city before it gets too congested."

"Okay." Jessie shut the car door and went through the revolving door into the office building. She stopped at the front desk to tell them she was there to see Neal Dempsey. She rode the elevator up to the fifth floor and stepped out. How many times had she performed the same actions when she lived here? There were some things she didn't miss. An elevator full of people for one. She smiled as she waited to see her old boss.

Jessie enjoyed the few minutes she spent catching

up with Neil. She even stopped by the old precinct where she often went for information. Neil and several of the officers she knew told her they would see her at the wedding. As she walked the long block to the museum, she was captured by the sights and sounds of the city. The constant noise of horns, sirens, and the crush of people jostling for space on the crowded sidewalks reminded her of all the reasons she used to love living in the city, which she didn't miss anymore. Blue Cove was home, but truth be told, she did miss all the museums and great restaurants. There were times when New York was the best place to be. Especially the theater and Broadway shows. She pushed her hair over her shoulder and enjoyed the moment.

In no time at all, she opened the doors into the museum and spotted Grams looking at a beautiful painting on the first floor. She gave her a brief hug and moved on to where another painting was displayed nearby. The artist had captured the seascape and cliffs beautifully, reminiscent of the cliffs of Moher in Ireland. Her eye was drawn to the water droplets that seemed to shimmer in the light. They were almost mystical. A metaphor for her life perhaps.

As she stood there concentrating on the painting in front of her, she had an almost spiritual experience. The clouds and the water in the painting took on a life of their own. On the sun rays shining through the clouds there seemed to be winged beautiful creatures ascending and descending the streams of light. Had the artist captured one of the thin places she had learned about through her ancestors? One of those special places where the veil between heaven and earth thinned and the viewer could see the invisible world.

What happened next took her by surprise. She found herself in the painting, standing on the cliffs as droplets of water tickled her face like effervescent bubbles. With her hands raised toward the sky, she danced over grassy cliffs with abandonment. All the excitement she should feel about her wedding took root, surfaced in her heart, and spilled over until she could no longer contain herself. Had she found one of the thin places where heaven and earth almost touch? She had no idea. All she knew was in that moment she was alight with a joy she hadn't felt in a long time. An unseen presence rested on her shoulder and smiled at her joy.

****

Mila sensed trouble headed their way. She heard the men whisper, and her eyes searched for their location. They were talking in front of the museum, and Mila knew the moment the man entered through the glass doors determined to do what he was paid to do. Concern vibrated through her tiny body, and she jumped into action.

She twirled her wand and slowed the man's forward motion while she set about to gather Jessie's friends to the area. Tapping Peyton and Katie, she caused them to observe what was about to happen. Mila wanted Jessie's friends to save her. It wasn't time for her yet. Removing the magical spell off him, she saw him rush forward, grab Jessie roughly by the arm, and pull her toward the door.

"You're coming with me," he snarled at her.

"Hey, you, take your hands off her." Katie and Peyton rushed toward the man who had pulled out a knife.

"Stay away or I'll slit her throat," he yelled.

Mila shook her head. The knife changed everything. She sent it flying from his hand before he knew what hit him. "Now, big boy, take what's headed your way without a weapon."

"Let go of me!" Jessie yelled as she came down from the high she had experienced.

"Let's go."

She kicked the man in the shin about the same time Katie smacked him on the head with the heavy purse that Sadie handed her. Peyton punched him with the heel of her hand across the bridge of his nose, which started to bleed profusely.

Between the well-placed kick and the bonk on his head, the man fell to the ground cursing. "Serves you right," Katie told him. "Sadie, what do you have in this purse? I came close to knocking this scumbag out."

"My mom always taught me to carry a heavy jar of cold cream in my purse for just this purpose." Sadie frowned at the man on the ground. "In this case, I'm glad that I listened. You stay right there, buster. That's my granddaughter you had your hands on." Sadie pointed at the man when he snarled at her.

People in the area erupted with cheers as two men rushed to help. "Stay put. You're not going anywhere." One of the men held the guy's legs, pinning him down.

Mila smiled. "Crisis averted," she whispered as she flew around the man's head.

****

"I'll take care of him for you, ladies." The security guard rushed toward the sound of the commotion. "The police are on their way, but you all need to answer some questions. Follow me, please," he told them after he cuffed the man. He led them back into the security area of the museum.

"For a minute there, cousin, I thought he would take you without you putting up a fight at all." Peyton leaned closer. "Where were you?"

"Lost in this painting." Jessie pointed to the beautiful painting as they followed the security guard. "Literally." Jessie told Peyton about what had happened to her. "Cousin, it was amazing. In that moment I was the happiest I've felt in a long time. The thought of marrying Matt made me dance with joy."

"Not to take that away from you, but maybe you should be concerned that someone tried to abduct you. I, for one, want to hear what the man has to say for himself."

"Jessie, you do attract all the kooks everywhere you go. I heard the guy tell the guard some guy paid him a hundred dollars to get you outside to their waiting van. What a crock. There's no van there," Katie said as they caught up to where she stood.

"It's possible the van drove away," Peyton reminded her.

"True, but I didn't see one, and you can't believe anything that guy says." Katie frowned. "Jessie, you really need to be more careful. Sometimes I think you're oblivious to your surroundings."

Jessie clenched her mouth to keep it shut. "I'm sure you mean well, Katie. I'll keep that in mind. But I'm not going to let that guy ruin my day." Jessie walked away from Katie and sat beside Sadie in the security area. In her heart, she knew there probably was a van and she needed to be more aware of her surroundings. She had been walking the streets of the city by herself for heaven's sake. She should be wiser than that. *Who thought that I would be dancing for joy in my heart right at the moment someone tried to take me?* Another item to add to the long list of crazy.

****

Jaxon shut off the belt sander to read the text from Peyton. "Matt, Peyton texted me that a man tried to abduct Jessie at the museum. She said they're sitting in security answering police questions and may be late getting home."

"Oh, hell. I should've have known I wouldn't be the only one that might have trouble." Matt lifted his roller from the pan to finish the place where he had stopped painting. "I'll be happy if we both make it to our wedding alive. How can you deal with an enemy you know nothing about?"

"I've asked myself that same question a few times over the past year. Somehow the suspect was always caught, and we both made it through alive, as you often told me we would. Now I'm going to say the same thing to you. Hang in there and do what you always do with a case. You'll solve this and be on your honeymoon before you know it, you lucky dog."

"Put me on the record—that day can't come soon enough for me." Matt continued to roll the paint on the wall. He wanted to get as much done as he could today. This would be Jessie's space when she moved in after they were married. His wife, what a mind-blowing thought.

Chapter 15

The car was much quieter than it had been in the morning when they started their trip to the city. Tired from answering questions, all Jessie wanted to do was get home and forget the museum experience altogether. After listening to Katie complain for the past hour about traffic, she was happy to be out of the city. Thankfully, Peyton started Katie on another subject and the two of them were chatting and laughing in the front seat.

"While your friend is occupied, I want to talk to you." Reba grabbed Jessie's hand.

"We were talking while the police questioned you." Sadie held her other hand.

"And what have you determined?" Jessie glanced back and forth at them.

"The guy that was arrested is only one of how many others who would willingly be paid to do the dirty work? We have no idea why, but we do know you are a threat to someone's plans, you are better with Matt, and you're stronger than you think," Reba reminded her.

"Remember the note you got with the pendant you wear around your neck. Which reminds me, you can't wear it around your neck on your wedding, but we've come up with a way for you to still have it on you." Sadie pulled a small box out of her purse. "Reba's sister had this beautiful necklace made for you to wear on your wedding day." Sadie handed Jessie the box. "Open it, dear. It's from the three of us."

When Jessie opened the box, her face registered her surprise. Against an emerald-green satin background nestled a small silver replica of her necklace encrusted with small diamond chips. "Oh, Grams, this is beautiful. I don't know what to say."

"The look on your face is enough, my dear," Sadie said, and Reba nodded. "Plus, Peyton had them sew a small pocket on the inside of your dress that zips. You can place your pendant from Johanna in there." Sadie squeezed her hand.

"You need to have your reminder on you at all times." Reba frowned. "You never know when you will be challenged and might need to be prepared."

"You mean like today?" Jessie shook her head. "I didn't see that coming."

"No, but with a little help, others did. It worked out the way it was supposed to." Reba smiled at her.

"What are you ladies talking about back there?" Katie asked.

"I gave Jessie the gift that Reba's sister had made for her to wear on her wedding day. At this moment, all talk is about the wedding, as it should be."

While Reba and Sadie talked back and forth around her, she blanked out their conversation. She knew Matt would be waiting for her version of what happened and have more questions for her to answer. It was the last thing she wanted to talk about. She'd much rather relive the amazing experience she had while viewing the painting. The artist had captured the Irish concept of the thin place—a place or moment in time where the space and veil between the ordinary, tangible, and physical world and the spiritual, mystical world becomes thin and one can experience or see what's waiting behind the veil of reality. She had such a powerful encounter that it was hard to feel anything but the sheer joy of the moment.

Reba was right; she'd had help, and she was thankful. Jessie leaned her head against the seat and closed her eyes. She didn't want to overthink everything but knowing herself she probably would. In her heart, she knew who didn't want their marriage to happen. She even knew why. But how many people he would use to put a stop to the wedding was where things got sketchy. She had no idea how many might line up for the job, especially if money was offered.

"It's quiet back there." Peyton turned to look at them. "Are you okay, cousin?"

"Thinking of Matt," she said. Which she reasoned was a partial truth. She had been trying to figure out what to say to him. All the while she could feel her phone vibrate in her pocket with incoming texts which were all probably from her hunky guy.

"He must be thinking about you too." Peyton chuckled. "Jaxon texted me and told me to tell you to please answer Matt. He says Matt is a bit anxious, and that's putting it mildly."

Jessie reached into her purse for her phone. One by one she read his frantic texts to her. She let him know she was fine and would call him as soon as she got home.

—*What took you so long to respond?*—

—*My phone was out of sight, and I was talking to the ladies.*—

—More like you're avoiding me. But I love you anyway.— He added a smile emoji and promised to call her if she didn't call him.

"Is he worried about you, dear?" Reba asked.

"Yes. He always seems to be." Jessie shrugged.

"You've got a keeper in that man." Sadie pulled a letter out of her purse. "I want you to read this when you're alone at a time of your own choosing. Your grandpa Max wrote each of you girls a letter to give you on your wedding day. Of course, he had hoped to give it to you himself, but such is life. I wanted you to have it early, so you could savor the message. This is a joyous occasion, and I want you to experience all the wonder of the excitement, passion, and magic you feel at this time. Young love is a unique and wondrous time in your life."

"Do you know what he wrote?" Jessie asked.

"No. I never asked him, and he never let me read the letter. But if he took the time to write it, I'm sure you will find the message worth reading. Your grandpa was a man of few words, but when it came to you girls, his heart was full. He couldn't have been prouder of each of you. He was able to see you often because your parents let him. It broke his heart that he didn't get to see Peyton and Madison more. He had words with his son more than once about what he was doing to his girls. We didn't even know the half of it then."

"At least my dad is changing, and so is Peyton's. Gramps would be proud of the fact they're trying, at least." Jessie squeezed her grandmother's hand. "I will not only read this, but I will treasure this gift from him." She placed the sealed envelope in her purse.

All in all, this had been a good day except for the

one blip at the museum. Matt wouldn't see it as a small bump in an otherwise perfect day, nor would she normally, but there was something magical about her experiences in the city, and the only way she could describe the incident at the museum was as a small distraction. The rest of the day had been perfect.

Jessie walked the path to her cottage with Peyton by her side. Filled with a sense of nostalgia, she realized she would only walk this path to her cottage a few more times, if any, with her cousin. This place had been home for over a year, and she loved everything about her cottage. Surrounded by beautiful gardens and the view out her front window made her transition from New York almost perfect. But it was all the special people whom she had met here that made Blue Cove home. Her love for the outdoors, especially being close to the path she ran most every day to the marina, was the added bonus that running through Central Park couldn't compete with. That path had one of the prettiest views of the cove. She had many memories from running that path. Some were good, and a few were downright scary, but she didn't want to dwell on those.

"I will miss this." She sighed and gestured with her hand in a sweeping motion.

"I would too. I loved my apartment in the city, but this place with its views and people is like a breath of fresh air. At least Matt's place has a lovely view too." Peyton linked her arm through her cousin's. "I know you couldn't say much in front of Katie. I did try to distract her, but she's nothing if not persistent."

"She is that. It's what I love most about her and get annoyed with on occasion too. She doesn't understand this part of my life. We've always shared everything, but she doesn't share in this area, and I think she feels left out. She strikes back by being snarky and lecturing me. I bite my tongue and try to imagine how I would feel if the shoe were on the other foot."

"That's why you've remained true friends. It's easier for me with Destiny. She's experienced the magic for herself. Plus, we rarely talk about it. Evan takes up most of the spare time she has, which is little. Being a lawyer for the city during this crazy time is keeping her busy."

"I can imagine." Jessie stopped walking and glanced at her cousin.

"Enough with the small talk, Jessie. What happened today?" Peyton asked. "How is it possible you weren't aware of the guy coming at you?"

"I'm not sure. Better yet, why were you?" Jessie grabbed her keys out of her purse. "Do you want to come in for a few minutes and talk? I'll tell you what happened to me, and you can tell me how you got there so fast." Jessie unlocked the door and turned off the alarm.

****

Matt kept busy as he waited for Jessie to call. She hadn't sounded concerned. Damn, he wished he could take some of what she took. He would try to take his cue from her as to whether he should be concerned or not. He ran his hand over the top of the desk he had been working on for weeks. It looked sharp. Glancing at the wall color before he turned off the light, he was sure she'd like the color. The soft glow in the room reminded him of her—full of light and sunshine.

He wanted his home to be her home too. This

bachelor would gladly accept some of her changes that he knew would be coming. At this point, he wouldn't even mind all the clutter that might come with her, although he had never noticed anything out of the ordinary in Jessie's place. Dylan had described all the bottles and baskets filled with Katie's self-described necessary items. Matt smiled. He had a lot to learn about living with a woman, which might be nice. Being a bachelor was highly overrated.

Where was she? She had to be home by now. He mumbled as he shut off the light and walked into the kitchen to fix something to eat.

He filled his plate with the microwaved leftover pasta and garlic bread. Now he was fortified to wait her out. Matt went to his lounge chair, turned on the TV to his favorite channel, and ate his lackluster meal. The microwave always seemed to ruin the taste for him. It never stopped him from using the darn thing, though.

His meal was finished, scores caught up on, and finally his phone rang. "Hey, are you home?" he said when he answered.

"Yes. I would have called sooner but Peyton wanted to talk."

"I'm coming over because I want to see for myself that you're okay. I'll be there in a few." Matt hung up before she could tell him no.

He grabbed his keys and rushed out to his car. The need to hold her and make sure she was good was upmost in his mind.

Chapter 16

Elida and Basil flew as fast as their wings could take them and zipped into the car right before he shut the door.

"Whew!" Elida wiped her tiny brow. "We are supposed to be with him every time he goes out." Elida settled down on the seat beside Matt. "That was too close for comfort. We can't afford to get distracted. No more of your silly games, Basil." She frowned at him.

"One of my shortcomings for sure. I have a hard time staying put and not letting my mind wander. I'm a daydreamer. I hope you can help me, or I will be in trouble for sure."

"Basil, it's okay to be your fun-loving self when you're at home. But here, this man's life depends on us being quick with our heads in the game. I'll stay on you until you learn this truth. When we're working, we have to stay alert. Celeste will demote us both if we let anything happen to him. He is important to the future. I don't know all the details, but both Celeste and my sister have told me repeatedly to stay alert."

"I'll work at it. I promise." He shook his head. "Yesterday was easy. I could see what had to be done. But today was quiet, and to be truthful, I got a little bored with the inaction. I know I should be happy, but I was born for adventure." Basil twirled up and flew around the car.

"Well you'd better get used to a few down times and learn to listen. Life isn't one big lark after all. We have important work to do, limited by the rules in the Intermediary Manual. Listening to your human is key. You'll learn about what might need to be done next. Magic is the last resort for us. Sometimes circumstances force us to become like one of them, but only with approval. Magic may be necessary in the preservation of life. I won't tell you again—stay alert." Elida pulled him down as he fluttered by her. "Give it a rest, would you, please?" He could frustrate her at times. Truthfully, there were times she'd like to bop him one. Neither Celeste nor Mila would approve. Why didn't Mila get the job of training him? She didn't have the patience for it.

****

Matt pulled into the parking space by Jessie's car. He walked the familiar path to her door. This was something he wouldn't miss. He smiled when she opened the door. Her curls looked like they had lost a war. He wondered how many times she had run her hands through them.

"Smart of you to hang up before I could tell you I'd talk to you tomorrow." She smiled at him. "What's so important that it couldn't wait until morning or another phone call maybe?" she asked.

"You know me; it's this addiction I have. I need to see you whenever I can. And more so after an event like today, I have to make sure you're okay." He waited for her to make the first move. "Do you want me to leave?"

"Of course not. I'm fine though." She pulled him in the open door and closed it behind him. "You're always welcome. She sat beside him on the couch. "I know I should be whimpering or something akin to it, but I'm fine." She frowned. "Next you're going to ask me why, right?"

"You've got that right. I know you well enough to know if you're not worried about a near abduction, you have a damn interesting reason for it. I need to know why." He grabbed her hand when she reached up for some hair to twist. "I'm ready when you are."

"I had a great day in the city. Besides my final fitting on my dress, I visited my old newsroom and the precinct I spent hours in getting info for stories. I enjoyed a great lunch and a trip to the museum with friends. Except for having to spend the last couple hours waiting for the police to let us go, it had been perfect."

"That's what you did, but it doesn't explain why you aren't taking this seriously." He applied light pressure to her hand with his thumb. "Fess up."

She told him about the painting. "Matt, it was amazing the joy I felt about our wedding. I wasn't about to let anything or anyone take the moment from me." She glanced at him. "I told you I thought we had help. I haven't seen a ghost, Mila, or her sister, but I know someone is here. Peyton and Katie weren't anywhere near me, but they stopped the guy. Peyton described the moment as a sense of urgency to find me and she had no idea why. She also said the guy seemed to be moving in slow motion. Like his feet were stuck in mud and he couldn't get them to move." She shrugged her shoulders. "Everyone in the museum seemed to be in some kind of suspended animation. It may sound weird but that's what happened. You can see why I think I had help."

"Works for me. If you're okay with it, then I am too." He lifted his arm over her shoulder and pulled her closer. "I can't help but wonder what this is all about. Why should anyone care if we get married except for one of your jealous old boyfriends?"

"I doubt there are many of those. I had few oddballs over the years, but I doubt that is what is going on." She laid her head on his shoulder.

"Do you care if I hang with you for a while?" He reached for the remote. "I missed you today." He winked at her.

"Hang away." She snuggled closer to him and sighed. "Before you get caught up in watching the sports highlights, what did you do all day?"

"Jaxon and I worked on a project. I think it turned out nice," he told her.

Later, as he drove home, he smiled to himself. Jessie tried hard to get him to tell her about the project. He could see why she was considered a good investigative reporter. He fielded more questions, giving as few details as possible, as he had at any news conference. He felt like some damn politician fielding questions by never actually answering one.

Then if that wasn't enough, she tried to get information out of him about their honeymoon destination. She never asked outright but kept asking about the weather. She had to know what to pack. His girl was good, and her tenacity was impressive. She wore him out. He almost gave in a few times, especially when she followed her question with a kiss. Jessie was a delightful handful, and she had made his life interesting and a whole lot better. No doubt about it.

****

Jessie stretched out on the bed and smiled into the dark room. She had to practice flirting. She thought for a moment Matt would give in and tell her, but the man was made of steel. The night turned out interesting. She figured out a few more reasons why she loved him. He wasn't oblivious to her charms, and more than once he had jumped up to get a glass of water. Their life together would be great, not without problems, but awesome, nonetheless.

What was today all about? Her thoughts took her down several paths. She wasn't afraid, but she needed to be smart. As the past year had taught her, all things were connected somewhere, and she had to find the connection between what happened to Matt and today. There were answers to discover if she would take the time to put the pieces together. She touched the envelope from Grandpa Max. She wanted to wait a few more days before she read the contents. Maybe a few nights before her wedding would be perfect.

Pulling her covers up, she closed her eyes, and with help from an unseen friend, she quickly went to sleep.

She stood at her favorite place gazing out at the cove. The cove appeared calm, the gentle waves slapped against the shoreline, and the sunlight danced across the water in an almost mesmerizing motion. Something important was happening out there beyond what her eyes could now see. She couldn't be fooled by the serenity she felt. *What am I missing?* she asked. Someone was listening; she could sense their presence.

The water in the center of her vision began to churn. Slowly, hypnotically the water moved first one direction and then the counter direction until a spiraling funnel came up from the deep and rose into the sky.

Dark and angry, the spout whirled across the water until it was out of her vision. What damage, if any, would it inflict?

As she stood there, the process began again. The waterspout twirled its way out of her sight once again. Over and over the same scene repeated itself. She had no idea what she was looking at or what it meant.

The next funnel that rose from the deep water took on the form of a dragon-like creature with glaring eyes making snarling noises as he flew off in a northeasterly direction. She shook her head to escape the mental picture. As the dream continued, she found herself in a large unfamiliar city. The cars and people moved about unaware of the menacing presence somewhere nearby. She didn't see anything, but her instinct told her he was close. Screeches filled the air before she saw him. Buildings swayed, raining glass and debris onto the unsuspecting people below. The earth heaved, cars flipped, and people ran in all directions screaming, and the same scene repeated itself in city after city until she awakened with a start.

Trapped in a continuous loop of an old Godzilla movie or better yet a new action sci-fi, she wrote on the notebook beside her bed. She had no idea if the dream meant anything or if she had eaten something that didn't agree with her. One thing she knew for sure—she wasn't looking at a real dragon. If the dream had any meaning, it had to be symbolic. She wrote down what she remembered, shut off the light, and went back to sleep.

****

Mila watched her charge fall back to sleep. "Symbolic, my foot," she muttered. "Think, girl. You know imagery. It's representative of what's happening in the world." She shook her head and flew around Jessie's head, waving her wand as she went. "If eating could open people's eyes, they would be open all the time." She landed on Jessie's cheek.

She tapped her forehead three times. "Now listen to what I'm going to tell you." Mila started by reminding Jessie of her time with her look-like ancestor Johanna. She moved on to the scrolls that Jessie still had stashed in her drawer and reminded her of necklace she wore around her neck. "You've seen this battle for a reason. There is trouble in the world, and you must figure out your response to it. Go back and read through the scrolls and learn what your ancestors learned about life in their times. Answers are waiting for you to discover. We will do our best to keep you safe during this crucial time, but don't stick your head in the sand or cover your ears. This is your time."

Mila continued to whisper her message into Jessie's ear as she slept. It wouldn't hurt to tell a few more things to inspire her charge at the moment. Mila knew better than anyone how hard it was to keep the attention of humans, especially when it came to things that had no logical sense. Jessie was more open than most, but she had to be coaxed into the areas that stretched her understanding. She needed encouragement to continue down the path she walked. Matt and her friends were important in her life to the process. She would need them all many times in the years ahead, including Jessie's best friend Katie Donnovan. Mila would be busy with her for years to come. That girl could be a stubborn one. It was the Irish in her. Mila scurried on her way. She loved a good challenge, and this night would be filled with them. A quick stop at Peyton's and then on to Katie's followed by a few whispers in the ear of one handsome bridegroom.

Chapter 17

Matt woke up several times swatting the air. The tickling in his ear kept coming back. He turned on the lamp and sat up. He was tired, and it was only three in the morning. The clock glared the number at him when he glanced at it. At least, he had no early morning tomorrow. He could sleep in if he could stop the infernal itching inside his ear. It wasn't an itch, more like someone blowing in it. A whisper-soft tickling sensation. Not unpleasant but annoying, nonetheless.

Damn, as if he didn't have better things to do than think about his ear. He was still troubled by what had happened to Jessie earlier. Peyton's description was a lot more intense sounding than what Jess had told him. Jessie wasn't concerned about the whole event, but he still was. Concern was always at the top of his mind when it came to her. He reached for his phone and sent Jessie a text about having brunch in the morning at the inn. Too much time had passed since their last time of eating there. They could use some time among their friends.

He shut off the light and let his mind work through what Jaxon told him. The FBI was following up leads on a shooting suspect, but they had nothing conclusive yet. Someone was fighting hard to keep him and Jessie from getting married, but he had no idea who or why. If only it was a jealous boyfriend from her past, he could at least put a face on the problem. It was not knowing that kept him on edge. At this point he didn't know if both incidents were related. Were they perpetrated by the same person or not related to each other at all? His second idea might be the worst-case scenario. A lone wolf acting on their own against each of them would be a nightmare.

He would run it by Jessie in the morning. He stacked his hands behind his head. At this point, any answers would be nice. His wedding was fast approaching, and he didn't want anything to mess with Jessie's big day.

****

In the morning, Jessie read Matt's text before she got out of bed. —*I'd love to go with you.* — she texted him.

She answered her phone a moment later. "Good morning." She pushed her hair away from her mouth.

"Did you sleep well after your eventful day yesterday?" he asked.

"After my strange dream, I did. I'll tell you about it later. I am looking forward to brunch at the inn, and I want to get ready." She lifted her legs over the edge of the bed. "I'll see you soon. Remember that we have to be careful what we say around Katie."

"I'll try. Hey, I asked Peyton and Jaxon to join us. I hope that's all right. I figure we could both use time with friends."

"Sounds good. I'll see you in a few." Jessie hung up and jumped in the shower.

An hour later she was ready. She glanced in the mirror. Her hair was behaving perfectly today. The curls were tame and lay in bouncy waves against her shoulders. She reached for her sweater that went well with her skirt. She would pass Matt's inspection. He seemed pleased with anything she wore.

She put her phone in her purse and opened the door when she saw Matt walking down the path. Stepping out the screen door she held open, she walked a few steps into his arms. "Good morning. I'm glad you came up with this idea."

"Me too." Matt reached inside the door, set the alarm, and locked the door.

"I will miss this place. The gardens are always so beautiful even at this time of year. The mums are gorgeous. Look at all the colors of autumn. I will also miss my favorite spot down by the cove and, of course, the running path."

"We'll make new memories together. I want our place to take its place in your heart and be home for you." Matt laced his fingers through hers.

"I'm sure it will. But as you know, this was my first place in town, and it will always be special to me." She glanced over at him. "I know we'll make many special memories together." She touched his cheek with her free hand. "Don't worry. I'm not having second thoughts. Along with my good memories here, I can't forget when Bristol, from our last case, destroyed many of my belongings with that stupid gun of his. I've had a few bad things come home to roost here, too, but I don't want to mar this beautiful morning with recalling those memories. It's a perfectly glorious day."

They walked around to the front of the inn and walked up the stairs hand in hand. Every time Jessie walked through the doors of the inn, she was reminded again how beautiful the place was. Everywhere she looked, it was a visual feast for the eyes. The wood was polished to perfection, the flower arrangements were always beautiful, and the food Katie served her guests was superb. Her friend was the perfect owner for the inn, and she took her guests' comfort seriously.

"Hey, you two. I reserved a table for us. It's been a while since we could all be together." Katie smiled at them. "I hope you are recovered from yesterday." Katie leaned closer to Jessie. "We need to talk. I had the strangest dream last night. I'll call you later," she whispered.

"What was that all about?" Matt asked as they followed Katie to their table.

"I have no idea." Jessie shrugged her shoulders.

"You two can fill your plates whenever you're ready. Peyton and Jaxon should be here any minute. Along with a few other friends."

"Sounds perfect. You have another yummy-looking spread, Katie. I don't know how you can be as small as you are, cooking the way you do. I want to try it all." Jessie turned her cup over for the staff to fill. "Decaf, please."

"And you, sir?" Katie's weekend helper asked.

"I want the real deal." Matt chuckled.

They were soon joined by Matt's brother, Evan, and his girlfriend, Destiny, along with Chad, Matt's friend, and Sally, Jessie's friend of many years. The last to arrive were Peyton and Jaxon. The morning was fun. Jessie laughed until she thought she couldn't laugh anymore, and then someone said something else funny, and they all began laughing again.

Her friends were simply the best for a good time, and she could always count on them to lift her spirits.

They talked about friendship, the town, and the great food they were eating. The guys razzed Matt about his limited days of freedom left, and the ladies talked about all things wedding. But the whole time Jessie wondered what Katie's dream was about. She couldn't imagine why Katie wanted to talk to her or what she had dreamed.

Jessie pushed the thought away every time it came, but in the end, Katie's dream won out. She wondered what Matt would say when she told him. He knew better than anyone how often Katie had lost it about the strange events in Jessie's life. She had walked on eggshells when it came to what she said in front of her friend. But now Katie wanted to talk to her. It might be nice to have her bestie at least be able to share a small part of her life in this area. Baby steps, perhaps.

Once Matt and Jessie walked out of the inn, Jessie knew Matt's inquisition was about to begin because he had watched her all morning with a perplexed expression on his face. "Before you start your questions, I know you have them. I have no answers about what Katie said to me. I can tell you about my dream, which at the moment doesn't hold a lot of answers, either, mostly questions."

"I do have questions but watching you this morning has me wondering how you handle it all with such grace. You enjoyed yourself as if you didn't have a care in the world, but I know you do. I am impressed. You never fail to amaze me." Matt slipped his arm around her and pulled her into his side.

"I misjudged you. I'm sorry." She turned in his arms to face him. "I thought you were going to do a formal inquest the way you were looking at me."

"How was I looking at you?" He lifted her chin. "Like I couldn't believe what I was seeing, or maybe slightly perplexed by how beautiful and calm you appeared when someone tried to abduct you yesterday? You impress me, and that's all there is to it." He grinned at her. "That doesn't mean that I don't have questions, but I promise you I wasn't going to grill you."

"You wouldn't be you if you didn't have questions. I thought maybe I displeased you somehow."

"No. Once again, you impressed the hell out of me." He leaned his head closer and kissed her.

"Hmm, that's nice to know." She took his hand in hers. "Thank you."

"You're welcome. I want to run some ideas by you if you have the time."

"I'm free the rest of the day." She glanced his way with a smile. "I'm all yours."

"Perfect. I get to have you to myself all day. Works for me. What more could a guy ask for?" He pulled her tight against him.

"Any plans you care to share?" she asked.

"Let me surprise you." He changed their direction and walked toward his car.

"I can live with that. I like your surprises." She slipped into the passenger seat and fastened her seat belt.

Her day with Matt was perfect. They talked about wedding plans, who might be trying to prevent the wedding, and her dream. They spent the entire day chilling at his place and then hers when he brought her home. His surprise was a trip to Hanover for an ice cream sundae at the nifty ice cream parlor there.

The day had been a relaxing one. They were comfortable together, and that was good. She loved Matt, no doubt about it, but better still, she liked him. She liked being with him and simply hanging out. Matt didn't ask any more questions about her dream, and she didn't volunteer more information. They stayed on pleasant topics. And no matter how hard she tried and cajoled him, he wouldn't tell her about the project he was working on. He kept saying soon she could see what he was doing; it still needed tweaking.

Now if only Katie would call and tell her about her dream, she could sleep in peace tonight. She got ready for bed and waited for what seemed like ages. Pulling back the covers, she slipped beneath them, resting her back against the headboard. She rearranged her position several times before the phone finally rang.

"I wanted to call you earlier but one of my guests wanted to talk tonight. They just went up to their room. I hope I didn't wake you," Katie explained.

"I'm in bed but not asleep." Jessie placed another pillow behind her back.

"What did you do after you left here?" Katie asked.

"Matt and I spent the day together. The day was perfect." She sighed, fanning her face.

"I'm putting off the inevitable." Katie paused. "After all the things I've said to you over the past year, many of which I'm not proud of, I find myself needing your help," Katie blurted out.

Jessie smiled to herself. "You know, I'm here for you."

"That makes me feel even more guilty. I was told in no uncertain terms in my dream that I hadn't been a good friend to you. I should be there to support you. I kept hearing over and over, 'You're Irish, after all. You should understand.' The thing is, Jessie, this stuff scares me. I feel out of control, and I don't like that feeling at all." Katie took a deep breath. "I told you and didn't ask you the first time we met that we would be friends. I've always felt in control of our relationship. I wasn't, but I liked the idea anyway."

"No, you weren't. But at least now you can understand what I've been going through. I didn't ask for any of this. Yet here I am. You know me better than anyone, Katie. I like to be in charge too. We've had many power struggles over this issue during our friendship. I've spent many years trying to control the circumstances around me. But I've had to face the reality that even with all the plans I make, life still hands me a large share of surprises that I can't manage or regulate."

"I know you're right. I hate being a coward, though," Katie said. "I want to support you and have the friendship we once had. Oh, I know you've been there for me even in the face of my stupid lectures. You took all my junk in stride, but I know you had to be biting your tongue."

Jessie laughed. "True, I have had to a few times, but our friendship was worth it to me."

"I knew it. I would have never let you talk to me the way I have you."

"That's what friends have to do sometimes to maintain their friendship. Katie, you're no coward. This is all uncharted water for both of us. We will take it one day and one step at a time."

"All I hope is I won't have to have a dream to remind me every time I slip up. My dream had fairies flittering about, whispers, and reminders of my Irish heritage everywhere. I'm not saying I'm ready to jump in where you are. I'm not, but I want to be there to support you with a listening ear." Katie paused. "I'm willing to try."

"I'm glad, and I'll try hard not to overwhelm you," Jessie said.

Katie continued to tell her more details from the dream, and by the time they had hung up, Jessie was happy to have her friend back in some measure. She had missed her.

"Thank you," Jessie whispered into the dark room, convinced that there were listening ears. She lay back and closed her eyes.

Chapter 18

"You're welcome, dear." Mila watched from her spot on the lampshade. She loved moments like this. Quiet, restful times with sweet acknowledgement even when the person wasn't even sure if you were there. Moments like this made everything she did in secret worthwhile.

There would be no dreams this night for Jessie. She'd had a few eventful days and needed her rest. Still, Mila had more than a few ways to influence and encourage her young charge. Mila rubbed her tiny hands together. Gold dust fluttered from her fingertips down upon Jessie's sleeping form. Spreading magic was simply one of her favorite things to do. From her friends to Matt, Mila's tiny hands and her trusty wand hand accomplished some great things.

Point one, she did a great job, if she did say so herself, with Jessie's friend. Katie, that stubborn girl, resisted almost everything she had tried up to now. Celeste gave Mila more leeway this time to work her magic. Jessie missed her friend's closeness and therefore a bit of magic was in order.

A few chosen words were spoken at the right moment and the story emerged in Katie's dreams. She responded well to phase one. But by no means was she done with Mrs. Katie Donovon Mitchell. There was much that girl needed to learn about her heritage. She wouldn't be like Jessie or Peyton, nor did she want to be. But she would be a strength to them and a force to be reckoned with. Mila smiled to herself. What was not to love about her job except when things didn't go as planned and, like her friend Aelfric, went to the dark side. Basil was in danger now, and thank goodness Celeste was doing her best to help the undisciplined prankster find his way. With the help of Elida, of course.

She raised the contraption Celeste wanted them to use to speak to her. Mila was not to leave Jessie's side for a moment, and after yesterday, she understood why. Still, she had important questions to speak with her superior about, and this was the next best way.

****

The sun shone through the crack in her curtain, hitting her directly in the eye. Jessie turned over to get rid of the offending light that had interrupted her peaceful sleep. But she was awake and pushed her prone body into a sitting position. She smiled, even though she was irritated by the sunlight in her eyes, when she thought of her conversation with Katie the night before. They promised each other to pick out their next book to read and discuss like they had done over many years. It would be great to do something normal with her friend once again. She had missed those conversations many times over the past several months. Jessie felt the loss inside where no one could sense how much she missed her friend. Jessie swung her legs over the side of the bed. *You may as well get moving; you're wide awake now.*

Jessie finished her morning routine and rushed out the door to work. Katie reminded her last night that her bridesmaids were giving her a personal shower on Friday night. She told her to come and be prepared to be embarrassed. Jessie didn't know what to think about Katie's statement, but she was sure Katie would make good on her promise.

Jessie started her car and drove past the inn, honking as she went by. She wasn't prepared for the tears that filled her eyes. This crazy action had been her routine every morning when she went to work since moving to Blue Cove. Now in a few short days, she wouldn't pass by the inn at all. No more honking. She wondered if Katie would miss this silly gesture as much as she would.

She found it strange the small things that came to mean the most to her. When she was hurt in their first case, the whole town brought meals to make sure she was fed. Of course, right up there at the top was meeting Molly on her first day in town and Reba soon after. Reba still amazed her, and Jessie couldn't imagine her life without Reba sharing one of her messages that left her thinking long after she left her store. Then there were her customers and the kindness of people who came and went in her life. The last few weeks, the gifts those wonderful folks brought her and Matt were stacking up. What meant the most were the people who stopped by to thank her for her help in solving a case. It made everything she went through since moving to the cove worth it all. And how could she top the touching surprise of a couple from one of their cases who named their first baby after her?

She began her morning routine in the store smiling at the ghost who remained in his usual place. She opened the doors into the coffee shop to say hi to Molly only to see Reba.

"I'll be right in with tea and scones, dear. We need to talk," Reba waved and called out to her.

"Of course, we do." Jessie shook her head. It seemed they were destined to be on the same wavelength. All she had to do was think of Reba, and she seemed to show up. What cryptic message did she have for her today?

While she waited, she straightened tables and dusted her countertop. Not much needed to be done because she always cleaned before she closed too. Busywork made her think her world was normal even when she knew better.

Jessie held the door open to let Reba in when she knocked. Molly followed with two cups of tea. "Good morning, ladies." Jessie closed the door behind them.

"I was just telling our sweet Molly that it's a beautiful day. I hope the day of your wedding will be this gorgeous." Reba placed a bag and her purse on the table.

"How are you feeling?" Jessie glanced at Molly when she asked her.

"I'm great. It's like I have a new burst of energy. I'm getting so much done. I hope the super tired days are behind me." Molly placed the mugs on the table and patted her baby bump. "I'd better get back to work. Enjoy your chat."

"I'm sure we will, dear. Don't forget to put your feet up whenever you get the chance. Better yet, have that nice, handsome husband of yours massage your feet tonight. You work hard." Reba pressed some money in her hand. "Buy yourself a treat. You deserve it."

"I know you're here for a reason," Jessie said as she sat in the chair beside Reba. She reached for the mug Reba pushed her way.

"I know you've heard the saying, 'Revenge is a dish best served cold.' Well, you are seeing the effects of it in action." She glanced at Jessie.

"What do you mean?"

"The idea of enacting their revenge on someone at a later date, taking them by surprise, is more satisfying to acting on impulse immediately. That is what is taking place with your and Matt's lives right now. Someone is angry from one of your cases and has chosen this time to get even."

"Well, isn't that just great," Jessie muttered. "All we have to do is figure out who that one individual among all the ones Matt's put in jail this past year to figure out who is mad enough to hurt us. That should be a piece of cake. Not!" She slapped her hand to her forehead. "Fred is a possibility, but he's too quiet. Maybe Bobby Angel who I knew in high school turned out to be a serial killer, or Stuart Adler who stalked me all through high school and beyond all because I watched his girls. There are too many to choose from." She sighed.

"Jessie, dear, don't be dramatic. You have help that may be working overtime or Matt would already be dead, and you would have been kidnapped. You'll figure out who the guilty person is, if not before your wedding at least by the day of. Think of it this way— your wedding will be the talk of the town for years to come."

"How can you make a plan against the unknown?" Jessie asked.

"You won't be doing it alone. As you've learned, the best way to take out hate is with love. Johanna stopped her enemy with her strength and life. She offered them honey and saved her people. And you have her gift, my girl." Reba took a sip of her tea and wiped her lips with the napkin from her lap.

Jessie told Reba about her dream of the dragon and the voice that seemed to whisper in her dreams. She told her about Katie's dream and how their relationship was being restored. "I'm cautiously optimistic. Katie's apology means a lot to me. We've been friends for such a long time." Jessie glanced at Reba's face, which had a huge smile on it.

"I think you have a wee friend at work." Reba's smile broadened.

"I know you're right. As for my dream, I need to go through the scrolls again. I was promised I would find answers there for today. Thankfully, I scanned them all so I can look at them on my phone or computer. I never know when they may need to go back to wherever they came from."

"I know you'll do fine. It's always a rough ride but imagine how nice your honeymoon will be. Time alone to relax with the man of your dreams and no interruptions." Reba patted Jessie's hand.

"From your mouth to His ears." Jessie pointed upward. "Let it be so. I like the sound of no interruptions." Jessie stood. "I need to open up, but don't go anywhere. I'll be right back." Jessie unlocked the front door and the doors into the coffee shop. She glanced at her guardian, as she liked to think of him, in his usual place on the stairs. She waved, smiled, and glared when he seemed to look right through her. Still, she had a sweet sense of security as he stood there. She would miss her sentry when he was gone. If he ever left. "You will go, won't you?" she muttered under her breath.

"Did you say something?" Reba asked.

"No. I was talking to myself." Jessie sat by her friend. They chatted for a while longer until her first customer.

A rush of cold air swirled around her when she walked forward to greet her customer. Something was not kosher. The man seemed normal enough. His mousy brown hair seemed wrong with the freckles on his face, or maybe it was simply her imagination. Jessie smiled at where her thoughts were taking her. He was young, familiar, and yet she couldn't place him. Her sentry was agitated, which wasn't good, but the man never did anything to draw the guard's negative reaction.

He looked around the store, purchased a magazine, and then went into the coffee shop. Jessie kept on eye on him from time to time in between customers until he left.

"You've had a strange but busy morning." Reba gathered her trash and cleaned the table. "I need to be on my way. I'll be thinking about what went on here this morning. I'm sure there is more to it than meets the eye." Reba slipped into her jacket. "Let me know if you come up with anything." She turned to leave but came back. "Did you feel that cold air rush through the store with your first customer?" Reba leaned close when she asked.

"Yes." Jessie nodded.

"I'm glad I wasn't the only one." Reba shivered.

"It wasn't natural is all I'm saying."

Jessie walked with Reba to the door and held it open for her. "I'm sure we'll see each other again soon."

Jessie walked to the counter and scrolled through the files on her phone. Darn. She wished she knew why the man seemed familiar to her. *Speak to me, my sweet sisters in time. I need answers about how to deal with this situation Matt and I are facing.* In each entry she read from her ancestors, the single connection for all of them was the person was moved by love and compassion to respond. From those who healed, mixed potions to those who could see the future, they were motivated by wanting to make a difference for good. Johanna had emphasized that many times in their conversations.

If anyone could see inside her mind and the conversations that went on in there, they'd think she was a bit weird at best. Her trip to Ireland over the summer had changed many things about how she approached the gift of sight handed down to many of the women in her family.

Thankfully, Matt took life with her in stride. And with help from her friend Reba and her cousin Peyton, she was able to also. Her evolution to acceptance had taken her long enough. One step at a time and one strange case at a time had changed her from always surprised to accepting this part of her life.

Yes, she was ready to marry the man of her dreams. She sighed. He was almost perfect, but she wished he would give her a hint about where their honeymoon destination was. The man had strength; she gave him that. She cajoled, flirted shamelessly, and begged, yes, she had done all three, but to no avail. The man held firm. There must be a way to find out. She tapped her finger against her forehead.

"Who was that man?" She frowned. "All I know is wedding plans shouldn't include dodging bullets," she muttered to herself.

Chapter 19

"What man?" Matt came up behind her and pulled her into his arms.

Jessie told him about what happened earlier when the man with the oddest brow hair came into her store. "I had the strangest feeling, Matt. I mean besides the unnatural chilly air that came with him, I'm sure I've seen him somewhere before. I need to take time to think about where. I'm not sure if his hair color was natural or if he had dyed it. If it was dyed, whoever had done it didn't do a good job. There were places on his head where red seemed to show through the brown. I'm not talking about just any red but almost carrot in color."

"How was he familiar?" Matt leaned his chin on the top of her head.

"I wish I had an answer for you. There have been so many suspects that have marched in and out of my life in the past year and half that I'm not sure." She pulled back to see his face. "But I know he is one of them, or a twin brother to one. Some I've tried hard to block from my mind. That's the only way I could move forward without fear."

"No twin, at least not the Johnson twins, because they're both in prison." Matt smiled. "I put them there, and they're not out. Believe me, I've checked, and Jason has someone monitoring their calls to each other and those on the outside."

"They're not in the same prison, hopefully. That would be nuts." Jessie shook her head.

"Not anywhere near each other." Matt shared details of where they were incarcerated.

"At least I know it wasn't Zach. Our past run-ins make me fully aware of what he looks like. The twins were handsome and buff men. This man was ordinary, nondescript, but seemed pleasant enough." Jessie turned her face to hide her smile.

"You think Zach is handsome? Really?" Matt frowned. "You did that on purpose, didn't you?"

Jessie laughed. "Matt, you're too easy. You were always a bit jealous of him in the beginning, but it was your charming lectures that won my heart." She laughed again and playfully swatted his arm. "Be serious. You have nothing to worry about. I will remember this guy. It may take a while, but I will. In the meantime, maybe I can look over the mug shots from some of our cases."

"I tend to lose my head when it comes to you." Matt grinned at her. "You're right. Mug shots it is. Still, I know you said that on purpose to get a rise out of me, and it worked." He shook his head.

"I'll never tell." She smiled at him.

"Do you remember Brewster who scared you outside of the church that night?" He saw her nod. "Well, Buddy is up for parole. I'm going to speak at his parole board hearing next week." Matt took her hand. "With any luck he'll stay behind bars for a while more."

"How is it possible he could get out? It's way too soon." Jessie asked.

"Gina's parents will be there, and you should be

too."

"Why me?"

"What do you remember about him? You'd only been in town for a while when you first met him."

"I wouldn't exactly call it a meeting." Jessie twisted a few curls around her finger. "When I came out of the church that night and saw his huge form dressed in black from head to toe, I panicked. I went running through the cemetery away from help with him in hot pursuit. That's when I tripped over the tree root and went flying through the air and down a small hill. His menacing voice calling down to me that he'd be back to play another day was beyond scary. And just so you know, you'll never have to worry about me calling him handsome." Jessie shuddered.

"I should hope not." He smiled and pulled out a chair for her. "He was smitten with you. He had several pictures of you in his house. I can't blame him for being taken with you," Matt said. "I feel the same way."

"Aren't you sweet." She patted his cheek. "Reba seems to think it is someone from your past who wants revenge. I tend to agree with her."

"Ah, the old revenge theory. We are checking files to see if anyone has been paroled that I didn't hear about. Some of the suspects who turned state's evidence got shorter sentences." He stood behind her chair. "I want lunch. I'll be back with something for us."

Matt ordered and watched Jessie as he waited. She was helping a customer. Who could the man be? She was right—there had been a lot of suspects over the past year and half. Most would be behind bars for a while. His talk with her had proved useful as always.

She constantly gave him a bit of information that sent him searching in the right direction. He needed to check through the lesser suspects in each of their cases. The ones in the background of the crime who stood to lose the most and wanted revenge.

Matt placed the bag with their sandwiches and two teas on the table. "I hope chicken salad works for you."

"Perfect." She unwrapped the sandwich and took a bite.

They chatted uninterrupted for the next several minutes and enjoyed their lunch. Matt cherished these special moments with her.

"I need to get back to work. Keep thinking about what made the guy familiar to you. In the meantime, be careful."

"I should say the same to you."

****

Jessie walked with him to the door and kissed him goodbye. Someone may have tried to abduct her but that was minor compared to what Matt had been through the past several days. She had seen the pictures of his car and knew that he should have been dead. Every kiss and their moments together were all the sweeter in her thinking. Jessie rubbed her arms to ward off the chill racing through her body. Her friends kept him alive, and she knew it. She didn't know how, but they had to be at work. She came too close to losing more than she had ever imagined possible. Matt's lectures and overprotectiveness both frustrated her and endeared him in her eyes. A therapist might call her conflicted. She wanted to believe she had finally awakened to his charm.

She needed him. The whole idea of a husband and

family was something she never thought she would want. Nevertheless, here she was and happy to be with the man of her dreams. Her hunky cop was the best thing that ever happened to her. That, along with a few friends who she was sure had to be around her somewhere keeping them safe. Which seemed to be a job that came with a lot of overtime.

Jessie reached for her mobile phone when it rang. "Hey, this Jessie."

"Hi, sunshine. I read about what happened to you at the museum. You seem to attract all kinds of strangers even while on a shopping trip to our fair city," Jeremy said.

"You read about it? Where?" Jessie tapped her finger on the counter. "I wouldn't think it was a major story."

"Well, you see the minute Peyton and Katie did their thing and the men rushed to your aid, the story became big news. You know the local hero angle, and everyone wanted to hear his version of what happened. I emailed you a copy. Can't wait to get your take on it."

Jessie spent a few minutes telling her friend about what happened. "Doesn't sound like a big deal to me. My friends kept the guy from nabbing me. To tell you the truth, Jeremy, what happened while I was looking at the painting was an almost spiritual experience."

"I figured there had to be more to the story. Tell me about the painting and what you call the thin places."

"I don't know a lot. Only what I've begun to learn through the scrolls and in my research. I wouldn't mind if you did a bit of research of your own. Still, I believe that Peyton and I have seen the invisible world beyond the veil but only when there is something we need to see. It wasn't until recently that I understood anything about what we were seeing."

"I will research more, if only to understand what is taking place in your life. You lead an interesting and strange life, my friend. Your life in New York seems tame in comparison to your life in Blue Cove. Traffic and millions of people is a piece of cake for you in comparison to what you've experienced since moving there. I'm not sure if you found your piece of heaven or hell." Jeremy exhaled. "I can't wait to see what your wedding will be like. It will be one for the record books, I'm sure."

"Matt told me ours would be a wedding to remember. I don't think he has any idea how prophetic that statement might prove to be." She laughed. "I need to go. I have several customers who walked in. I can't wait to see you. I've been thinking about who I might hook you up with while you're here. You're too good of a guy to leave on the open market for long. I want to entice you to move here. Matt could use you on his team."

"Don't get your hopes up," he told her. "I'm a big city fella, and it would take more than a pretty face to get me to leave the Big Apple." He chuckled. "We'll talk later."

Jessie got busy taking care of the ladies along with the one man who had come in behind them. Her afternoon flew by. When she finally had time to read the article Jeremy had emailed her, she had a good laugh. Boy, could people exaggerate the truth to make themselves appear even better than they were. She did appreciate all those who helped her, but at no time did she remember their lives being in the kind of danger they described. By the time they had rushed to her defense, Peyton and Katie had things under control with a little help from a friend. She whispered her thanks with a smile.

****

Mila smiled. It was getting hard to put anything past that girl. Jessie seemed aware whenever they were around. Maybe with some fancy talking, Mila could use Jessie's knowledge when she talked to Celeste about being actual human guests at the wedding. Celeste was more than fair about most requests, and she listened to their reasons. She was getting more reluctant to let her fairies appear as humans on a whim. Basil could be a problem. She could only hope that he didn't mess up this time. That prankster could worm his way into even the hardest heart, but his lack of focus had blown more than one assignment. No one wanted to work with him anymore. Celeste had a soft spot for him, but even she was ready to crack down on him if he blew it this time.

Mila found herself short with him on more than one occasion, but the boy made her smile and lifted her spirits. Elida gave her an earful when they last met. Basil, the little imp, was driving her nuts. There was a fine line between love and hate, and Elida could cross over that line with a bit of a push.

Chapter 20

Matt was busy all afternoon. Sneaking in the time he had with Jessie at lunch was nice, plus he always learned something when he took the time to be with her. A guy that looked familiar to her meant he was someone from one of their earlier cases, and all he had to do was figure out which one. He needed to have her look over the mug shots from the past year and a half. He could be any one of many. For some reason, Matt's gut told him it was probably one of the lesser-known suspects. He had to be one who was sentenced to less time in prison. That was where he needed to begin. Those who could be paroled after a year or got time off for good behavior. There weren't many, but there were some.

Matt mentioned his theory to Dylan and got Gary down in tech to go through the digital files. Gary emailed him a list with close to fifty names on it. Damn! The number surprised him. He had no idea there had been that many over the past eighteen months who might now have a vendetta against him. Still, it didn't make sense that someone serving such a small amount of time would be angry enough to kill him.

Was it possible he was someone who hung around the edges and didn't serve time at all? Better yet, had they made a plea deal to stay out of prison? He would know soon enough. He had Gary check for anyone who might have pleaded out.

"Matt, Jaxon is on line one," Joe Collins, the desk sergeant, told him.

"Hey, what's up?" Matt asked when he answered the phone.

"Were you able to finish your surprise for Jessie? I have some time the day after Jessie's shower if you want some help," Jaxon said. "Don't forget that the same night is your bachelor party at Patterson's."

"Keep it clean. I have an image to maintain." Matt chuckled. "Besides, Jessie would have my hide if I did something stupid."

"It'll be nice enough for a choir boy to attend. Peyton would have mine, along with all the good citizens of Blue Cove. You're the police chief after all."

"A fact I'm reminded of on a daily basis." Matt turned his chair to look out the window. "I stopped in to see Jessie at lunch, and she shared something with me that has me thinking." Matt went on to tell Jaxon what Jessie had told him. "I put Gary to work on going through the digital records looking at suspects that might fit into either category. I was taken aback by the number of names that could be active now. I'll be doing some follow-up on each person on the list."

"Sounds like a plan. You never answered me about if you want help to finish your gift to Jessie," Jaxon reminded him.

"Help would be nice. I haven't done much since our time the other day." Matt slipped his glasses on. "I won't be able to get around to working on the room until after the party Friday."

"Before I forget, we are still working on our end. Send me a copy of the names, and I'll help you search.

We have a few more resources at our disposal."

"Will do. See you Friday."

"Have a job ready for me to do Friday night later or even early Saturday morning. I can do both if necessary." Jaxon ended the conversation.

Jaxon was a great friend. Matt looked over the list again. Three names stood out to him. He needed to find out any information he could. One of these men tried to kill or hired someone to do the job for them. He opened his computer and started searching through their files. Well, hell, that was no help. All three were still possibilities. He added more names and files to his search, which added more names to the list of three. At this rate, he'd never narrow down the number of potential suspects. "I could use a little help," he muttered aloud.

****

"That's our call to action." Elida shoved the sleeping Basil stretched out beside her resting his head against the book on the shelf.

"What? Where?" He jumped to his feet a look of confusion on his face.

"It's time to wake up. Our human has asked for help and that's why we're here. And to keep him safe, of course." She frowned, pointing her finger at him. "You're either goofing off or sleeping. Get your head in the game, Basil. This is your moment to make something more of yourself and do something great in the process."

"Did anyone ever tell you that you're a bit of Debbie Downer and a nag?" He swatted at her pointing finger.

"I don't care what you think of me. I'm the one

who's going to save your sorry backside from being demoted and to live up to your potential. Call me all the names you want, but I'm determined to make you a hero among the fairies at home." Elida flew over and landed on Matt's shoulder. "How can we help? I'm listening." Elida's tiny, pointed ears got close to Matt's mouth.

"Good grief, what are you doing now?" Basil flew over and landed beside her on Matt's shoulder. "Are you trying to kiss him?"

Elida shook her head in disgust. "What do you take me for? He's a human." She frowned. "I'm listening. He's speaking even if you can't hear his words out loud." She jabbed her finger on Basil's chest. "You might try being quiet and listen for once. I can hear what's in his thoughts and speak ideas to him. This is another way to communicate besides dreams. Didn't you learn anything in your class, the Art of Communicating?"

"There might have been something. I don't remember. I'm not a classroom sort of fairy. I like action." He twirled up into the air and shot around the room.

"Well, I never. How will you ever help anyone? You know the rule—we can only do magic when the human believes it's their idea. Keeping him alive falls under another category. Matt hasn't finished his work and we're helping him find his way and come up with a plan that will work." Elida swatted at Basil as he flew by in another one of his energetic maneuvers. "No wonder no one wants to work with you." She huffed.

"I want to learn. Really, I do, but it's hard for me to sit long enough to absorb anything. I want to move, spin, and fly about. All the rules make me feel trapped. The Intermediary Manual is a boring read, and I can't seem to get past the first chapter every time I try reading it. How do you deal with all of it? You're a free spirit." He plopped down beside her, his face scrunched in defeat.

"I'm no different than you. I love action and the thrill of adventure. The difference is, I've learned to have my adventures within the rules we live by. To do otherwise is to eventually find yourself on the dark side with Aelfric, our once illustrious leader. He's a sad testament to one of us gone bad. The trick, Basil, is to learn the rules and see the freedom that they give you to make a difference. It's quite exhilarating." She touched his arm. "Now hush." She put her finger to his lips. "Listen and you'll discover. Tell me what you hear him saying."

A huge smile lit up his face. "You're right. I can hear him."

Ecstatic that one lesson had finally got through to Basil, Elida wanted to zip around the room herself. Instead, she patiently waited for the silly boy to tell her what she had already heard Matt say. How she became Basil's teacher she would never know although she could feel the pride of the simple accomplishment deep inside her stirring her to keep trying. She might help him make something of himself yet.

She smiled, making a note to tell her sister Mila later about her small measure of success with her charge. In the meantime, they needed to get down to business and plan how to keep Matt alive.

Chapter 21

Jessie leaned against the counter tapping her fingers on the smooth surface. With ten minutes to closing time, there were only two people left in the store. "Did you find everything you were looking for?" she asked the couple when they approached her.

"She always finds more than what she needs." The man smiled at the woman standing beside him. "She's an avid reader, and if she's happy, then I am." He placed a stack of books on the counter.

"All my friends have told me this book is a must read." The woman pointed at a book by one of Jessie's favorite authors.

"I just put that one on the shelf. She is one of my favorite authors. I love her easy style of writing. In fact, Corrine was the guest author at this store's grand opening. This novel is her latest, and I can't wait to dig into it myself." Jessie rang up their purchases, placing several books in the bag. This was by far her largest sale of the day.

"Does she have more books if I like this one?" She handed Jessie her credit card.

"Yes, several. I think you'll enjoy her writing." Jessie handed the woman back the card and placed several bookmarks into the bag along with a pamphlet listing the book clubs that met at the store. "Thank you for coming in."

"I'll be back. We're new to Blue Cove, and this is such a lovely store. The owner did a nice job with the décor."

"Thank you, I'm the owner. My name is Jessica Reynolds, but everyone calls me Jessie. If you like great coffee and food, then Joe's Coffee Shop next store is the perfect place to go. She has wonderful scones."

"We'll have to try it then. My name is Louisa, and this is my husband, Bill. I look forward to becoming a part of this community. He has an interview at the police department tomorrow."

Jessie smiled. "I know the chief of police, and he is a real nice guy." She walked with them to the door and locked it after they left.

She went about her closing routine. They seemed like a nice enough couple. She closed the doors into the coffee shop, waving at Molly who had her purse and was slipping into her coat. "Put those feet up when you get home." Jessie smiled at her. "Better yet, have Kenny give you a foot massage."

"I plan on it." Molly waved at her.

"Goodnight, my guardian," Jessie said to her ghost standing guard on the stairs. "You seem perfect being there. At least to me it seems a natural place for you to be." She shut off the lights and locked the door when she left.

Most of the day after Matt left her was consumed with trying to figure out why the man's face seemed familiar. His name would come to her even if at the moment it proved elusive. What she needed to do was stop thinking about him for the moment. She took a quick look at her calendar for the rest of the week. Her bridal shower with her friends was Friday. Tonight, she was open unless Matt wanted to hang out. She sent him a quick text, started her car, and headed for home. How many times had she driven this same way over the past eighteen months? She swiped at the tears trickling from the corners of her eyes. Darn, she wished she weren't nostalgic about everything at the moment. She wasn't moving from the cove for heaven's sake. She never had this many emotions leaving home for college. Marriage was a huge step, but Matt wasn't her father. Their life together would be good, unlike her parents' until recently.

Her parents were a constant surprise of late. They were almost lovey-dovey if they thought no one was watching. Her dad was even paying for all of the wedding costs. She hadn't asked him or expected him to. Truthfully, when he told her, she had no words. Her known world was turning upside down or maybe it was right side up. Only time would tell.

Her mother had flown to New York to go dress shopping with her and paid for the dress the same day. All the venues and caterers were paid for, including Molly, who was creating a fabulous pastry tray to go with her wedding cake.

The cake she had on order could be described as a masterpiece of five different luscious layers with a lovely stream of flowers flowing down one side from top to bottom. Her mother was the one who found the bakery. She read all the five-star reviews and was convinced that this was the happening place to get a wonderful wedding cake. The baker took a sample of the green material from the bridesmaids' dresses to match the light blue-green in the flowers. The light green intermingled with white lilies and deeper green leaves would be beautiful. Jessie was impressed. After the cake-cutting ceremony, her hunky guy would probably opt for one of Molly's decadent brownies. She wondered if guys appreciated all that went into making the day special. She doubted they did, but she sometimes wondered herself if all the expense and work was worth it for one day.

All Matt seemed to care about was getting married and the honeymoon. Her friends and now her mother were the ones telling her all the details along the way that simply must be a part of the wedding. She landed somewhere between Matt and her friends. Still, when she allowed herself, she could get into the spirit of the details and the day.

She turned into the lane leading back to the inn and her cottage. Her phone rang as she pulled into her parking space.

"Hey, sweetheart, I'm on my way over with dinner. I hope your evening is clear," Matt said when she answered.

"I was going to text you when I got home. Nothing is on my schedule tonight. Dinner sounds good."

"I'll be there in a few. I have to stop and pick up our meal."

"Sounds good." Jessie disconnected the call and walked the familiar path to her cottage.

She collected some of her photos of wedding details. Matt was going to see them tonight. Everyone told her the day of the wedding would be a blur and it was hard to remember anything. The way her mind worked she decided to keep a record with photos before the big day. Of course, he wouldn't get to see the wedding dress—that was reserved for the special day.

Come to think of it, the dress seemed like another big expense to wear only one time. "There's more of your father in you than you like to admit, dear girl," she muttered and went to open the door for Matt.

****

"Dinner is served." Matt kissed her cheek as he walked past her into the kitchen. "I see you're ready for me." He placed the carryout bag on the table. "How was your day?"

Jessie told him about Louisa and Bill. "She said he had an interview at the station tomorrow."

"Yes, Harrison does." Matt dished up some salad on his plate. "What?" he asked when he saw her facial expression.

"I can't believe you went for the salad first." She smiled at him.

"I'm following you. Besides, I can eat rabbit food when I know it's only the beginning of the meal. I've got the manly food coming soon." He held up his knife and fork.

"How was your day?" she asked her mouth turning up at the corners.

"Quiet. Which has me worried. Several days in a row I was shot at and now silence. It has me rattled. I'm not sure what to think. Are they going to turn their attention to you like on Saturday? Or are they looking for an easier target that would hurt us equally? That shakes me the most. I wish I could get my mind to stop."

"I hadn't thought of that. I guess I'm too invested in wedding plans and the fact that I think we have help. At least at the moment, I'm not concerned, but maybe I should be."

"Truth is, sweetheart, the fact you think you recognized someone is a good start. But I have this sense that it won't be one suspect, or one simple answer. That would be too easy."

"You're right, of course. But I can remain hopeful, can't I?"

"Be my guest. It never hurts to hope." Matt stood. "Let me help you with these." He picked up his plate and loaded it in the dishwasher. "Let's talk wedding. You need to catch me up on what's in the works."

"I'm glad you said that." She reached for his hand and pulled him toward the couch. "Someone else needs to hear about the details that threaten to swallow me whole. I thought a wedding in two or three months would be simple to plan. Enter Katie and my mother, and all bets are off." Jessie pulled out her wedding notebook and began to fill his head with all things wedding.

"The colors of the frosted flowers on the cake have to be dyed to match the bridesmaids' dresses. Is that some kind of fast rule or something?" Matt glanced at her.

"According to my mother it is. You haven't heard half of it. I doubt we'll remember any of the essential items for a perfect wedding five years from now." She leaned into his side.

"I should hope not. I only want you to think about how perfect we are together." He draped his arm over her shoulder and pulled her tight.

"Although, it's been kind of fun to see my mom so happy and my dad paying for all of it. Something I never thought I would see. Maybe I didn't give my parents enough credit over the years."

****

Mila was excited to see her sister and Basil come in with Matt. She wanted to hear about what they had found out and tell them all about what she knew. Celeste warned the next several days up to and including the wedding might be hard for them. They would have to keep their tiny ears open and be ready to move at a moment's notice.

"Have you both listened to what Matt said?" Mila sat on the back of the couch by her sister and Basil.

"We heard. He's right about being quiet. It's easy to get bored and not pay attention." Elida frowned at Basil. "Especially when this one gets easily distracted."

"They may be adjusting their strategy, and we might need extra help protecting Sadie, Reba, and family coming to the wedding."

"Will you speak with Celeste?" Elida swatted at Basil as he flew in front of her face. "You might mention my patience in dealing with the little problem she gave me." She tapped her fingers to her chin. "Well, maybe I'm not patient exactly, but at least I'm trying."

"I know you are, sister, and you have to admit he did a good job chasing down the bullets the other day and helped to keep Matt alive."

"If he could focus for longer than five minutes, he might turn out to be a great fairy." Elida shook her head.

"Hey, what do you mean I can't focus? I'm as good as anybody about keeping my head in the game." Basil stretched out his tiny legs and leaned back on his arms.

"You can dispute the merit of that statement at another time. Right now, we must listen in on their discussions and make our plans alongside of them." Mila wiggled her ears and wings together. "We don't want to miss anything."

"Yeah, Basil, like we almost missed Matt when he left the other day. I had to get your attention once again," Elida chided him.

"Enough!" Mila tried too hard to hide her smile but was failing miserably.

She could remember a time when Celeste had to separate her from Elida. They were fighting too much. It was the best discipline to happen to them. Elida was adventurous, while Mila loved to spread gold dust and wear all kinds of glittery dresses. They were total opposites but best of friends now.

They had even drawn a line down the room that they shared. Elida threw her clothes and anything else on to Mila's side, which was always neat and tidy. It wasn't that they changed much since those days, but they had learned to appreciate their uniqueness and differences with a little help from Celeste.

Mila understood that given time, Elida and Basil would become the best of friends, or at least she hoped that would be the case. "Quit your woolgathering and pay attention," she said under her breath. She moved to Jessie's shoulder and listened as they discussed their concerns about the days leading up to the wedding.

Chapter 22

Jessie walked Matt to the door when he was ready to leave. He pulled her into his arms and kissed her. "Promise me you'll be careful," she whispered in his ear.

"I'll do my best and you do the same. This may get harder before it gets better." He kissed her again. "This is a big nuisance interrupting more pleasant thoughts." He leaned close and whispered in her ear. "Right now, all I want to think about is how much I love you and our life together. I fantasize about what it will feel like to hold you in my arms at night and fall asleep with you by my side."

"You're such a romantic. Keep those thoughts and I will too. Hopefully, they'll carry us to our wedding day no worse for the wear." She hugged him tight.

"Whatever works, I'm in." Matt kissed her one more time.

"Text me when you get home. I need reassurance that you made it home safe and sound. I'm committed to our life together, and I want you in one piece for our wedding. I love you," she told him as he walked out the door with Elida and Basil sitting on his shoulder.

Matt's warning earlier hadn't sat well with her. She knew he was right. Reba had been warning her also. What she wanted was an uncomplicated relaxing couple of weeks before her wedding. What she was probably going to get was anything but.

Turning on her computer, she reached for her vibrating phone. Matt arrived home safe. Now she could breathe easier. Being in love made her feel more vulnerable than ever. How that sense of vulnerability must compound when there were kids in the picture. Life was filled with too many complications—something she was beginning to understand. Knowledge which was changing her views on too many things to count.

The first thing she had to own up to was that she probably hadn't given her parents enough credit growing up. She spent too much time thinking they didn't understand her or her problems. She thought they were rather indifferent, stern, and unloving. That idea was crushed a few cases ago when both of the Reynolds brothers changed dramatically after a family curse was broken.

That case had taught her there was a lot more to life than what was in front of her. Everybody went through personal challenges that could change them for good or bad. Anybody could change, as she had seen firsthand several times since moving to the cove. People didn't remain static but went through constant evolution based on the circumstances that came and went in their lives. A positive, as far as she could see. One could, if they chose to, continue to grow as a person every day of their life or not. The power rested in their own hands.

Jessie sent a quick text back to Matt and got ready for bed. —*Goodnight, sweet dreams.*—

She smiled when he sent her a heart emoji. She would never have guessed that Matt would be such a romantic guy. Not her when she first met him. His rugged good looks went with his gruff personality and were a turn-off, or so she thought. But he could turn on the charm. She had fallen victim to his gorgeous deep-blue eyes and lopsided grin more than once over the past year and a half. Now she could look at his handsome face all day. She sighed. She was no match for him. She especially loved him in his glasses. They made him look intelligent and quite sexy. She sighed again. There wasn't anything she could think of about him that wasn't a turn on. Maybe he had a bad habit of dropping his dirty clothes on the floor. She chuckled. She was looking forward to discovering all things Matt.

Jessie saw the envelope from her grandfather on the nightstand. She was tempted to open it but wanted to wait until it got closer to the wedding. Reaching for the envelope, she held in her hands, turning it over. She ran the length and the width of the envelope through her fingers. Tears filled her eyes as her grandfather's face came into her mind. He appeared as she remembered him whenever she went to their house. The words he would say to her when she felt flummoxed by a problem came to her in his grainy voice. "Use your head, girl. You're an intelligent one and you'll see the right path forward. Use the brain you were blessed with." She placed the envelope back where she found it. She'd wait. Shutting off the light, she stretched out on the bed and let the tears flow. "I miss you, Gramps. Why must death separate us from those we love?" she said into the empty room.

She didn't expect an answer although it would be nice to understand life's meaning more clearly at times. Grandpa Max was in her memory and heart. As far as she was concerned, he'd be at her wedding. She smiled. *I hope you don't mind that Grams has a new friend coming all the way from Ireland to the wedding.* Ronan Fitzpatrick was a nice lively fella who was quite taken with Grams. She sniffed and wiped the tears forming in her eyes. Somehow she knew Gramps would be okay with whatever his Sadie did because he would always be her first and one true love.

"Okay, Gramps, I'll use the brain I was blessed with." She began to think through recent cases looking for a connection and a face until she went to sleep.

****

Mila waited until she could hear Jessie's steady breathing. Her charge needed a memory refresher, and she was the one to help her. Taking her wand, she swirled gold dust around Jessie's head and tapped three times on her forehead. She pursed her tiny lips and blew her a kiss filled with the magic of her memory.

Mila knew the moment Jessie's walk through the past began. Her charge tossed and turned and twisted herself in her bed covers. Mila perked her pointed ears to listen to the words Jessie mumbled in her sleep. She could rest now. All would be well. Mila closed her eyes and slept.

****

Matt took off his glasses and placed them on the nightstand. Rubbing his eyes, he tossed the open file aside. He hadn't found anything that called to him. He knew he was missing something simple but to this point every lead was a dead end. What he wanted was a nice tidy answer that tied both the shooting and the attempted abduction together. There didn't seem to be any link, or suspect, for that matter.

Jessie seemed almost cavalier about what had happened to her New York. He wanted her to enjoy the next couple of weeks as family and wedding events began in earnest, but at the same time, he didn't want her to let her guard down. Hell, this shouldn't even be an issue for their celebration and the start of their lives together. This seemed to be par for the crazy world in which they found themselves living at the moment.

Matt stacked his hands behind his back and stretched out. He couldn't wait until she was beside him every night. No more leaving her on cold nights. They could snuggle in front of the fireplace. When she needed space, she could retreat to her newly renovated office space—his special surprise for her. As long as she was under the same roof, he'd be one happy man.

He closed his eyes and conjured up the face of his blue-eyed angel who simply took his breath away when she wasn't causing him a major headache. Life with her could never be called boring.

Matt reached for his ringing phone. "Hey, brother, what's up?"

"I'm called to see how you're doing. I took the photos of your car. Let's just say I'm glad you're still with us," Evan told him. "I hope Dad and Mom never see them."

"I hear you. I'm fine. We're still trying to find a suspect." Matt frowned.

"And is Jessie okay after her ordeal?" he asked.

"You know Jessie; she handles it better than I do."

"Are you ready for your big day?" Evan chuckled. "Forget that. I know you've been ready for months."

"You've got that right."

Evan told him about the plans for his bachelor

party. "It'll be aboveboard, fit for the chief of police. We might have to smack our younger brother to keep him in line."

"You know the last time I talked to him, he seemed like he might be growing up a bit. We'll see how long it lasts. Jason isn't much different than we were at that age."

"Really? Were we that girl crazy?" Evan laughed.

"Yes, brother, we were. It takes the right woman to tame us."

"Yeah, well, for me it was Dad. I wanted you to know I haven't forgot my best man duties. Get ready to have a good time. I love you, man. Do your best to stay alive, will you?"

"I'll do my best. Goodnight, Evan." Matt disconnected the call.

He'd like to have a good time with his friends and not have to worry about whoever it was that wanted him dead. Damn, he wished he had answers.

Chapter 23

"Sister, we need to talk." Mila flew into Matt's room and plopped down beside her sister and Basil on the footboard.

"I was thinking the same thing a few minutes ago. Somehow, we have to come up with a plan for our charges to be able to enjoy the days leading up to the wedding without the fear of dying. I have no idea how we can make it happen for them, but we have to try." Elida nodded and swatted Basil's hand pulling her hair. "Would you stop, please?" she muttered.

"I agree," Mila said. "We have to refresh their memories while they sleep each night until they can put the pieces of the puzzle together. We can keep them safe as they solve the mystery. At least for now that's what Celeste says we can do. She wants them to solve the problem with little interference from us." Mila folded her hands in her lap.

"I guess I understand, but it would be much easier to force their enemy out into the open." Elida scrunched her tiny face.

Basil doubled up his tiny fists. "I would give him give him one of these followed by another." He twirled around, boxing the air.

"Nobody is hitting anyone at the moment." Mila pulled Basil's leg to bring him back to eye level. "We have to do this right. Who knows? Maybe Celeste will give us more leeway in the future. But the real magic is within them." She pointed at Matt. "We can stop the bullets meant for them, but they must follow the trail of evidence for themselves."

"How can that be? They hardly believe in anything." Basil pursed his lips and scowled.

"It's simple, really. When they believe, a desire to live kicks in. Matt wants to marry Jessie. He's been waiting for this moment, and it keeps him moving toward his dream. He may not understand we are helping him, but he's not fighting us either. He believes he will make it to the wedding, and that lets us operate beside him. For the moment, Elida, you do what you can with Matt. I will do the same with Jessie."

When Mila left them, Elida swirled her wand around Matt's head and she, along with Basil, stood guard at the foot of his bed.

****

Jessie awakened early and wrote down any details she could remember from her dream. She understood the person who tried to abduct her worked for someone else. He was a small part of the tide of discontent and an enemy from the past. The attack on Matt was in some way the same. An enemy from one of his past cases was angry and bent on seeking revenge. All she had to do was figure out who the mystery man was, or men were, whatever the case may be.

Many odd pictures had filled her dreams, and they didn't seem any clearer this morning. She fingered the pendant under her nightshirt. Her studies of the scrolls had made some truths more understandable, but there were still many questions about what the gift she had could and couldn't do. What good did a gift do if you couldn't help those you loved with it? She shook her head and sat on the edge of the bed.

Peyton told her the same thing a few days ago. They had much to learn and were novices like each of their ancestors were when they first discovered their gifts. Jessie knew in her heart she wasn't alone in this journey, yet some days she felt like no one understood her at all. The incident at the museum and Matt's car proved to her they were not alone. No doubt about it, help intervened, and had more than once, in the most unusual ways.

Rising tides, ghosts from the past, magical beings, and who knew what else. Jessie lifted the pendant into her hand. A warm sensation started at her fingers and made its way up her arm. Some warrior she had turned out to be. She had no idea if she could hold her own. Would she always need another entity to rescue her, or would she reach deep inside herself and rise to the occasion on her own? Jessie wanted to believe she was stronger than she gave herself credit for, but in moments like this, self-doubt crowded her thoughts, and she felt like she hadn't grown at all. "Face it, Jessie girl, you have room to grow. The question is, are you willing to?"

She stood up and headed for the shower. A little over an hour later, she was out the door and honking as she passed the inn. Another morning ritual that would soon come to an end, but she was ready to move on. Now that her friendship with Katie was back on somewhat solid footing, she could hang with her without fear that she'd say something that would earn her another lecture. She had her fill of reprimands this past year. There had to be a bit of magic involved for

Katie to apologize. Jessie knew her friend and the change hadn't come easily. Hopefully, the new Katie would stay around through the wedding and beyond. Jessie smiled.

"Hey, you're getting an early start," Katie's cheery voice came across the line.

"I was up and thought I stop in Joe's before I open the store. You know how I like Molly's scones." Jessie turned from the lane at the inn onto the street leading into town.

"I'm looking forward to your shower Friday night and being with all the girls. We always have fun when we get together. Dylan will be with the guys for Matt's bachelor party. He told me Jaxon has promised it will be aboveboard and befitting the chief of police." Katie laughed. "I have no idea what that means."

"I'm sure we'll find out soon enough," Jessie said. "I'm excited to see my friends on Friday night too. Next weekend more family will be arriving, and then all the wedding festivities will be in full swing. It's hard to believe I'll only be single for a short time more."

"Are you ready? Cold feet or doubts?" Katie asked.

"No doubts and I'm ready. And if I'm being honest, I know there are a lot of unknowns, but I'm ready to discover them with Matt."

"It's different, not bad, but definitely different answering to someone else in your life. After leaving home, I made my own decisions without consulting with anyone else. It was a bit of a wakeup call when we realized we needed to consult each other, and some decisions had to be made together. You know how I can be."

"*Take Charge Katie* is what we used to call you."

Jessie laughed.

"You'll find out soon enough, stubborn Jessica Lynn."

"I'm sure I will." Jessie pulled into the parking space at the back of her store. "I'm at work. I'll catch you later."

"Sounds good. Stay out of trouble and be safe." Katie hung up.

Staying safe was her plan. She would do her best to. She unlocked the back door and locked it behind her. Placing her purse on the counter, she waved at Molly through the glass doors. She turned on her computer. While it loaded, she went into the coffee shop to get her scone and coffee.

"Hey, Molly. How are you feeling?" Jessie asked.

"Besides the fact I have a little person doing somersaults inside me and using my insides for a drum, I'm doing well."

"All I know is you look great. I bet you're getting excited to greet your little one. It must be pretty amazing having that wee fella moving inside you."

Molly smiled. "There is nothing like it." She patted her stomach as the baby kicked. "See what I mean. But I have a feeling our lives are about to change in a major way." Molly handed Jessie her bag and a cup for her coffee. "I've heard stories from many customers, and it has me wondering if I can handle the changes."

"Change is inevitable for all of us as we grow older, I think. Marriage seems like a big enough one to me, much less a baby. You'll have to keep me in the know each step of the way." Jessie filled her coffee cup with decaf and lots of cream. She waved as she walked through the open door into her store.

With time to spare, she got on her computer while she munched on her scone. "Too bad you can't eat," she told her guardian on the stairs. "I think you would love this." She winked at him and noticed a slight curve to his lips. She might win him over yet.

****

Matt wanted to feel good about no more shooting incidents for the past few days. Instead, he felt jumpy. Something was off and his gut told him it wasn't over yet. He pulled into the open spot in front of the coffee shop.

When he stepped up to give Molly his order, he could see Jessie working on her computer. She was early. He'd call that a win for him. He grabbed his coffee and his breakfast sandwich and tapped on the glass in the door.

He smiled when she turned to look his way. Matt walked through the door she opened for him. "You're here early this morning." He placed his coffee and bag on the table.

"I awakened early and thought I may as well come to work. I need to place a book order."

"Did I interrupt you?" he asked.

"No, I was catching up on emails and chatting with Jeremy. In other words, I was procrastinating." Jessie laughed and sat beside him. "How are you?"

"I should be happy that I haven't been shot at for a few days, but my gut tells me that might not be good. I don't want any surprises at our wedding."

"You don't think there might be a possible shooting at our wedding, do you?" Jessie jumped up. "I don't want to put our guests at risk."

"All I'm saying is that in my line of work, quiet

isn't necessarily a good thing." Matt pulled Jessie down into his lap. "I'm going to do everything I can to keep us and our guests safe and so will all my officers with help from Jaxon." He rubbed her back. "Don't worry. Aren't you the one that told me we had help and everything would be okay?"

"Yes, but I'm also the same person that finds it's easier to say it to you than to actually believe the words myself." She slipped off his lap into the chair next to him. "Eat your breakfast and I'll sit here while you do."

"I'm happy to have you by my side for whatever reason. I want to keep you there. It might take all I have keeping you content by my side, but I plan to do my best to make you happy for as long as we both shall live. Isn't that what we say?" Matt glanced at her between sips of his coffee.

"Speaking of what we say, remember, you have to write your wedding vows. I've been working on mine."

"Mine are done. I've been working on them for a while. Every time I've thought about why I love you the past few months, I wrote them down, and what I want to promise you seemed to flow straight from my heart with ease. You, my love, make it easy for me."

"Who would have thought that Matt Parker, Chief of Police, is a true romantic at his core?" She playfully squeezed his bicep. "My hunky tough guy cop has a soft lovable side." She fluttered her lashes at him.

"You know, sweetheart, I enjoy moments like this with you. Times we can let down our guard and relax with each other, but as much as I enjoy being here, I have to get to work. I leave you with reluctance." He reached for her hand as they walked to the door. "Is your friend still guarding the place?"

"Yes, he's still doing his job." Jessie glanced at her guardian still at his post.

"As strange as this may sound, I'm happy he's watching you when I can't." He leaned close and said softly to her, "I think you'll be safe under his watchful eye."

"I'm glad too." She let go of his hand when they got to the door.

"Catch you later, sweetheart." Matt gave her a quick kiss as he went out the door.

He signaled and did a U-turn on Main Street toward the station. When Jessie told him she didn't want anything to happen to the guests at their wedding, she had no way of knowing he had nightmare scenarios in his head about just that. When he uttered the words about a wedding to be remembered, he had envisioned a beautiful event and day surrounded by family and friends ready to celebrate with them. Now he wasn't sure getting a large group together in one place was such a good idea. Only time would tell. He sure as hell hoped this nagging feeling in his gut was wrong.

****

"Basil, what's on your mind? You are too quiet for my liking." Elida sat beside him on the dashboard as they observed Matt.

"I like this guy. He's one of the good ones." Basil tapped his finger on his chin. "What can we do to keep him and her safe? He's troubled, and I can sense he's not sure what to do. We need to speak into his dreams and whisper ideas into his thoughts."

"Well goodness, look at you thinking like a fairy ready to do his job. All I can say is that I'm proud to have witnessed this moment in your transformation.

Before you get too excited, remember that you have to be always thinking ahead to what might happen next and be prepared to act." She smiled at him. "Let's put our heads together and come up with the ideas he will need to take him safely through to their wedding and celebration with family and friends."

The two began to speak quietly to each other. Plans began to formulate which could easily with a touch of magic be slipped into Matt's dreams and thoughts. Basil had come up with some great ideas, and Elida knew she needed to remember to tell Mila. Her sister would, of course, report the good news to Celeste.

Elida didn't want to be too giddy, but even she had to admit this was a good beginning for Basil. Maybe he would be one of the great fairies, given the time to grow. She also enjoyed working with him even if he was a bit of a pain. He reminded her that there was still a fun side to what they did, and she liked laughing. Yes, Basil might be okay after all. If they managed to get through this case successfully, she wouldn't mind working with him again. Time would tell if it was a possibility or wishful thinking.

Chapter 24

Jessie watched Matt as he drove away. She was troubled after their conversation earlier. Matt had good reason to be concerned that things were too quiet. His instincts were too good not to take them seriously. Her dream seemed to point her in the right direction. She hadn't zeroed in on the right person yet. But he—and she was sure their suspect was a he—was at the edge of her mind, and she knew he would be revealed in time.

Now if only she could figure out who was behind her attempted abduction. If the dreams were true, the scheme had roots dating back to Johanna, which is why the ghost still guarded her store and she wore the medallion around her neck. All of the writings on the scroll talked about a war that ensued in each generation with the same entity who adjusted to changing times. How he maneuvered through each new generation but lost most of the time. The only ones he seemed to advance against were angry people who blamed others for their woes and those who did what Johanna said not to do—use the gift for their own purpose or neglect it altogether.

Jessie rushed back to the door a few minutes later when she saw Reba get out of her car and walk toward the store.

"Good morning, sweet lady," she said, holding the door open for Reba. "I can't say that I'm surprised to see you."

Reba swept through the open door and patted Jessie's cheek as she walked past her. "I'm sure you aren't. We seem to be on the same wavelength most days, are we not?"

"I'm beginning to believe we are. We are simpatico." Jessie smiled at her.

"How long before you must open the store?" Reba asked placing her coat on the back of the chair. "Do I have time to get tea?"

"Of course, and we will still have about twenty minutes." Jessie motioned for her to go. "I'll be waiting."

Jessie rushed through her morning routine, so she'd be ready to spend time with Reba. Her friend always showed up when she needed her most. And at the moment, she needed to talk to someone.

"I brought you tea too, dear girl. The world's problems can be solved with a nice cup of tea."

"Thank you." Jessie sat at the table beside her friend. She had her doubts about the power of tea to solve the world's problems, but who was she to argue a moot point?

"Ah, just what I need to calm me." Reba sighed after she sipped her tea. "I feel better already. Now we can get down to business and the real reason I came this morning."

"Sounds good to me. You rarely come here and do not have a purpose to your visit. I'm listening whenever you're ready."

"First, I think you need to tell me something that is troubling you, don't you, dear?" Reba glanced over the top of her cup at Jessie.

Jessie told her about her earlier conversation with Matt and the dream she was still trying to put together. "I'm concerned for Matt and for the guests coming to our wedding."

"I can understand why you needed to talk to me. We can't let anything mar your special day. Where should we begin?"

"I have no idea," Jessie said.

"Let's start with you. I believe you know more about who is behind your attempted abduction than you think. If you think about the details, the puzzle will become more clear." Reba sipped her tea. "You were having a spiritual moment when the man approached you. That tells you something very important. I believe you will have no trouble reasoning out the instigator working behind the scene. As for Matt, you will see clearly soon who is seeking revenge."

"I hope so." Jessie exhaled.

"I know it to be true. My purpose for coming here this morning was to tell you there will be as many unseen guests at your wedding as family and friends. They will be there to celebrate the one who gave them a voice when they had none. I wouldn't want to be the one who tries to do anything to hurt you or Matt with them around. Can I guarantee nothing will happen? Not at all, but I can say in the end you'll be heading on your honeymoon with the man you love."

"I guess that's about as much as I can hope for at this point. I also believe I have a few friends helping out. I haven't seen them, but I know in my heart they have saved Matt's life already. At least twice, and maybe more times than I'm not aware of."

"That's my girl. You're thinking in the right

direction. Keep on track, my dear. You won't be led astray. These criminals may be from your past, but they are both two sides of the same coin. What I mean is the two incidents are closely related although to the casual observer they seem different."

"Hmm, that gives me something to chew on. What you've said makes sense to me. I knew I could count on you to point me in the right direction." Jessie sipped her tea. "Your visits always bring wisdom along with a wonderful conversation. I look forward to them, although there was a time I dreaded them." Jessie chuckled.

"Why?" Reba's brows rose.

"Truthfully, you scared me. You were a bit like a white tornado. You would come in and give one of your ominous warnings, and I wasn't quite sure what to expect next. But now, I look forward to them because they usually confirm what's on my mind."

"That's nice to know. Sounds like I'm doing my job right." Reba continued to chat while Jessie listened to her friend.

Reba always gave her a lifeline to hang on to. Even though the discontent in the world seemed overwhelming at times, there were so many reasons to feel hopeful. Jessie went through them in her mind as Reba seemed to speak her exact thoughts aloud. With Reba, hope constantly made a comeback in her life. There were good people everywhere doing their part to push back against the tide and giving people reason to hope.

She needed to remember this conversation to tell Matt. Reba's bit of wisdom made her realize the two events were related. She could see it more clearly than before. What appeared to her as two separate incidents were tied together by both of their pasts.

Jessie walked with Reba to the door. "Thank you for stopping by."

"This is one of my favorite spots in town to visit. And by the way, even your grumpy inhabitant seems to have a lighter spirit these days. See you later, my sweet girl." Reba patted her cheek as she rushed out the door Jessie held. She waved as she got in her car.

Jessie got ready to unlock the doors and open. The day was off to an interesting start. She couldn't help wondering what the rest of the day had in store for her. Maybe it was best to keep her thoughts to herself.

****

Matt's morning was busy talking on the phone and with his officers. He hoped Jaxon had some new information for him. He made a note to call him as soon as his department meeting was over. He handed out the duty roster for the month. Dylan would be acting chief when he was on his honeymoon. The guys had plenty to say and didn't let up teasing him the entire meeting. Matt knew it was all in good fun, and he had done his share of ragging on the other guys getting married over the years. Including Dylan, who took it all in stride.

As soon as the meeting was over, Matt went to refill his coffee. Waiting never sat well with him. He felt like he should be doing more to solve the case. He didn't like to have to let others take the lead. In the case of his shooting, he was obviously too close to the situation. But it wouldn't stop him from investigating all he could on the side. He couldn't sit on the sidelines. It didn't sit well with him. He had to have his skin in the game. That's how he rolled.

"Matt, you have a call on line one." The desk sergeant Joe's voice came over his phone intercom.

"Thanks, Joe." Matt pushed line one.

"Hey, Parker," Jaxon said when Matt answered. "We've ruled more out than in at this point. We checked on Johnson's and his twin brother's activities in prison. Both of them are quiet and model prisoners according to our inside sources. No new outside activities. I'm trying to find out if anyone from the Harvest Club has had an early prison release."

"As you know, our old police chief messed with and covered up some cases. He was paid under the table. I can't help but think this might have something to do with him or one of his many mishandled cases. We've been going through files of his back cases and found plenty of irregularities. So far, I haven't found a reason why some of his cases would interact with me at this point, but we'll keep searching." Matt leaned his elbows on the desk. "There are quite a few characters when it comes the Harvest Club, starting with Anderson's flunky, Fred, Buddy, his hired thug, or Gordon Stockton, who promised the chief thirty-five percent of the club's earnings to turn his head, which totaled into the millions. Greed was their motivation, and the gravy train went away when the club was exposed."

"That's a good theory to consider. I'll do some checking myself," Jaxon told him.

"By the way, I talked to Tom Maxwell about you being on call if Dylan should need you while I'm on my honeymoon. He gave the idea his full support, which means you'll be busy the way Blue Cove has been lately. Peyton, I'm sure, will be happy to help if needed." Matt chuckled.

"Don't get your hopes up. I'm sure all will be quiet while you're away." Jaxon laughed. "Who am I kidding?"

"We can talk more at my bachelor's party. I'm looking forward to a night with my friends."

"Did you get Jessie's surprise done?" Jaxon asked.

"It's almost finished. I worked on the trim last night for a while. Most of the major things are done, but I have a few last-minute touches to add. With your help, her surprise will be ready for the big reveal soon."

"When will you show her?

"I want to show her before the wedding. We'll be moving a few of her belongings in this Saturday. I think that will be the perfect time." Matt turned his chair to look out the window for any activity in the park. "Which means I will have some work to do after the party on Friday."

"I know she'll love it. I'll stay in touch and see you Friday night. Peyton and I have dinner plans tonight. I'm looking forward to it. We'll talk later."

Matt turned his chair around to look out the window. Dinner out sounded like a perfect idea. He reached for his phone and texted Jessie about a night out. The rest of the week and weekend would be busy with family and wedding preparations.

—*Yes, lets. I have lots to talk to you about.*— Jessie answered his text and added a heart at the end.

He smiled to himself. She always had plenty to talk to him about, and he could count on her to come up with more than a few more answers. More than any of that, she had a way of making him hopeful and happy. He believed in a bright future together, although not perfect. After all, he was nothing if not a realist, but secretly he was beginning to believe there was magic in the universe even if his logical brain found it a bit over the top. Matt turned his chair around, opened the file on his desk, and got to work going over another one of Chief Anderson's old cases. There had to be an answer in there somewhere.

****

Basil sat on one of his shoulders and Elida on the other keeping watch over their assignment. Basil watched the outside while Elida whispered thoughts and tapped images into his thoughts to help Matt along in the discovery process.

"Do you see anyone in the park outside that looks like they shouldn't be there?" Elida asked.

"No one. The open area seems to be empty, but I'll keep watching." Basil flew over near the glass to get a better look. "You know, I can understand his frustration. The waiting can get to you and take you out of your game. You can forget to pay attention and miss something important when nothing happens for a few days. What happened to the person bent on killing him?"

"A question we would all like an answer to. Maybe he felt the police were starting to close in on him, and he went underground for a few days. I wish we could explore the possibility further, but our orders are not to leave his side."

"I get it. We've had to help save him a few times, but I'm with you." Basil pressed his hands against the glass and pushed off into the air. "I wonder if there's anything we can do to bring the guy out into the open." He landed and placed his face close to the glass.

"I'm sure if we put our heads together, we could come up with something." Elida smiled at him. "At least for the moment, we have found a way to stop fighting and start working together. Maybe I can give Celeste a good report of our time working together if we continue on this path."

Elida turned to watch Basil who seemed to be concentrating on something outside. He never turned away from the window even when she spoke to him. "Is there something outside we should be worried about?"

"Nope, I'm thinking is all. We have to help our friends, and we need a good plan."

With that said, they both stared out the window and concentrated on trying to come up with a plan to get the two of them married. It was important. Basil caught what Elida had been telling him all along. The smile and warmth inside her grew and came out in a sigh.

Chapter 25

Jessie spent her afternoon thinking about her conversations with Reba the past several days. Her friend always had something to say that stimulated her thoughts. What she needed most was a long chat with her cousin. Besides missing Peyton around the store every day since she was back at the school, she wanted to remind her that any strange happenings in Blue Cove would be hers to hold back while she was gone.

At this point, any destination away from the cove sounded perfect as long as Matt was by her side. Was she content to find out the day of the wedding where they were headed? No way, but she had tried everything to worm it out of him to no avail. It wouldn't stop her from keeping the pressure on him though. She smiled.

The bell rang, and a new customer she had never seen in the store before walked in. The man was shorter than her and a bit on the stocky side. His full head of dark hair didn't seem to go with the rest of him. He strolled over to the book table and began to read the back of one the books he picked up.

"Let me know if I can help you find something," Jessie told him. An uneasy feeling settled over her.

"I will. I'm just looking." He placed the book back on the table and picked up another one. "Has this place been here long?" he asked glancing around the store.

"I opened it over a year ago."

"You've got a nice place. Does it do well?" he asked.

"Well enough." She didn't like his line of questions.

"I wouldn't think you'd turn a good profit. I guess having the coffee shop next door helps. I like the building and all. You wouldn't be interested in selling it would you?"

"No, this is my happy place." Jessie sensed something off with the guy.

"Do you have other employees?"

"Yes, I do. One of them should be in soon." Okay, she fudged a bit on that answer, but the guy was starting to make her genuinely nervous.

"Well, I hope you'll think about my offer to buy you out. I wouldn't want to see you lose everything in, let's say for practical purposes, a sudden downturn in your luck. Not many people are buying books these days. You might be able to get extra protection from my company if you insist on keeping it." He smirked. "You know, a bit of insurance for a price."

"You gave me no offer, and I'm not selling or buying anything anyway. I'll take my chances on keeping my business here and safe." Jessie reached for her purse when the man started walking toward her. Several women came in from Joe's, which seemed to stop his progress.

"I'll be back to check again another day. I hope you reconsider the offer. Things have a way of going south quickly."

Jessie greeted the women as she walked past them to check on his retreating form. He was nowhere to be seen. *Well, that's not good, girl.* She shook her head. *I think he might have been threatening me*. She glanced at the guardian on the stairs. He wasn't there. If he had been solid, she would have bumped into him. Instead, she walked through him. Which she would describe as more than a strange sensation.

When the last of her customers left and the clock said five, she was ready to close the store. Simply thinking about the odd man kept her on edge all afternoon. She wanted to go home. Before she closed the doors into Joe's, Molly rushed through them.

"I know it's time for you to leave, but I had the strangest little man in my store. I thought I saw him in yours too."

"Did he ask if you wanted to sell with a veiled threat attached to it?" Jessie asked.

"Yes, and I've already told Kenny about it. Did he give you a card or tell you his name?" Molly frowned.

"No, he offered nothing but told me he didn't want to see me lose everything in a sudden downturn. I had a strange idea that he would make that happen if he wanted to. I know that sounds odd, but that's how it sounded to me."

"To me also. I didn't like the man and thankfully there were lots of people in the coffee shop, which seem to make him nervous. It got me thinking about you all alone over here, and I wanted to check on you." Molly took Jessie's hand. "I do have a good photo of him on my security camera. Kenny had it installed after my kitchen was being messed with. Of course, I didn't tell him it was a ghost. That wouldn't have gone well at all." Molly laughed.

"At least, Matt takes all my baggage in stride. He grumbles and talks to himself a lot, but he doesn't rule anything out anymore. He's a keeper." Jessie grinned.

"Are you going to tell him about this?"

"You bet I am. He didn't only threaten me; he did you also. Which makes me wonder if any other store owners on the block got his interesting offer. I would like to get a picture of the guy to see if he has a record anywhere."

"Not a problem. Kenny taught me how to freeze a frame and download it to my computer. I'll send you a copy in a jiffy." Molly turned to leave. "Hurry up and close. I'm going to do the same. I don't particularly want to see the guy again today. Once is enough for me."

"Sounds good. I'll see you tomorrow." Jessie went to lock the doors behind her and finish her closing routine.

What was it about that man that spelled trouble? Matt would know. Gone were the days of trying to keep information from him. He was the first one she wanted to run things by. Her guardian didn't seem to like the man either. She was glad he was still in her store. Some warrior she had turned out to be. She closed and locked the back door behind her and got into her car, heading for home.

She could swear someone was following her, but the car drove past when she turned into the inn. She parked in the back but walked around to the front. The same car must have turned around and now drove by the inn slowly. Yep, she had been followed all right.

****

Mila had watched the afternoon unfold from her vantage point on the guardian's shoulder. They had come to a meeting of the minds in some odd way. He didn't talk and she didn't want to. But he kept watch over Jessie and cared for her like she did. Mila would have stepped in to help, but he restrained her. This time Jessie hadn't needed anyone's help.

Mila didn't like the man. As a matter of fact, the way he talked had made her fairy blood boil. Even now she wanted to stamp her foot. She knew all too well when something didn't feel right about a person. That man was up to no good. If he even was a man. Like Aelfric, her fairy friend who went bad, Mila could sense this man headed in the same direction. Which made her wonder if he was sent here as part of a larger mission. She would need to run this news by Celeste. Maybe she could tell Mila what was going on. Celeste was up on all the latest news, and she would know what his real purpose was.

Mila settled on Jessie's shoulder and followed the car with her until it was out sight. Jessie didn't move and neither did she. They watched together as the car moved slowly by the inn one more time and then sped off.

Not good, old girl. Not good at all.

****

Matt knocked on Jessie's door. "Hi, sweetheart. I hope you're hungry. I know I am," he said when she opened the door. "I hope you don't mind if we meet Jaxon and Peyton for dinner."

"Not at all. I've missed seeing Peyton at the store since she's back working at the school again."

"Maxwell said Dylan could call on Jaxon if anything comes up while we're gone. I thought we should get together a few times before the wedding." He kissed her. "I should have done that when I first came in. Blame it on a preoccupied mind." He kissed her again. "I hope that makes it right."

"Almost." She smiled at him. "You'll have to try again later. I might still need a bit more convincing."

"I can live with that, sweetheart. I don't mind doing my best to convince you." He held her jacket for her to put on.

"I noticed the air is getting a little chillier in the evening. I hope the weather is beautiful for the wedding. Fingers are crossed because it is fall after all."

"If it's important to you, then it's important to me too. But truthfully, all I care about is marrying you."

She patted his cheek. "Aren't you just the sweetest guy!" She pushed past him when he turned to check that the door was locked.

He grabbed her hand before she could get far. "Oh, no, you don't. I'm not letting you out of my sight." He pulled her into his side. "This is where I want you."

"You might change your mind after I tell you about my day, but I'll wait until we are with the others." She latched her seat belt. "How was your day?"

"Let's just say I'm getting tired of waiting and I want some answers. That's nothing new when it comes to me. I want this puzzle solved before our wedding because it's messing with my mind."

"I hear you." She glanced out the window. "The answers are waiting to be discovered."

Chapter 26

As soon as they got to the restaurant, Jessie got out of the car and went to stand by Peyton. "Long time no see." Jessie smiled at her.

"My part-time work has turned into full-time the last few days. I'm helping in an art class because the teacher has been ill the past few days. She'll be back tomorrow or the next."

"We have a lot to catch up on," Jessie told her.

After they ordered, Matt talked with Jaxon for a few minutes and then turned to Jessie. "Now is as good a time as any to tell us about your day. I want answers, and Jaxon needs to know what he might be up against, looking for our possible suspect."

Jessie began by reminding him about the idea of the revenge factor and then moved on to Reba's visit to her store earlier. "She told me that what happened to you and to me were two sides of the same coin. They are related." Jessie went on to tell them about the man who came into her store. "He also went into the coffee shop and told Molly basically the same thing. I felt it was a threat and so did she. We both wondered if we were the only shops in town or if there were others."

"I know of two others on Main Street because they called the station to tell us about it. The problem is I got several descriptions of the man. There was no consistency at all." Matt shook his head.

"Well, it happens that Molly's new security got a picture of him, and she was able to send me a copy of him, which I will now send to you. Hopefully, this will help." She pulled the photo up and sent it to Matt's email.

"Thanks. I can run it through the system and see if we get a hit." Matt took a sip of the tea the waiter placed in front of him.

"What did Reba mean by the two coins phrase? Did she explain it to you?" Peyton asked.

"Yes. Although the situations may seem different, the two incidents are closely related to each other. At least, that is how she explained it to me. And I think the man today, who seemed like mobster to me the way he talked, fits into the scenario somehow. No facts, only guessing." She placed her napkin on her lap and thanked the waiter who placed her meal in front of her. "All I'm saying is somehow they all interconnect despite their different situations."

"Makes sense to me," Jaxon said.

They talked through dinner about the theories they had to this point. Jessie kept going over in mind the revenge factor. A clue too important to let go by the wayside. Someone from the past was angry and seething in his plot for revenge. The rising tide of discontent was possibly the catalyst to set him along with others into action.

When Matt and Jaxon got into one of their job conversations, she turned to Peyton. "I hope you realize that while I'm gone, you'll be watching over Blue Cove." She thanked the waiter when he placed their desserts in front of them.

"I've been thinking about that, of course. Maybe

it'll be quiet. One can hope." Peyton took a bite of her chocolate cake. "Yum, this is the best. Patterson's cake is to die for. I probably need to find a different way to say that. How about it is to live for?"

"Works for me. I would have to agree with you that it's the best." Jessie licked the chocolate frosting off her lips. "I don't want to miss even a morsel of this treat."

"If you think this is good, you should see what Katie has planned for your shower. Man, can that girl cook. It's hard to believe she was ever as bad a cook as you said she was, but Sally told me the same thing and so did her brother. I guess the old adage practice makes perfect is correct in her case." Peyton took a sip of her coffee. "You simply must have coffee with such a rich dessert." She smiled when Jessie shook her head. "Are you getting excited for Friday night?"

"I'm looking forward to seeing my friends. I'd be even more excited if I knew Matt had caught those involved in this mischief making."

"Is that what we're calling it now? Someone tries to kill him and abduct you, and that's mischief. I would call it attempted murder and kidnapping." Peyton glared at her.

"Well, when you put it that way, I guess I was being a bit tepid in my categorization of the suspects, but hey, I'm trying to keep things on a lighter note. I would rather be talking about my wedding instead of revenge. I've always been a somewhat nice person, and I can't figure out why people seem to dislike me so much." Jessie frowned.

"I don't dislike you." Matt grabbed her hand. "Who doesn't like you? Give me names, and I'll have a little chat with them." He raised her hand to his lips and kissed her fingers.

"Spoken like a lovesick soon-to-be husband." Jaxon laughed. "I'll set them straight. Let me at them." He punched Matt playfully on the arm.

"You know what I mean. I can't believe anyone dislikes Jessie. Except for maybe the criminals who have to worry about her knowing they are there. What's not to like about you, sweetheart?"

"All I'm saying is, since I've moved here, I've been shot at, chased, abducted by someone in an RV, and the list goes on. No one ever did that to me before. They found me when they got out of prison and tracked me here of all places. How can that be?" Jessie shook her head and took her hand back. She wanted another bite of cake.

"I can see how it might make you wonder, and I'm right there with you. Maybe it's not so much the place as the guys we're with." Peyton chuckled.

"Now there's a theory I can embrace." Jessie popped another piece of cake in her mouth.

"You're not going there. I don't see ghosts or have dead realities showing up for visits and dropping off their belongings in my attic," Matt said.

"Me either," Jaxon added.

"They do have a point, you know." Peyton patted Jaxon's hand. "But on the other hand, none of that stuff happened to us either until we got near our guys and moved here."

"How right you are, dear cousin." Jessie laughed. "Let's face the music. It's us, this town, and these guys."

After Matt paid the bill, they walked out of the restaurant to a chilly evening. Jessie took a deep breath.

The evening had been fun, and at the moment, things were as they should be. Two young couples in love enjoying a night out without a care in the world. Laughter and, of course, chocolate made the evening extra special. Matt's chivalry didn't hurt either. All things considered, the good in this moment outweighed the bad.

She latched her arm through Matt's as they walked to the car. "I love you," she said as she slipped into the passenger seat.

Matt leaned close to her before he closed the door. "I love you too."

****

"Young love." Mila sighed. "I love this part of my job."

"I wish they'd keep their minds on what's important although they do make a nice couple." Elida plopped down on the headrest beside her sister.

"Sheesh, why did they have to get all mushy?" Basil slapped his tiny hand to his forehead. "Love, is that all you girls think about? What about the thrill of the chase? Where is all the action I was promised?"

"Come now, Basil, this is one sweet moment among many. You've had all the action you can handle for now. And believe me, they need this tiny respite because the next several days will be hard on them and keep us busy. Kick back and take it easy while you can." Mila tugged his foot as he flew by her.

"More action sounds good to me. I forget humans are not as resilient as we are. They have a limited life span." Basil sat beside the sisters.

"Falling in love, so I'm told, is quite nice." Elida smiled at Mila.

"You're right, sister." Mila could remember the feeling as though it happened yesterday and sighed inwardly.

****

Matt walked Jessie to the door and took the keys she held in her hand. Unlocking the door, he held it open for her to walk in. He almost pushed her aside when a flashback came racing through his mind. If she had walked in that night, she would have been dead. It was strange how certain memories would sneak up on him when he least expected them. That gun, the sound, and the smells that came along with the helpless feeling still had the power to stop him. There had been too many close calls, his therapist told him. He couldn't disagree with him there. But that time, with Bobby Bristol hiding in her cottage and shooting at them from the inside, had messed with his mind more than any other time. He had no idea why. They had other close calls, but that one had impacted her deeply.

She was right on some level tonight. He had brought some of this trouble into her life. If he were smart, he would step away to keep her safe, but there was no way he'd ever do that. He would have to find some other way.

"You're quiet. Is everything all right?" she asked.

"Sorry, I'm thinking is all." He helped her out of her coat. "You mind if I turn on the TV?"

"Be my guest." She handed him the remote once he sat down. "We won't have many of these quiet moments before the wedding. All my family will be arriving soon. My mom is flying in for the shower. She and Dad will be staying with Sadie."

"My dad and brothers will be here for the party,

and my mom will be at your shower too. She's looking forward to seeing your mom and grandmother again. It's kind of amazing how fast the past few months have gone and at the same time seemed like a lifetime."

"I can see you are packing." Matt looked at the stack of boxes up against the living room wall.

"I've been sorting through what I want to take and what I don't. It's kind of sad that I finally got the place furnished after Bristol shot it up, and now I'll be leaving most of it here. At least, I don't have any attachment to most of it yet."

"We should probably start moving some of your belongings on Saturday. The ones you don't need the next couple of weeks anyways." Matt placed his arm around her shoulder.

"Sounds like a plan. Everything would be perfect if this other matter could be settled. I worry about my family being here with this going on." She pursed her lips.

"I hear you, but I think I'm catching some of your optimism. I believe it's all going to work out perfect at the right time." Matt flipped through the stations until he reached the one he wanted. "You know, sweetheart, it's moments like this with you by my side that I like best. I love you." He kissed her and then watched the scores.

Chapter 27

Whew, somehow, they had managed to make it to Friday with no more attempts against Matt or her. Tonight was her shower and Matt's bachelor party, which should be fun. Jessie tried to picture it in her mind as rushed out the door headed for work. She had overslept and was running behind. She honked and waved when she passed the inn. When she turned onto the road into town, she noticed the white car that had followed her home the other night was a few cars behind her. At least, it looked like the same car. Had the car followed her, or did they simply live up the road? Either way, she had forgotten to tell Matt about it. If only the car would get close enough for her to see the plates.

One of the cars in front of the white one turned off, which left only one car between them. They were too close to town for the other car to turn anywhere before her store unless they pulled into the church. Instead of going to the back of the store, she did a U-turn and parked in front, hoping to see the plates as the car passed by. It didn't work but at least, she tried.

She waited in front of the store to see if the car would come around again. But after ten minutes she drove around back to her usual spot and got ready to start her day.

Today was the mystery book club's usual meeting

day. Ever since they had moved to their new morning time, they got her day off to a quick start. She loved it when they were here. The store buzzed with laughter and conversations. It was the best part of the week along with when a tour bus came to town and filled her store with book lovers. There were plenty of those with all the fall tours. Her sales had been brisk the last few weeks, which would be nice to show her picky dad on the spreadsheets.

In some ways her father had changed a lot, but in others he was still the old grumpy control freak. Not unlike her store guardian who never smiled. A good spreadsheet filled with positive numbers would keep his lecture at bay. Thankfully, Sadie knew how to keep him in line. His newest soft spot was his mother. He treated her with the utmost kindness and respect. Jessie wondered if he would totally freak out when he found out a special gentleman was coming all the way from Ireland to dance with his mother at the wedding. It might make for a few interesting moments.

She unlocked the door and rushed in to find her guardian near the back door.

"We need to talk," he said. He looked menacing to her.

"All these months you've been here never saying a word and now you choose to talk. Ghosts can't talk."

"I beg your pardon. Johanna is a spirit, and she talks. Up to this point, I had nothing to say."

"I can't at the moment. I'm late and need to open for business." She brushed past him only for him to hover in front of her again.

"Fine." He frowned, his arms folded across his chest. "But before this day is over, we will talk." His voice was commanding.

"Why not? But at the moment I need coffee because I can't believe this is happening to me." She saw him smile as she moved around him once again. Grabbing her wallet out of her purse, she opened the doors into the coffee shop and ordered a coffee and scone. She had less than ten minutes before she had to open the store.

"Hi, Molly. I'm late this morning. Could you have someone bring this in when it's ready? I have to open." She glanced through the open doors to see the guardian watching her.

"Sure thing. I know how you like your coffee." Molly took her money and handed her the change. "Get going. I wondered what had happened to you today."

"The truth is I overslept." Jessie waved while rushing back into her shop. With no time for a leisurely morning opening, she went to unlock the front door and turn the sign around. She couldn't imagine the odd conversation that awaited her. Hopefully, he would tell her why he remained in her store,

The church parking lot was full. Her dress rehearsal would be there two weeks from tonight. The church looked beautiful in the sunlight. Her mother was happy Jessie had chosen to be married in a church and loved Pastor John. Of course, her mother had no idea about all the abnormal things that had happened to her when she worked there. Yes, that place was the beginning of her unexpected new life.

A cold chill moved down her arm. She knew without looking her stalwart champion apparition was nearby. Thankfully, the ladies started to file into the store with their coffees, and she had a morning reprieve.

"Good morning, ladies. Your table is ready. Enjoy your meeting." Jessie went to stand behind the counter. She loved listening to their chatter until they got into the book discussion. Sometimes they never got around to the book at all. Their gatherings often turned into local gossip sessions as much as about the current book they were reading. If they only knew all the unseen eyes that had observed them over the past year or the strange beings that had paraded through the store during the weeks they met here. Jessie smiled to herself and turned on her computer.

As the ladies' group broke up and began to leave, Jessie could see the store's ancient guardian headed her way. An earlier promised conversation was about to take place and actually she was intrigued by what he might tell her. Maybe she was about to find out the reason why he still remained even though Johanna hadn't been seen in weeks.

Jessie checked out two of the women who found some books before they left the store and waited for what was sure to be an enlightening chat. It was sure to give her something to tell Matt if she saw him today. Maybe she should mention the white car that followed her home. He wouldn't be happy that she hadn't told him right away. At least, she had made it to Friday, and a fun night with friends was just what her therapist would order.

****

Friday, and still the suspect hadn't shown himself. Matt wasn't sure if he was pleased or not. He was glad to be alive for sure but not knowing when the next attempt would come was a tad unsettling. After studying several of their past cases, his gut told him he was getting close to figuring this one out.

Anderson had dealt with some shady characters and was up to his head in corruption and kickbacks. The whole world he walked in made Matt sick when he saw the extent of how badly his hero had slipped. What makes a good cop go bad? A question he asked Jaxon, and others. Money seemed to be a common answer. The other fact that he found as he studied several similar cases was the quest for power and control. To be able to operate outside the law while making others toe the line was a strange phenomenon to Matt's way of thinking. He didn't understand how they could live with their own hypocrisy. The same held true for spiritual leaders, politicians, and anyone else who could see an easy way to serve their ego while making money at another's expense. A man's ego could make him lose his moral footing fast. His dad used to tell them they needed to figure out what kind of person they wanted to be before they found themselves in situations that would test their staying power.

He'd had plenty of times over the years that tested his resilience. The one time he messed up bad, he got rip roaring drunk after graduation. The next day, sicker than a dog, he had to listen to a lecture from his father. His mother wiped her tears and shook her head, sniffing every time she glanced at him. All the while, his dad seemed to speak every word, in what sounded like to him, a shouting mode. Both his brothers, Evan and Jason, laughed while his parents constantly told them to be quiet. The chaos of the morning imprinted itself into his psyche and he never wanted to repeat it. Later he learned his laughing older brother Evan had already lived through his own version of too much to drink at a graduation party. And Jason followed, having learned nothing from his older brothers' poor example, and had to find out for himself.

The one sentence his dad said repeatedly over the course of that morning stuck with him through college and beyond.

"Matt, drinking too much doesn't make you a man, but it does make you lose control and act like a fool." He had no idea what he had done that night, and he still didn't want to know all the details although he had heard enough rumors that circulated among his friends to have a good idea. Call it a hard lesson learned.

He turned his chair around to look out the window. What was Jessie up to at the moment? He should call her. With his bachelor party and her bridal shower, he wouldn't see her tonight unless it was late. Tomorrow he would move some of her boxes to the house and show her his surprise. He wanted her to feel like his house was theirs and not only his.

He called but she didn't answer. "I'll bring you lunch. See you soon." He left the message on her voice mail.

He received a text back from her. —*Too busy to talk now. Lunch sounds good.*—

Matt turned when someone knocked on his door.

"Sorry to bother you, Chief." Dylan leaned against the door frame. "Jaxon asked me to meet him here in ten minutes. I can see that I beat him. He told me to tell you we both needed to hear what he has found out." He walked into Matt's office and sat in the chair in front of the desk.

"Great. I would like to have any information I can

get my hands on. I've looked over several old files from some of Chief Anderson's cases, and we may have a few more messes to clean up in the next few months. I will leave the files I've read for you to go over. I want to know what you think about them. Maybe I'm looking for trouble and am too close to the whole Anderson episode to think clear. But my gut tells me that guy trying to bully shop owners may have something to do with one of his old pay-to-play cases."

"If anything, you would be more likely to give him the benefit of the doubt. I'd be happy to check them out. That guy turned out to be a snake, and those who he turned a blind eye to were too."

"Hey," Jaxon said as he walked in and closed the door behind him. He sat next to Dylan. "We need to keep this under the hat for now. I don't want anyone to get wind of what I'm about to tell you."

"I'm all ears," Matt said. "And as I've found out before, information has a way of leaking out of the station. A closed door is probably a good idea.

"I have no idea who we are looking at yet, but we're closing in. I can tell you this could go back to a revenge motivated by you taking down the Harvest Club or the arms dealer in Palm Springs. Those were both big cases and took out a lot of people. I heard your suspect was extreme in that one."

"True. Damn, I forgot all about him. He was a real gem. Reba Thompson said the shooter was motivated by revenge. There were quite a few men taken down when both those groups were put out of business." Matt tapped his pencil on the open file. "Some high-profile people were involved in each case, which I'm sure didn't do me any favors or win friends."

"I read over the list of them. It gave your career a boost but made you a target at the same time," Jaxon said.

"Is Zach Johnson or his brother involved in some way?" Matt asked.

"Not according to our inside source. No, this is a lone wolf who is on the outside. We're trying to go through the list of people from each case recently released or on parole. There were quite a few, as you know. This guy had to be one of the lower-level members to get out this early. Nondescript and low-keyed might best describe who we're looking for."

"At least that narrows down the field of cases a bit." Dylan leaned forward in his chair. "I'll start going through the case files."

"I will too. Between the two of us we should be able to figure out a possible suspect." Matt reached for one of the files on his desk. "I pulled one of the club files today. I hadn't got around to reading it yet. I plan on doing it after lunch."

"I wanted you both to be aware. I don't believe he's done. But having said that, we are still looking at a couple of other suspects that have made threats against you. Whoever it is, they're serious about taking you out and may be behind what happened to Jessie in New York."

"Like two sides of the same coin." Matt muttered what Reba had said to Jessie under his breath.

"Something like that." Jaxon nodded. "I was thinking we should have eyes on the party at the inn tonight. In case someone decides to be a party crasher."

"A good suggestion. I'll mention to Jessie to be alert and not to let her guard down. Of course, that seems a bit sad when this is supposed to be a happy time for her." Matt shook his head.

"It never hurts to be careful, but let's not tell Jessie. Instead, let me talk to Peyton. She'll be happy to keep an eye out, so Jessie can have a fun evening."

"That sounds like a good idea. I want her to have some good memories of this time."

"Katie is already in high gear with preparations for tonight. I doubt I'll say anything to her, but I'll check the grounds around the inn before I leave to be with you all tonight. There are too many places to hide with all those trees." Dylan frowned.

"I'm not saying he'll try anything, but I can't rule it out either." Jaxon stood. "I need to get to another meeting. I'll see you two tonight."

"See you later." Dylan also stood. "You can give me one of those files to look over if you want."

Matt handed him one of the files out of the pile. "Catch you tonight."

Matt glanced at the clock. He still had thirty minutes before lunch. He slipped on his glasses and began reading over one of the files on the Harvest Club and Johnson's other criminal projects.

Chapter 28

Matt went first to Joe's to pick up the lunch he had
ordered. He could see Jessie standing near the counter
her hands on her hips, but he couldn't see her face. It
was the same stance she often took with him when she
hadn't agreed with something he said. Matt knew there
was a story in there somewhere, and he couldn't wait to
hear it.

"Thanks, Molly." He placed a tip in the jar after
she handed him his change. "How much longer do you
have to work?"

"I start maternity leave the Monday after your
wedding. I'm looking forward to putting my feet up for
a few days and finishing the baby's room."

"I bet. With the Family Leave Act, Kenny will get
some time off to be with you once the baby is born."

"I know, and I'm looking forward to it. Thanks for
being such a great customer." She gave him his order.

"My pleasure. Your food is good and that's the
reason. The owners are nice too, which is a plus."

"It doesn't hurt that Jessie is next door either."
Molly chuckled.

"Yeah, that too." Matt winked at her.

Matt walked into Jessie's store, went to the table to
sit down, pulled his order out of the bag, and placed it
on the table. She still hadn't noticed him. He had no
idea what she was up to.

He cleared his throat. "Hi, sweetheart."

"Oh, Matt, I didn't see you come in." She walked over to where he sat.

"I noticed." He smiled at her. "I wonder why that is." He placed her lunch in front of her.

"I was having a somewhat one-sided chat with my resident ghost. It would seem he's here for a while." She pursed her lips and plopped down on the chair beside him.

"What makes you think that?" Matt asked.

"He told me. Before you say anything, I'm as surprised as you that he talks. He hadn't said anything up to this point. He told me in clear terms it was because he had nothing to say until now." She glanced to where he stood guard.

"What important message brought him out of his mute state?" Matt took a bite of his grilled chicken sandwich.

"In the fewest words possible, he told me he was here to stay for the duration of my life and Peyton's and anyone else who came along with the same gift."

"Did he say why?"

"That's where it gets a bit more detailed. Johanna once nursed him back to health after he was wounded by the dagger upstairs. Her family was kind to him. He made a vow to protect her family and anyone else who followed in her family line with a similar gift and heart." She sipped her tea. "I tried to get more out of him, but that's all he gave me. He must have been a man of few words."

"Anything else of importance?" Matt knew there was more.

"Well, there is one more thing which I guess you

could say is an important detail. The past has come to the present to enact revenge. You know, the whole two sides of the same coin." She ate a bite of her lunch. "And before I forget to mention it, a white car followed me home the other night. I'm not sure that has anything to do with this, but I thought you should know."

"Seems like an important detail to me. I guess I need to ask you more often if you have any other important information."

"I tend to move on in my mind so fast that I don't always remember the small details."

"Jess, no facts are small when it comes to you. Reba told you something similar. I'm sure there's an important piece of information in there to help solve the case. At this point, we need all the help we can get. I would like to leave for our honeymoon with nothing left unfinished." He took her hand in his.

"Honeymoon. Heck, I want it solved before our wedding. I'm nervous about my family getting too close to us with someone running around wanting to kill us." She frowned. "Could we change the subject? I still have hope that besides him—" She pointed at the stairs. "—there are others who are looking out for us."

"Sounds good to me." He lifted her hand to his lips and kissed it.

They spent the rest of their lunch going over the pieces that had happened up to this point. The close calls that Matt had already had. Her near abduction.

"I agree with you that we've been lucky so far." Matt gathered the trash from the table to throw it away.

"No one can be that lucky." She walked him to the door. "Try not to think about the job tonight and have a good time." She kissed him. "That's what I'm going to

A Wedding to Remember

do. I'm excited to be with my friends tonight."

"I'll do the same." He kissed her back. "I'll see you tomorrow."

"You can always call even if it's late to say goodnight. I'll be up."

****

Jessie watched him until he drove away. "Ever the optimist," she muttered under her breath. She wanted to believe that everything would be fine, but they both had had too many close calls since she moved to town. What she needed at the moment was a break from it all. Not that the powers that be seemed to listen to her complaints, and she could complain with the best of them. Matt would have his hands full when it came to her. Not that she would intentionally cause him trouble, but she was bound to inadvertently.

Her empathy often made her seem naïve and easy pickings, but this year had taught her that she was stronger than she ever imagined. She used to walk into the middle of trouble without sizing up the situation and think nothing of it. How radically her life had changed in a single year. She held her special locket in her hand, which glowed and got warm to the touch. Something new to ponder. The way the light shimmered through the stone mesmerized her as she turned the Celtic locket over in her hand and studied it. Matt was her destiny, and she wanted to help to her future husband like her ancestor of old and not hinder him.

What she hadn't told Matt was her resident ghost told her this was only the beginning. Now that she knew who she was, the challenges she would face in this life would be constant. In truth, she understood she couldn't run away or take a vacation from who she was

203

meant to be. It was better to wrestle this out now. Like anyone else who lived, there would be good days and bad days along with highs and lows. She wasn't here simply for herself.

She was happy to see Reba walk in and even happier when she said she was only there to look for something to read. Jessie pointed her toward a section with a few new books that her customers were loving. Jessie loved how Reba took time reading the blurbs on the back of the books. Something she always did too.

"Hey, cous." Peyton walked in. "I got off early and thought I'd stop by and do what Reba is doing. I want new reading material."

"Look in the section with Reba. Several of my regulars love those books," Jessie told her.

"Are you getting excited for tonight?" Peyton asked as she stood beside Reba.

"I am. I can't wait to see everyone. It's been a while since I got to hang out with friends and have fun."

"At least since we got back from our trip, it's been all work and no play. But not tonight. We get to talk, laugh, and eat to our heart's content." Peyton smiled. "I for one am happy to celebrate something good for a change."

"I'm happy to give you a reason for celebrating. I wonder what the guys have planned for tonight." Jessie pulled a book off the shelf and handed it to her cousin to check out.

"Jaxon said it would all be on the up and up. Matt is after all the chief of police, so they can't get drunk, rowdy, or have any girls. He added the last part to assure me that there wouldn't be any." Peyton laughed and Reba chuckled.

"Smart man. I know Matt wouldn't go for any shenanigans. He has his professional reputation to maintain, although I've been working with him to surprise our wedding guests at the reception. It's out of character for him and way out of his comfort zone. I'll go on the record as saying, he's quite talented."

"You can't leave us hanging. What are you planning?" Peyton asked.

"If I told you it wouldn't be a surprise, would it?" Jessie smiled. How she had ever convinced Matt to take part in her plan still amazed her. They had fun the past few weeks working out the moves and details. "I'm happy you finally agreed to sing with Destiny at the wedding. I love your voices together."

"She had to promise me a lot to convince me to do it, but I've enjoyed practicing with her. I'm not sure about singing before all those people, though." Peyton handed Reba the book to look at.

"You mean all our family and friends. You'll be singing before a friendly crowd. Relax." Jessie pulled a sequel to the book for them to look at. "These are the first two in the series. They should keep you busy for at least a couple of days if you read like me."

"If a book is good, I can read for hours. I'll try these two." Reba handed the books to Jessie. "I'm waiting for the next one by one of my favorite authors. She can't write them as fast as I can read them. And when I hear the date of her next one, I go back and read the series over from the beginning. I always find new details. I think I must be odd."

"I do the same thing." Peyton handed Jessie copies of the same books.

"I'm guilty too." Jessie rang up their purchases and placed the books in bags for them. "I hope you like them. I bought the same two a few weeks ago but haven't started to read them yet. I've been too busy."

"What's the latest news in town?" Peyton asked. "I need to catch up."

Jessie spent the next thirty minutes telling them what she had told Matt earlier. She let Reba explain her part. When it came to the resident ghost, she told Peyton he would be around for a while and why.

At five, she closed the store and rushed home to get ready for her night out. Her bridal shower. She knew one day she might get married, but it was the last thing on her mind when she first moved to Blue Cove and especially to Matt. Their first introduction hadn't gone well at all. Now she couldn't imagine anyone else to be the one. Matt was a keeper. Though he couldn't understand most of what went on with her, he did his best to support her. At least he put on a brave face. How she loved the man. And because of her, his life was at risk from anyone who didn't want the two of them to stand together. How weird was that? She could not see this part of her life coming, but she couldn't image it being any other way.

****

Matt closed the file on his desk. He rubbed his temple as he took off his glasses. His gut told him he was narrowing down his list of possible suspects. When he glanced at his watch, he stood and slipped his glasses in his pocket. Chilling with his friends sounded great at the moment.

Jaxon promised him a relaxing evening with good food and friends. A card game or two, pool, and darts with a group of competitive males, and you had a party as far as he was concerned. With both of his brothers together in the same room, it was bound to turn into a major rivalry and contest complete with bragging rights. He was looking forward to it.

Matt arrived at Patterson's and was ushered to the back room where several of his friends and family were waiting. The staff was arranging the trays of food, with the famous chocolate cake among the dessert temptations.

"You ready, bro?" Evan, his older brother, slapped him on the back. "Your days of freedom are coming to an end."

"With a stunner like Jessie, do you think he minds?" Jason walked up beside him.

"You're right about that. How are you doing, little brother? Have you grown up at all, or are you still chasing anything in a skirt?" Matt glanced at him.

"A bit of both, I guess. At least, with you two as my example I'm learning to be more discerning. Between Jessie and Destiny, I have dreams of what might be." He laughed.

"Good to know. Dad will be happy to hear it." Evan clapped Jason on the shoulder.

"Happy to hear what?" Dad Parker asked. "Never mind. I don't want to know. I'm happy to see the three of you together and nothing is broken. That's good enough for me."

"Geez, Dad, we weren't that bad." Jason chuckled.

"The three of you were knuckleheads. You were in one scrape after another. Let me enjoy one of the rare moments of parental pride when it comes to you three. You've all turned out fine." He turned to Jason. "The jury is still out on you—" He pointed at his youngest son. "—but I'm seeing some progress in that department."

"Thanks, Pop." Jason grinned. "At least Mom doesn't cry as much and call the priest."

"Never fear, Jason. She did that with us too," Evan told him.

"Truth is, I couldn't be prouder of you boys." Dad swiped at his eyes.

"In case we haven't told you often enough, you're the best dad." Matt put his hand on his dad's shoulder.

"You've got yourself a real gem, son. Jessie is a lovely young woman. Your mom and I are happy to have one of you boys ready to settle down. And Evan, after meeting Destiny, I hope you'll soon follow your brother's lead."

"I'm considering it, Pops. I'm not getting any younger." Evan laughed. "Should we join the others? I'm ready to eat and play some cards."

"Food is always good. I challenge you both to a game of pool and darts. May the best man win." Jason got into the buffet line and started filling his plate.

Matt realized once again how much his family meant to him. He needed to spend more time with each of them. Matt glanced at his father in line in front of him. *He's a good man, and he's right—we were knuckleheads growing up. How can you repay love?*

"Hey, brother, you're way too serious. Let's party." Jason handed Matt his plate. "The night is young and you're only single for a few more weeks."

Matt lost at pool and darts to his brothers. His heart wasn't in it. Chad, Kip, and Dylan were being set up to take their challenge and the competition was on. It didn't take long before the whole room was lined up on one side or the other cheering on their favorite competitor.

"Before you get caught in the fun, Matt, Sally wanted me to give you a copy of this letter she got from her ex. I think you'll find it interesting." Chad handed him the letter.

Matt glanced over the contents. "Something worth checking into for sure. I wonder if he is still in prison. Thanks."

"It's time for you join in the fun. I'm going to take Jason on." Chad laughed.

Matt soon forgot his concerns and joined in the comradery. He accepted Evan's challenge a second time and finally got his own bragging rights. He won.

Chapter 29

Jessie couldn't believe all the amazing detail that Katie had put into creating the atmosphere for her shower. From the beautiful display of her culinary creations, the floral arrangements, along with the games and prizes, everything was perfect. The colors of the plates, down to the ribbons on the gift bags, all matched her wedding colors.

Matt's mom and hers were chatting happily. Reba and Sadie sat side by side deep in conversation, and the room was filled with some of her favorite friends. Jessie smiled to herself. This would always remain in her thinking as one of those perfect moments to be remembered. She took her phone and snapped several photos of those in the room. Many would end up in her wedding remembrance album. Katie told her she must have one because details were often forgotten in the excitement of the time.

"My friend, this is perfect." Jessie wrapped her arms around Katie. "You're so gifted. You should add *wedding planner* to your Inn's Wedding Destination resume."

"You really should. I could put that piece of information in the town's tourism brochure. This is all so beautiful, and I can't wait to taste all of this wonderful looking food," Sally said. "It is so great that the three of us are together again. I never imagined I could be this happy ever, and I have you two to thank for it." Sally hugged them both.

"Jessie, you and Sally fill your plates, and I'll tell the others to do the same." Katie motioned them toward the table.

"How do you even begin to choose?" Sally asked softly. "That quiche looks wonderful, and so do all the salads. Don't even get me started on the desserts."

"I know. It's almost too pretty to eat, but I'll manage." Jessie cut a wedge of the spinach quiche. She reached for a spoonful of the fruit salad and a blueberry muffin. "I'll have to come back for dessert later." Jessie carried her plate to the table and placed it near her name card. "Grams, let me help you carry that." She took Sadie's and Reba's plates to the table for them.

"Thank you, dear girl." Grams patted her cheek. "You look beautiful tonight. That dress makes your eyes seem even bluer if that's possible. Did you read your grandpa's letter yet?"

"I was saving it until a few days before the wedding," Jessie answered. "I want to savor it."

"Don't wait too long. He wanted you to have it. His words might give you comfort." She grabbed Jessie's hand. "Reba and I were just talking. We don't believe there will be too many more twists and turns in this case. It's straight-up revenge, and once the culprit is found out, you'll be married and on your way to your honeymoon destination."

"In other words, don't chase rabbit trails. Think retribution and someone who is angry." Reba patted Jessie's hand. "Have some fun, dear."

Once Jessie reached her chair, Sally sat across from her. "I want to give you this. Chad is giving Matt a copy too. You don't need to read it right now, but maybe it will help you in solving the case. If not, he might become a problem later."

"Is this from your ex?" Jessie asked.

"Yes, and it's not nice either." Sally placed her napkin on her lap. "This is a night for fun."

With all of her bridal party sitting around her, they chatted and talked all things wedding, marriage, and guys. At least until the games began and then laughter became the order of the evening and luscious desserts, of course.

Jessie received all kinds of lingerie—pretty, sexy, and thankfully some practical ones too. The color trend seemed to be red with a few pinks and blues thrown in. Jessie smiled to herself. She wasn't a fan of black; the colors suited her fine.

Reba's sister, Barbara, gave her a beautiful painting for her wall. The landscape reminded her of the view from her cottage window. One which had brought her a sense of peace every time she looked out her front window. She would find a special place for it to hang.

Sadie handed a gift to her granddaughter from her. "Lingerie is nice for the honeymoon, but mine is for your wedding day."

Jessie opened the small box to find a replica of her necklace made into a bracelet with several diamonds circled around an emerald in the Celtic symbol. "Grams, this is beautiful."

"A little something to remind you who you are every time you look at it." Sadie hugged her.

"I will cherish this always," she said as she took the tissue Katie had in her hand to wipe her eyes.

Later on, as she lay on the bed, she thought about all her friends and how blessed she was to have them. Her mom and Matt's mother were touched as well. Blue Cove had brought many changes to her life, and one of them was the special people who had celebrated the evening with her. Another, of course, was the special man she was about to marry.

****

Mila sighed. She had been a silent observer for most of the night except for her occasional whispers in the ears of a few of guests. Special human moments still caught her off guard and made her wistful. She wasn't sure why, but it was almost as if she were missing out on some unnamed emotion she would never quite grasp. Still, she was proud of the work she had accomplished in Sally's life to connect her with Chad. Destiny along with Katie's sudden change of heart were two of her other projects.

She found herself daydreaming when she was supposed to be paying attention. What if Aelfric had stayed the course? How foolish she was to even think in that direction at all. He was lost to them forever. Her work had to be enough for her. She sighed again and waited for her charge to fall asleep.

"Mila, don't castigate yourself." Celeste settled down beside her.

"Oh, my. What are you doing here? I should have come to you." Mila glanced at her.

"You have worked tirelessly for good, and I wanted to tell you in person. It will not erase your memory of the past and Aelfric's descent into darkness, but you'll be free to give your heart to another in time. In the meantime, keep spreading your good magic.

Kindness always finds its way home." Celeste touched her hand to Mila's cheek. "May the good you've shown others come to rest upon you."

When Mila turned again, Celeste was gone. She blew a misty kiss toward Jessie and smiled to herself. Wow, Celeste, the fairy queen, had come to her. She would remember this moment always and work extra hard to live up to her words. Speaking of work, she needed to check on Basil and Elida. A quick peek to check on Katie wouldn't hurt. A second dream might keep the change percolating inside of her. Yes, this had been a wonderful night indeed.

Mila wrapped Jessie in a fog of her protection as she went about her job for the night.

"Sleep tight, my beautiful girl. Dream sweet and great dreams. You also have a lot of work to do. Tonight, dream of your handsome man and how you might best help him." Mila tapped her finger three times against Jessie's forehead and waited for the dream to begin. Mila floated up into the air and moved toward the inn to where the sleeping Katie rested.

****

Jessie reached for her ringing phone as she placed another item in the box she was packing. "Good morning, Peyton. You're up early for a Saturday morning."

"I wanted to talk to you before you and Matt start moving your belongings to Matt's."

"What's up?" Jessie asked.

"After Ireland, we both understand our family connection to the gift of sight with all its variations, and that it came down to us. Through the scrolls and writings of the women in our ancestral line, we've learned of the different methods and ways it has been used over the years. Johanna made it clear it had to be used for good. All of this has me thinking. Especially after your shower last night. It would be great if at some point the gift could be used to prevent a murder from happening."

"You mean instead of solving the crime after the fact, it somehow could prevent it. What got you thinking along those lines?" Jessie closed the box, sealing the seam with packing tape.

"A few things. Reba always gives us clues and warnings ahead of time. You were able to help Sally Mansfield before her husband could kill her. Isn't part of using it for good like Johanna standing up against the invading Normans in her day? These are all simmering ideas and questions in my mind."

"I get you. I've always thought it's not that we are special, but that everyone is meant to walk in this world aware of others and what is happening around them. It appears to me that secrecy can hide a plot to commit or perform an actual crime only until a tiny awareness by someone acts like a light and brings it all out into the open."

"Okay, following your line of reasoning, how do you apply that now in your situation?" Peyton asked.

"Reba gave us a couple of hints. The idea that our suspect is seeking revenge, and two sides of the same coin, says to me we are looking at one individual who is angry at both of us and is caught up in the rising tide in our generation. Can knowing this prevent him from being successful? I sure hope so, with a little help from our tiny friends." She paused, scrunching her lips. "I know they must be nearby. Let me get this straight. I believe what you're saying is that Reba has tapped into seeing the plot before it becomes a crime." Jessie nodded thoughtfully. "Hmm."

"I guess I am. I know we both have had small moments when we experienced the sense of hearing, but we have a long way to go to be where she is. As she says, we only can see what we see.

"Moving is never fun, but Matt has roped in a couple of guys to help. He didn't want you to have to lift the boxes. He told Jaxon he only wanted you to arrange your items the way you want them at your new house. I thought that was not only thoughtful but kind of romantic."

"Matt can be quite charming when he's not grumbling or shaking his head. Which is an often occurrence when it comes to me." Jessie laughed. "I'm not moving everything today. I'm also leaving the cottage furnished for whoever is going to live here next. I know they'll love it as much as I have. I will miss my cottage by the sea as I've come to think of it. At least your sister, Madison, will enjoy staying here for a few days while we're on our honeymoon."

"I know Matt and the fellas will be there soon, and I don't want to keep you. I wanted to tell you where my thoughts have been traveling before I forget them. It gets crowded up there somedays." Peyton chuckled.

"How well I know that." Jessie smiled to herself.

"I love you, cous. We'll talk later, I'm sure."

Jessie closed her last box that she would be moving today and stacked it with the others in the living room. Peyton had been thinking along the same lines as she had, only Jessie found herself questioning everything. She also thought back over the many cases she had gotten embroiled in since moving to the cove.

Hearing in her thoughts Abigail's cries for help had sent her on a race with time to save some children who had been abducted. The moment they rescued the children was a great highlight in her life. She still saw Abigail from time to time. She was growing into a pretty young teen and full of life.

Sitting across from Sally last night had reminded her of the condition she had been in when she first came to visit Jessie and Katie. The three had been inseparable growing up and had got into plenty of trouble, led by Katie's crazy plans.

Their once happy friend arrived overweight, beat down by the words of a controlling husband who often followed the words with physical abuse. She came to them because she had left Bruce Kingman before he could kill her.

In her heart, Jessie knew Bruce would track her and he did. His ego wouldn't let her leave him no matter what. Matt got her out of town to a safe house, but somehow Bruce had found her. After shooting her—thankfully she survived—he ended up in prison. That's why the letter Sally showed her was disturbing. He promised retribution on anyone who had helped Sally leave him. From her parents who had given her money, to Jessie, Katie, and anyone else who helped her.

Sally was doing well now. After recovering from her injuries both physically and mentally, she had arrived back in the cove, thinner, healthier, and like the friend that Jessie had always remembered. Along with a bit of Christmas magic, Sally met Chad Richards, Matt's best friend growing up, and they were slowly evolving into a couple. Sally was on the cautious side, and who could blame her after the abuse she had endured?

Jessie found it strange that all of a sudden Bruce wrote to her out of the blue a vengeful letter. He even knew Chad's name, which meant someone was feeding him information in prison. Could Bruce be the one they needed to look at? He seemed like a possible suspect to her. Maybe a bit too convenient, or maybe not.

Jessie rushed to the door when she heard male voices and laughter. "Good morning. The boxes are all ready for you," she told Matt. "If I would've known you were all coming, I would have had coffee and scones for you."

"I've taken care of the food, sweetheart. As soon as these are all loaded, you're riding with me." Matt grabbed a box, hefted it on his shoulder, and gave her a quick kiss as he walked through the screen door she held open.

Chapter 30

Matt arranged for Kip, who was driving the truck, to stop to pick up what he ordered from Molly and give him at least thirty minutes alone with Jessie at the house. It was time for him to share the surprise he had been working on to make her feel this was her home too and not his alone. After the party last night and early this morning Jaxon helped him finish the last few details.

"You're too quiet. What's on your mind?" Matt asked.

"I had an interesting conversation earlier with Peyton, and it got me thinking about all the twists and turns in my life since moving here. Don't get me wrong—most of them were good ones. That would be you." She pointed at him. She told him about her morning conversation. "It got me thinking about the people we helped. Those we were able to save and those who could only be helped after the fact." She glanced out the window. "Sally let me read Bruce's threatening letter."

"Chad gave me a copy too. I have someone checking on him in prison and any connections he might have on the outside. What do you think?"

"He knew Chad's name, which is a bit concerning. It means someone is feeding him information, which is never good. I'm not sure what to think. The letter fit the revenge factor, but I'm not sure."

"I hear you. Let's put it aside for the moment and enjoy a nice Saturday morning." He pulled into the driveway at his house. "I have something I want to show you. First, you have to close your eyes and promise not to peek,"

"Sure, why not." She closed her eyes and let him lead her.

"Take a step up. That's a girl." He held her arm tight so she wouldn't fall. "Just a little farther. Keep them closed a little longer." He opened a door. "Okay, you can open them now. This is my gift to you. I want you to feel at home here. I thought you could use this space to write or do whatever it is you liked to do without me underfoot."

"You did all this for me?" Jessie glanced around the room. She ran her hand over the beautiful desk. "Did you make this? The craftsmanship is exquisite."

Matt nodded. "I even chose the room color with a bit of help from Peyton. I didn't want it to be dark but something you might like. Do you?"

"I do. The room is perfect. I wouldn't change a thing. I see you even hung my favorite painting. Sadie painted this one for me, and I love the colors and movement in it." She kissed him and leaned her head on his shoulder as they stood side by side. "I love it all the more because you created the space. Thank you." She noticed he had hung the painting Barbara, Reba's sister, had given her. Seeing it there also made her wonder how he came to have the painting.

"You're welcome." Matt smiled to himself. "Do you think you can help me turn the rest of this place into our home? I want you to be happy here." He gave her one long delicious kiss.

"As long as you're here, I'm sure I'll be happy," she said when he let her catch her breath. "I have one question for you though." She glanced at him.

"Ask away," he said.

"How did you get this painting? I only opened it last night." Jessie asked pointing at the piece of art leaning against the wall waiting to find its final space.

"I'll never tell. I have my ways." He chuckled. "Let's meet the others." He took her hand and tugged her toward the kitchen.

****

Matt had surprised her. Later she wandered by herself into the office. Her new room was beautiful with its cream walls, soft bluish-green accent wall, and beautiful lamps and accessories. The desk, credenza, and bookshelves were art in themselves. He had put so much loving thought into all of the details. Each done to make her feel like this was her home too. On her first glance at the interior, she hadn't seen the gorgeous painting on one of the walls across from her desk. The painting reminded her of the one she saw at the museum. She read the card and brochure Matt had placed on the desk about the artist. When she read about the artist, tears came to her eyes. The painting was from the area around Kilkenny. The artist's love for Ireland showed in each detail of his work.

Jessie sighed. She would have this beautiful reminder of her trip any time she wanted to look at the beautiful landscape. She found herself pulled into its wild beauty until a pair of sturdy hands settled on her shoulders.

"I hope you like this painting. When I read your

journal about Ireland, I knew I had to get you a painting for your new home office from Kilkenny."

"It's absolutely beautiful. I can get lost in the detail. It's almost like I'm standing there for real. How did you ever find it?" she asked, taking her eyes away from the painting long enough to glance at him.

"I went online. I saw this artist and her work. I had several conversations with her personally, and I bought the painting directly from her." Matt continued to tell her about their many conversations and how he had come to choose this particular painting from the woman. "She told me it was one of her paintings of the few places people had described as Ireland's thin places. I knew you would understand." He pulled her into his arms and hugged her tight.

"I can't believe you did this for me. I will cherish your sweet gesture every time I walk into my room." She rested her head on his chest. The love she felt for Matt seemed to explode within her. They were meant to be. And she wanted to be here with him at this time and in this town. No wonder someone didn't want them to get married. Together they could be a formidable team, and she had no doubt this was her home.

Later, after Matt dropped her off at home, Jessie reflected on her day with him. He had gone out of his way to make her coming transition to his house as smooth as possible. She pulled the throw from the back of the couch and covered herself. The air was a bit nippy with the wind blowing today, and she could still feel the chill in her bones. What she wanted now was warm and cozy along with a cup of tea. Matt wanted her to feel like his place was her home too. He mentioned the fact at least a dozen times. She smiled.

Endearing was the word that came to mind.

For the second time in weeks, she found herself anticipating her wedding. The dress, the celebration with family and friends, literally the whole shebang. She glanced at the bag containing her dress hanging in her closet. Most of her belongings that she wanted to keep and her shower gifts from the townspeople were already at their house. She had taken several boxes with items to give to a drop-off box in town a few days ago. Her cottage looked less like her home and more like a place to stay for a few days.

Her suitcases for the honeymoon were partially packed but since she had no idea where they were going, she would have to rely on Peyton to put the right outfits conducive to weather where they were headed. Matt hadn't given her a clue, and he refused to tell Katie. Peyton was his confidante of choice. Jessie couldn't get her cousin to budge. Still, she was excited to go anywhere with Matt and get to know him better. In this case, she would have to trust Peyton's sense of style and, of course, Sadie and her mom's gifted wedding trousseau. The shopping trip with them had been one of the highlights of the whole wedding experience to date. She got some really awesome clothes.

With the tea kettle whistling, she went into the kitchen to make her tea. Each step seemed important at the moment; routine gave her a sense of peace. Placing the hot tea on the table by the couch, she rushed to her bedroom and picked up the envelope. She ran her finger gently across its length, imagining her grandpa who had lovingly written the contents. This was her moment to read his letter. She leaned her head against the back of the couch, closed her eyes, and her grandpa's face was all she saw.

****

Matt thought the day went well. Jess had loved his gift. Her face lit up, her eyes were glistening with happy tears, and the look she gave him made all the work worthwhile. He would have never finished without Jaxon's help. He glanced around the room one more time before shutting off the light. He could still see her standing there with her hand running the length of the desk admiring the beauty of the wood and his handiwork. He'd never tell anyone else, but in that moment he knew with her by his side, he could do anything. Did every man feel this way when he was in love?

Enough with the mushy stuff. Matt went to his favorite lounge chair and turned on the sports channel. But his sweet fiancée and soon-to-be bride wasn't far from his thoughts. Neither was the fact that they still had a suspect out there who opposed their marriage. He hoped Jaxon would have some information for him about Bruce Kingman soon. He wasn't sold on the idea Bruce was involved, but his threatening letter made him stop and think about the possibility.

Matt took a swig of his beer and reached for his ringing phone. "Hey, Jaxon, I was just thinking of you."

"I promised to call you as soon as I learned something about Bruce. Our inside sources say he's up to something and someone we need to keep our eyes on. He has a man on the outside that is feeding him information about his wife. As well as a possible future indictment in the wind from his old boss. I'm running a check on it now to see if there is any truth to the rumor."

"Do you think they would kill for him?" Matt asked.

"Our insider is getting close to getting a name for us and we'll pick him up and question the man. Who knows if he'd be stupid enough to kill for Kingman. One thing we do know—Bruce definitely is nursing a lot of anger still. He can't get over the fact that Sally left him."

"Never mind the fact he abused her their whole marriage and tried to kill her after she left him. I guess she is supposed to simply forgive and forget. Man, he's a piece of work." Matt used an expletive under his breath. "I'm glad he's behind bars for what he did to her."

"I hear you. After hearing what Peyton and her sister went through growing up, it makes me wonder how she turned out to be the great caring person she is. I'll let you know if we have more. In the meantime, our suspect has gone suspiciously quiet. Which makes me think we may need a security plan for the day of the wedding," Jaxon said.

"I've been thinking the same thing. I don't want to leave anything to chance. You saw what he did to my cruiser. I can't imagine how many people could be injured if he gets through our security. Hopefully, we'll get to him before the wedding."

"Amen to that," Jaxon replied. "I'll be touch."

Matt put his feet up and changed the channel. He wished he could change his thoughts with a remote. He closed his eyes only to rest them, but he dozed off with the TV still blaring the scores.

Chapter 31

Basil zipped across the room to sit beside Elida. "I can see from listening to Matt's conversation with his friend that there is a lot more to this assignment than chasing a few bullets. Who knew I would have to use my brain too." Basil shook his head, and his wings fluttered with the motion.

"Using our reasoning ability and designing plans are a major part of each job. The key is we must encourage our charge in such a way that they believe it's their idea. This one," Elida pointed at the sleeping Matt, "is smarter than most. All we have ever needed to do is give him a well-placed nudge and his mind does all the rest. He's a bit distracted right now, but even so he's always thinking and analyzing facts and comes to the right conclusion in the end."

"I like him. He's tough, smart, and still manages to have integrity. A great combination for a human."

"How do you know that?" Elida asked.

"I've watched how he treats those under him. He's a good leader. He works as hard as those who work for him. Much like Celeste. I'm sorry I've given her fits all these years. Her patience has been boundless, but she was starting to lose it when it came to me, she told me. That's why I'm here with you. I wonder if I can change enough to make her proud of me." He spun up into the air and darted around the room. "I find it hard to wait and be still. A lot of this job is about patience and being able to chill. I wonder if there is something a bit more on the exciting side in our world."

"What can be more exciting than doing enough magic to change someone's world?" Elida tugged on Basil's leg as he flew by.

"I guess you're right. But they never know we helped them, and we don't get the credit we should." He puffed out his chest.

"Aww, but we know, and there's a great feeling that comes along with that understanding. No one can take that from you. Not to mention when you complete a job well done, we grow a tiny bit in stature. Plus, sometimes we get to show up like one of them. Mila's successes have been written about in the Intermediary Manual for others to read." She tried to grab him as he flew by again. "Would you please sit down? My head is spinning."

"Sorry. You can see what I mean about energy. I find it hard to be still. I want to do big and great things, but I can't seem to slow down long enough to do them." He landed once again, resting his head on his hand.

"Celeste used to tell us when we were younger to practice. Practice and discipline are the keys to being a successful fairy and climbing the ladder in our world. Mila took it to heart and dragged me along in her wake. Eventually, I caught on, and you will too." She landed softly on Matt's cheek. Elida tapped his head with her wand, sending gold dust flying across his sleeping face. "Here's to thoughts that will lead you in the right direction, and may you follow the path you devise."

"What do we do now?" Basil asked.

"We rest and stay alert." Elida leaned against the

lamp on the nightstand, stretching her tiny legs out. She closed one eye and kept the other on Basil until he was snoring quietly beside her. Shaking her head, she frowned at him. "He never listens to anything, I say," she whispered.

****

Jessie opened her eyes. The lights were on, and she still clutched the envelope tightly in her hand. A glance at the clock told her she must have dozed off. She ran her hand along the seal of the envelope but decided to get a letter opener. Walking to her desk, she found the one Sadie had given to her when she went to work in New York.

That was her first office—more like a cubicle—and Grams wanted it accessorized with a few special touches. She still had them all, and they would follow her to the beautiful office Matt created for her. Simply thinking about all his hard work brought tears to her eyes. Which didn't bode well for her getting through her grandpa's letter. She'd most likely be a tearful mess by the time she finished his words to her.

She slid the opener along the seal and carefully opened the envelope. There was another sealed envelope inside. She took out the letter and unfolded the handwritten pages. Reaching for a tissue, she dabbed at her the tears. She hadn't read a word yet. The fact that he wrote this with his own hand made the pages priceless to her. In her mind she could see him hunched over the desk in his office laboring to get the words the way he wanted them. She would cherish the pages for the rest of her life.

"My dear Jessica Lynn,

"You'll always be Jessie Lynn, my curly-headed

moppet, to me. I have no idea where the years have gone, but watching you grow into the beautiful, fine young woman you've become has been a joy to me. You spent lots of time in the naughty chair when you were little because of that stubborn streak, your mama would say. I never saw that as a flaw, my sweet girl. I always knew you were strong and would use it to help others in some way, just like my Sadie in that regard.

"The fact you're reading this means I'm no longer with you and you're about to get married. How sad it makes me even to think I might miss this special day in your life, but we have little say over our lifespan. You can only grab ahold of and cherish the moments you are given. Besides my own dear Sadie, you grandkids were the joy of my life, and you, Jessie, have that special something extra like your grandmother. I like to think of it as tenacity. You'll will search for the truth and hold on until you are sure you've found the answer you're looking for.

"I know your fella has to be a special man because there is no way you would stand for anyone but the best for yourself." Jessie sniffed and wiped the tears running down her cheeks. She remembered the many times Gramps put his hand on her head, tousling her curls and calling her his little moppet. She scanned the page, reading more of his message as she did. Her lips turned up at the corners. Memories of him were hers to keep and kept her grandpa close to her.

She began to read the second page. *"You need to know some things about me, things I always wanted to tell you so that you could better understand yourself. My father died when I was going into high school. He had been the disciplinarian in my life. With his death, his influence was gone. In my hometown, friends, beer-drinking, and football were the big things. I began to drink heavily when I was fifteen. I also began to fight and had a mean disposition."* Jessie paused. This didn't sound anything like the man she knew.

"One day when I was drunk, I hit my brother in the head with a heavy jar. He was taken to the hospital and required stitches, but I felt little or no remorse. I couldn't seem to stop the anger pent up in me. My mother was broken-hearted. It severed the relationship with my brother for a season, although many years later we became best friends, I'm happy to say.

"Around that same time, the drug scene was about to get popular in the nation. It hadn't made it to the small town where I lived, or so I thought. In my quest to stop drinking and fighting I got turned on to the drug culture by a young man in town whom we thought of as a pacifist because he didn't want to fight like the rest of us. I was attracted to his calmness. I started to experiment with drugs. I started by smoking pot and thought of myself as being enlightened. Along the way I found myself in Haight Ashbury along with thousands of people like me. Jessie, it was a strange time. I lived hand to mouth and traveled wherever the winds took me.

"Jessie, the reason I'm telling you this story is because along the way, I had some profound and deeply spiritual experiences. Some people would think of them as bizarre. How I met your grandmother, the whole hippie movement, and the things I experienced in my life taught me life isn't always simply black or white with simple pat answers. There is often the unexplainable, the profound, and the times of

enlightenment in our life. I don't regret those times. They made me who I am. It seems we are always on a journey to find ourselves or to unlearn who we aren't supposed to be. From the time I met Sadie, we traveled that road together. There was never a doubt in my heart about her.

"Jessie girl, ever since you were a little, I recognized something different in you. I had experienced such moments in my life too. Your grandmother saw it too. You are destined to change your corner of the world with a strength that revealed itself early on in you.

"I can remember the day like it was yesterday when I was reading a story to you, and before you went to bed you reached up and touched my cheek. 'Grandpa, who are all the beautiful people in the room?' 'What people, sweet pea? I don't see anyone.' Your tiny finger pointed in every direction all around the room. You described what they were wearing and what they looked like. In that moment, I knew you had described my father, and you had never seen him before. Do you remember that day?" Jessie paused as a long-ago memory surfaced in her mind. She pictured that moment as though it was yesterday.

"I wish I could be there to meet the young man who has won your heart. I'm sure he didn't have an easy job. I'm sure you gave him a run for his money." Jessie chuckled. Yes, she had. *"With you he'll have his hands full, but he'll also have his greatest champion. I hope he is worthy of your love and loyalty. I have to believe he will be."* No worry there; he is. She pulled the comforter up around her shoulders, reading through several more pages to the end.

"As you start down that aisle on your father's arm, hold your head up high, look your groom in the eyes, knowing the amazing woman you've become. I'll be watching even if you can't see me. But then again, knowing who you are, you might see me after all. The sealed envelope, save for the day of the wedding. It is my gift to you, my darling granddaughter. Love you."

Jessie dabbed at her eyes. She left the second envelope sealed to be opened and read on her wedding day like he requested. "Thank you for bringing back a memory I had forgotten," she whispered. "Even then, I was different. I wondered how early in my life this gift had shown up."

She needed to remember to tell Matt the story about how her grandfather was a draft dodger, lived in a tree house, and on a commune in New Mexico. He went out the back way when the Feds were coming in the front looking for him. He wrote how he went into the mountains to a cave that he had found earlier on his explorations of the area. He had sought to be protected and stayed there in meditation, something he had learned from the Native Americans in the area. Several days later on his way back to the commune, he saw a pair of new moccasins tied together hanging over a branch of a tree. He needed a new pair. His were worn and had holes in the soles. When he tried them on, they fit perfectly, and he knew they were a gift to him. She wondered why he had never told her that story before— or maybe he had, and she had forgotten.

She couldn't believe the stories he shared in his long letter. They sounded like some of the oddities in her life. Had he also experienced one of the thin places? Not everyone finds meaning in the same way, but everyone desires to find purpose. Her grandfather had lived a truly unique life.

Jessie turned off the lights and curled up on the couch under the warm throw. She didn't want to mess with going into the room and getting ready for bed. Her mind was buzzing with what she had read. How she missed her grandpa. He was more of a dad to her growing up than his son. Her dad was distant, busy, and had no time to read stories or take her to get ice cream like Max had. On the rare occasions when Peyton and Madison could be at their grandparents' home, they had such a fun time with him and Grams. She never lacked for love because of them. And now she knew he was like her. Which had to mean somewhere on the male side of her family there were others.

****

Mila had learned something new about her charge. She had come into her gift as a child, which was often true but not always. Sometimes it took years for a chime baby to grow into the gift and understand what its purpose meant.

"Jessie, Matt needs you to think clearly at this time. Your memory will bring back the face of the one who is filled with anger and seeks revenge. You will save the man you love and will save yourself along with him." Mila spoke the words in Jessie's ear. "Dream your dreams and awaken with a thread of knowledge to unravel in the days to come." Mila touched Jessie's head and blew her a misty kiss. She settled herself on the back of the couch to rest her eyes as her charge slept. Mila crossed her tiny feet and spread her lovely dress to cover her legs. She wasn't above doing a bit of dreaming herself. There was a wedding coming up and, of course, the annual Fairy Ball. Sighing, she let herself relish in some wonderful girlish fantasies she had in her youth.

Chapter 32

Matt awakened to the TV blaring and lights. He had fallen asleep in his chair. For someone who rarely dreamed, he had his fair share of them lately. The darndest thing is they seemed to be real and lifelike, but he couldn't remember most of the detail. He'd never be like Jessie, and he was happy about it. She saw too much. Only once had he seen a ghost. He still wasn't sure if he wanted to believe that's what he saw. She hovered around Jessie right before he killed Chief Anderson. She glowed with an incredible light until she was gone as suddenly as she had appeared, but he had seen her. Once was more than enough for him. Matt shut off the TV and lights on his way to the bedroom.

Why was he reminded of that now? It seemed that all the bits and pieces he could remember were like parts of a puzzle, and they all somehow fit together. As soon as he placed one into place, another one would pop into his memory. They were important in some way, and he would figure out why. He never told anyone but Jessie that he had seen Gina's spirit. Who would believe him anyway? Hell, he hardly believed it himself. Saving Jessie was uppermost on his mind when she appeared. Seeing her apparition had stunned him. At the time, he hadn't known if she was there to take Jessie or save her.

Even at that early stage in their relationship, he

would have fought hard to keep Jessie alive. He knew she was the one he had been waiting for. He smiled. She fought the attraction, but his charm had prevailed. What a chase it had been.

Matt stretched out on the bed and leaned his head back on the pillow. He went over all the details for their honeymoon. He hoped she loved his plan as much as he did. The tickets were already packed in his carry-on bag. Not that he was in a hurry to be out of here or anything. Maybe a smidge. He wanted to see any place with her and spend time, just the two of them, day and night. He had stored up lots of vacation time, and he arranged for Jessie's store to be covered long past the two weeks he had told her.

Hopefully, he hadn't crossed a line asking Peyton for help. The closer they got to Thanksgiving, the more Jessie's store would be busy for the holidays. That's why he planned to be back a few days before the holiday, which was later this year. It gave them a cool three weeks for their honeymoon. He wanted everything to be perfect and a total surprise.

From the first moment he had laid eyes on her, he was captured. Sure, he had fought the feeling along with her, but it never changed the fact that the day she walked into his office ready to do battle, she also walked right into his heart. Matt rolled onto his side and went to sleep.

He jumped up when he heard the glass break followed by the alarm. He reached for his gun and went slowly toward the front of the house. One of the big windows in the living room had a gaping hole in the center of the glass. On the floor Matt saw the guilty culprit, a brick with a white paper held firmly in place by several pieces of twine.

Matt put on his gloves and carefully removed the note. He opened the page, careful not to tear the paper, and read the bold letters in black marker.

Two strikes you've had and there's only three. After that you'll face me.

He placed the paper, brick, and twine into an evidence bag. Looked like he had another window that needed to be replaced. Wide awake, he showered, made coffee, and went to the station early.

He glanced at his watch when he arrived at the station. He needed to tell Jessie about the note. He sent her a text asking to meet at lunch.

****

"Well, Basil, was last night exciting enough for you?" Elida followed him and Matt out of the car.

"I guess you can't let your guard down around here. It can be boring and then, *bam*, exciting happens all over the place." Basil flipped and zipped around Matt's head. He winked at Elida as he passed by her for the umpteenth time.

"That's the way of it when you are on assignment. Some days are endless tedium, and others keep you on your toes with action. We are waiting for the word from Celeste where we need to go from here. Their wedding is fast approaching, and I think the note holds a clue that will stir a memory in both of them."

How could she rein Basil in? Truth was, she didn't want to change him. He was happy but wouldn't be if he lost his place among the fairies. Mila could help— she was smart when it came to troubling situations. Her sister had a good head on her and seemed to know what to do to help. She had helped more than one fairy in her day. She tried so hard with Aelfric but not even Celeste could help him. Elida sighed. He was a lost cause.

"Basil, keep watch over him. I'll be back." Elida flew off when Basil nodded. Elida enacted her plan, hoping that Mila would think it was a good idea.

Elida flew away and backtracked to a hiding place while Basil wasn't looking her way. Hiding among the books, she would give him time to be in charge but be near enough to jump in and help if needed. Her plan was a sound one.

****

Jessie arrived at her store and got right to work. She had answered Matt's text earlier. She always liked to see him. She waved at the spirit watching her store as she walked back from putting a few new books on the table. She had one more load of new titles to add to the display, and she wanted them perfect enough to attract the customers' attention. It was nearing the peak of the fall tours, and she wanted all the sales she could get before the big holiday push from Black Friday to after-Christmas sales.

Her store had turned a nice profit up to this point, and she wanted to keep the trend going. Thanks to the coffee shop sales, both businesses were doing well. Jessie finished her morning routine and turned on her computer. She checked her phone messages and got ready to open.

She wasn't fooling herself. This was the calm before the storm, and she would take each quiet day as they came. Two sides of the same coin, Reba's warning rang through her mind often enough. The past and the present on the same coin. She wished her mind would come up with their suspect. He was there lurking in the back of her mind, familiar, and yet something about him was new. How could that be? Jessie confused even herself. While she was thinking, how could she forget the threatening man who had come into her business?

Wedding guests were starting to arrive at the inn, and it was paramount that they kept them safe. She knew Matt had been thinking about their safety and would have a plan. For her part, she wouldn't mind if their entire family remained oblivious to the danger around her and Matt. "Hopefully—" She looked at the ghost. "—you can arrange that for me. Or at the very least, send help." She smiled and opened the doors into Joe's.

The first person through the door when she turned the sign around was Sadie. "I couldn't wait to ask you if you'd read your grandpa's letter. I have no idea what he said. He was hush hush about it."

"I read it all, except the last part, which was sealed in another envelope. He asked that I save that one for my wedding day, and I will do that. Grandpa was a colorful character. He told me many stories from the life he lived. I learned he had been robbed at knife point in Balboa Park and made digger stew to help feed all the hungry hippies that had converged in San Franciso. His explanation of how they made digger stew from dumpster diving was a bit too much for me." Jessie laughed.

"He had a pretty wild youth, it's true. I heard new stories every time he shared them with someone else. But he was the very best husband any woman could have. He wanted you to know that you and he were more alike than you knew."

"He mentioned more than once how much he loved

you, Grams. You were the best of the best as far as he was concerned. Your love story is what finally convinced me that Matt and I could be happy together for a lifetime."

"I think, dear, he'll be watching over you on your wedding day. There's no way he'd miss seeing his little moppet get married." Sadie reached for the tissue Jessie handed her. "Are you any closer to finding a suspect?"

"I feel the answer is lurking in the back of my mind, but I can't pull it out." Jessie pursed her lips and frowned.

"We all have times like that." Sadie patted Jessie's hand. "Reba's sister is in town for the wedding, and Reba couldn't make it here this morning. She wanted me to give you a message from her." Sadie reached in her purse and pulled out a piece of paper. "Read this when you get a chance. I have a bit of shopping to do and will talk to you later. I see you're about to get really busy. Put that in a safe place." Sadie stood and kissed Jessie on the cheek. "Love you, sweet pea." She waved on her way out as several customers came in the store.

Sweet pea, that's what grandpa had called her too. They were two of a kind. How blessed she had been to have them as her grandparents. She greeted her customers and helped a young woman armed with a list looking for several specific books. The first moment she had a break she read the note from Reba.

"Remember, Jessie, this is not a complicated case. Someone from your and Matt's recent past is out for revenge today. He has been prompted by grievance egged on by the ancient spirit who has risen again to test your generation. Flip the coin either way and you'll

see the same face. It will come to you."

Well, that helps a lot. Jessie shook her head. *Not really, but I'm sure it will soon. Reba always gets it right. Maybe it's the idea of it being simple that makes this one seem tough to me, or perhaps it's because I would rather think about my wedding than the person trying to kill the man I love. There'll be no wedding if anything happens to either one of us. I'd better get my head out of the clouds and back in the game.*

Her store continued to be busy all morning and was still hopping when Matt came in. She was the only one working the store, with Peyton back at the school and Audrey only working a few hours a week until Jessie's honeymoon. She waved at him and continued to wait on a customer. She followed his progress into Joe's and knew he'd be back soon with lunch. She could only hope that she would catch a break long enough to eat with him.

Chapter 33

"Has it been like this all morning?" Matt asked Molly as he gave her his order.

"It's been crazy busy. Two busloads of tourists and the normal lunch crowd, and I've not been able to sit down once. I'm not complaining because it makes for a nice profit at the end of the day." She smiled. "Although, I am looking forward to my maternity leave."

"You've earned it."

"I sure have." She handed him back his change. "I'll have the new guy bring your lunch over to you when it's ready. It might be a longer wait than normal."

"Sounds good." Matt dropped several dollars in the tip jar.

"Matt, before I forget, a man was in here earlier asking a lot of questions about you and Jessie. I didn't think anything of it at first. He asked about your wedding, but then he wanted to know how well I knew both of you and some other more personal questions."

"Like what?" Matt asked.

"Questions like do they still live in the same place and do they plan on making the cove their home. I told him I was too busy to chat at the moment, and he lingered a while, but when the customers continued to come in, he left. I hope I did all right. I don't think I said anything I shouldn't have."

"You did fine, Molly. Don't worry about it. Probably one of the locals that is just curious is all."

"That's the problem. I've never seen him around town. Of course, I don't know everyone, but I don't remember him."

"Was there something about him that you would remember?"

"That's the issue. The guy seemed forgettable, if you know what I mean, although I couldn't get a good look at his face. He seemed to be turning away or covering some part of it with his hands. He kept throwing your names around, which is why I found it strange he was asking questions. Those who know you wouldn't need to ask about you."

"True. Thanks for letting me know. Do you think your security camera got a close-up of his face?" Matt asked before he walked away.

"I'll check and see when I get a chance. I doubt it will be a good visual, but who knows."

"I'd appreciate you checking whenever you can. You can always send it to me." Matt walked back into the bookstore and sat in one of the comfortable chairs. He watched his soon-to-be wife rushing around the store.

Wife, a word that both excited and terrified him. He could never have imagined a better partner to share life with. She was his equal in every way and far surpassed him in others. They would be great together.

Damn, Matt wished he could have got a look at the man asking those questions. He was the one they were looking for. His gut told him. He had spent the last week checking on Bruce Kingman, who was still behind bars. He still had a lot of influence on the outside and anger toward him and Jessie both. Was he responsible? Maybe this was Bruce's hire, but Matt wasn't sure of anything at this point.

Kingman seemed too easy to be true, but maybe this time would be different. Logic told him there was more to the threat than what they could see and yet somehow straightforward at the same time. Which made no sense even to him. They needed to come across a possible suspect soon. Their wedding was coming up at the end of the week and he wanted no incidents at the church.

"Here's your order. Molly told me to bring it over to you." The young man placed the bag and two drinks on the small table beside Matt. "She wants you to know she'll get on what you asked as soon as the lunch rush is over."

"Thank you, and tell her thanks too." Matt handed him a couple of bucks.

"Whew!" Jessie kissed Matt's check and went to plop down in the chair beside him. "I've gone nonstop all morning." She took off her shoe and wiggled her toes. "I'm starving." She scrunched up her face. "Not literally, but it is a perfect word to use at the moment." She chuckled.

"I hope you have time to talk too. I got this note on a brick through my living room window in the middle of the night last night." Matt handed her a photocopy of the original note.

"Well, that settles it," she said after reading the contents. "Do you remember I received a similar note like this during our first case? Buddy Brewster was hired to scare me off. Does that mean it's him or a copycat? That is the question that we need to answer."

"I do recall that now that you mention it. There were a lot of suspects in that case. How do we narrow down the field?"

Jessie took a bite of her sandwich. "Let me throw something else into the mix." She handed him the note she had received earlier from Reba.

"Okay, that's another piece. I'm not sure what it means, but I'll consider it." Matt took a swig of tea.

"Let's eat our lunch while I can. Hopefully, I will get to finish every bite." Jessie wiped her mouth with her napkin. "Can you hang out tonight? The next few nights will be busy for us with family in town."

"Yes, as long as it's only the two of us." Matt waggled his brows at her.

"Works for me." Jessie jumped up when a customer came in. "Don't throw my sandwich away. I plan on eating the whole thing." She took a sip of her tea and scurried off to help.

Matt smiled. He would never throw away good food. He would eat it himself first. That's what growing up with brothers would do to you. Matt placed the bag with her sandwich in it on the counter along with her tea. He walked up behind Jessie and gave her a kiss on the cheek.

"I'll see you tonight," he whispered in her ear. He loved watching the blush tinge her face. He couldn't help kissing her again in front of her customer.

"You're a rascal, Mr. Parker." The woman laughed as she told him, "Oh, to be young and in love again. You've got a keeper there, sweetie."

"I know." Jessie fanned her face playfully. "I'll be right back," she told the older woman. She walked Matt to the door. She pulled him close and kissed him soundly.

"I think you're learning, sweetheart, how I like to be kissed." Matt smiled when he heard the customers clapping in the background. "See you later."

"You might need to get a bit better yourself." She laughed as she waved goodbye.

"Challenge accepted." He got in the car and left.

****

Jessie took a deep breath and smiled. How she loved that man. She walked back to the customer she was helping before Matt kissed her. "Now where were we?"

"I was looking for a good romance. Who knew I would see a real life one?" The lady chuckled. "Still, I'd like a suggestion."

Jessie took her to the romance section in the store. "Do you like contemporary or historical?"

"I like historical."

"How about heat level?" Jessie asked.

"It doesn't have to be sweet but no erotica please," the woman told her.

"This section will be perfect for you. I'll leave you to your search. If you need me, I'll be helping the man over there." Jessie pointed in the gentleman's direction.

After taking him to the section with nonfiction political books, she left him to his quest. She mentioned some of the new titles and walked with him to the book table for him to look and pointed to the section on the shelves where he could find more. While they shopped, she rushed over to the counter and took a quick bite of her sandwich while she had a minute to enjoy it.

Jessie thought more about the note Matt had shown her and what Reba had written. She could definitely see the two sides of the coin with the same face starting to emerge. All that was left to do was to see the face. This week was a full one, what with a family dinner—both hers and Matt's—at the inn. Add in the wedding rehearsal, the rehearsal dinner, and of course, all the preparations Katie said were absolutely necessary to look her best, she wouldn't be spending much time with Matt alone. She was determined to enjoy tonight with him.

The "necessary" was a trip to the spa for facials, a mani and pedicure with her bridesmaids, and hair and makeup done before the wedding. How did brides ever do it before all the detailed wedding books came out telling them what they simply had to do? There was something to be said for a low-key wedding, but she could never have had one as long as Katie was her friend. And Katie would always be her best friend.

The change in her friend was profound. She had suddenly become her greatest champion and an expert of all things Irish. Jessie smiled when she thought of their many conversations lately. Katie told her she needed to get in touch with her Irish heritage. Katie had been born a Donovon, and Jessie thought that might be a great idea for Katie.

Peyton walked in. "Hey, cous, you look like you can use some help."

"Thanks." Jessie checked out the older woman, who had found several books to read.

"This should hold me over for a few weeks. I do love to read," the woman stated.

"I'm with you there. That's why I bought a bookstore." Jessie smiled. "To help support my habit. Thank you and please come again." Jessie handed the woman her bag after putting some bookmarks in the bag. "Have a nice evening."

While Peyton waited on a woman with a rambunctious child, Jessie finished her sandwich and sipped her tea. What a day this had been. Her father would be impressed with her balance sheet for the week. Knowing him, he would ask to see it. She glanced at her guardian, who rarely moved from his place on the stairs.

"How was your day?" Jessie asked Peyton.

"You know how I love my kids. Every day is a good one. They were all super good today." Peyton smiled. "It was perfect. I was thinking all day about your wedding. Madison will be here tomorrow, and I can't wait to see her. She'll be staying with me, and we always have so much fun together." Peyton paused. "I'm also curious to see if she will end up with the same gift that we have. Knowing now that the gift expresses itself through each person in a way that fits who they are."

"I've wondered the same thing. We may not have long to find out." Jessie spent the next hour filling Peyton in on details of the day. In between customers, that is. She was happy to hear any ideas that her cousin had. She also told her about the beautiful room that Matt had made for her.

"I saw it before Matt put the final touches on the room. Jaxon told me he helped the Saturday we went to New York and after the bachelor party."

"It's perfect. I can see myself spending many quiet moments in that room. I can spread the scrolls out and read over them to my heart's content." Jessie pulled up a picture of the finished room on her phone. "See, isn't it pretty?"

"He did a great job." Peyton scrolled through the pictures Jessie had on her phone. "Matt made the desk and shelves himself. They are better than most you see in the stores. He could make custom furniture, which might be a safer line of work."

"As if that would help, being married to me." Jessie laughed. "Looks like our moment of leisure is over."

A small bus pulled in the open space in front of the store, filled with smiling seniors from the local assisted-living home. Jessie loved it when they came to shop. They were always polite, funny, and loved to tell her stories about when they were young. They also came armed with their book lists, and those books found their way into the home's library for others to read. Jessie often donated a few books herself.

"How are the wedding plans coming, dear?" Marilyn, one of the regulars, asked. "We are excited that you invited us girls to come. Did I tell you I bought a new dress?"

"The plans are finished. I'm glad you are coming, and every girl needs a new dress for a special occasion. I can't wait to see yours." Jessie took her list and helped her find the books she was looking for.

By the time the ladies left, it was almost time for her to close for the evening. She started totaling up the sales for the day while Peyton straightened the chairs and cleared coffee cups left behind.

Jessie closed the doors into Joe's while Peyton locked up. She had no complaints about the day and looked forward to her evening with Matt. Hopefully, they could put a few more pieces together and make it one day closer to their wedding with no suspect in sight.

She wanted to hear what Jaxon found out when he went to interview Bobby Brewster in prison. The parole board was weighing his release. According to them, he had been a model prisoner. All she remembered about him was that he was one big scary dude. She rushed out to her car and followed Peyton home.

Chapter 34

Jessie glanced at the bag with her wedding dress in it. She knew the moment she tried the beautiful gown on that it was made for her. It suited her perfectly. She unzipped the protective bag and peeked inside. She smiled. She couldn't wait for Matt to see her in this dress. As a girl, she used to dream of the look on the man's face as she walked down the aisle. She sighed. Matt looked at her sometimes in a way that turned her inside into mush. She could only imagine what she'd see on his face in that moment. She couldn't wait to see and only hoped she would remember the details. Dylan's expression when he saw Katie made her weird bridezilla moments worth enduring. She hoped her day wouldn't start like Katie's with a murder in the woods. Thankfully, Katie never knew that tidbit. Her day turned out perfectly, as would hers. She knocked on the wood door frame before she walked out of her bedroom.

While she waited for Matt, she searched the files in her computer regarding the Harvest Club. She found a copy of the note she had received like Matt's. She had scanned the paper and placed it into one of the folders about the club. The two notes were word for word the same. The same threat, and they were running out of strikes. Which meant they could see something happen again soon. Part of her wanted that to happen and part of her didn't.

She read over the list of suspects, prison sentences, and the dates of their possible parole. From Bobby Brewster to Pastor John's son, Rick, who killed himself, they were caught in a web of murder and organ trafficking while the cove's chief of police took money under the table to look the other way. How many lives had been impacted by the greed of the group was still being discovered. Gina's life was one, and all the people who her life had touched, including her parents and the church. Was their suspect on the list or a copycat?

She hoped to know more soon. If Jaxon ruled out Bruce Kingman, which seemed likely, then the suspect had to be someone on the list or at least know the particular details of the case. The first scenario would be much simpler. Otherwise, it could be anybody from any of their previous cases. And how did that mob-like guy who came into her store fit in? More than one daunting idea to her way of thinking. Her fingers were crossed for a break in the case soon. She would rather her parents knew nothing about this side of her life. Knowledge of this kind would freak them out.

Shutting off the computer, she waited for Matt to arrive. Where would he take her tonight? She laughed to herself. It seemed their life consisted of complex questions every night that needed to be answered, like what should we eat and where do you want to go. And they weren't even married yet. Of course, their marriage would have tougher questions to answer when you threw in a murder or two.

****

Matt pulled into the spot beside Jessie's car. His

days of having to pick her up here were numbered. Soon she would be by his side right where he wanted her. Not that he hadn't enjoyed his trek here on a regular basis; it was the leaving that he hated. He wouldn't miss that part at all. Matt walked the path to her door. Even with all the leaves falling from the trees, Katie's gardener managed to keep the grounds at the inn immaculate. Who would live in this little cottage next? Whoever it was would hopefully love the place as much as Jessie. He raised his hand and knocked on the door.

"Hey, sweetheart, are you ready?" He helped her slip into her jacket.

"I'm ready if you are. I was thinking earlier we will spend a lot of our lives together figuring out what's for dinner." She chuckled as she walked out the door that he held open.

"True. It was one of the questions asked and repeated most frequently in my house growing up. Maybe we can come up with a unique way to ask it." He held the car door open for her. "I'm not going to ask you tonight though." He smiled when he latched his seat belt. "I've already made reservations." Matt adjusted his rearview mirror before he turned on the road into town.

"Did you have a nice day?" Jessie asked.

"I had an informative day." He glanced in his mirror. "Did you say you thought a white car followed you a few times? Take a look in your side mirror and tell me if that's the same car. There are lots of white cars on the road."

"The one I saw had a dent in the front left bumper like the one behind us now." Jessie studied the car behind. "I think it's the same one or a clone of it."

"Okay, good to know. We're going to play a few games to see if we can shake him." Matt made a quick turn without signaling first. The car followed and continued to follow after several more quick maneuvers on his part. "I think he's definitely a tail." Matt pulled int a parking spot in front of a small boutique. The car drove past him and didn't stop.

"Did you see the plates?" Jessie asked.

"I got a couple of the numbers. I learned two things tonight. Someone is following us, but I'm not sure he's who we're looking for. He could have shot from the car if he had wanted to when he passed us."

"What else did you learn? You did say two things."

"Whoever was driving the car has done this before. He was good and stayed with me the whole time. I couldn't shake him. I have no idea what that means, but I need to put that information with the other puzzle pieces."

"Who knows why? Most of the time these people rarely make any sense."

"That's just it, Jess. When you get to the core of their motivation, their grievance makes perfect sense to them in some weird way."

"I know you're right. As we saw in our last case, as unrest rises around the world, people get caught up in the waves. It doesn't have to make sense. It simply happens. People like to feel like they're not alone and that someone feels the same anger that they do. It feeds their strength. There is always a greater strength in numbers, even if it's misplaced."

When they arrived at the restaurant, they followed the host to their table. They could watch the boats coming and going in the cove. It was a beautiful place to spend time getting to know more about each other. Matt smiled when Jessie talked about her Grandpa Max. His love for Bob Dylan and his life experiences had Matt thinking he had to be a colorful character as well as a remarkable man to accomplish all that he had.

Matt told her about his grandparents, who would be at the wedding. "Family, you got to love them." Matt thanked the waiter who placed their food in front of them. "This looks good." Matt was hungry, and the steak on his plate was cooked to perfection.

"Oh, darn." Jessie bent over to pick up the napkin that had slipped off her lap.

Matt ducked his head to see what had happened. The sound of breaking glass sent Matt flying to the ground, and he pulled Jessie from her chair onto the ground with him. He shielded her with his body as glass rained down around them.

"Damn." Matt reached in his pocket and called for backup with the sound of screams in the background. He motioned for everyone to stay down and showed his badge while he pulled out his gun. "Promise me you'll stay down, sweetheart."

She nodded. "Promise me you'll wait for backup and stay safe." She touched his face between her hands.

With the sound of approaching sirens, more bullets hit the windows, and the glasses on the table broke, pouring water onto the floor around them. They remained low to the ground and motionless for a moment. Matt gave her a quick kiss and slowly crawled toward the kitchen and out the back door.

What infuriated him was he knew the guy would be gone before he got to where the bullets came from.

With help from officers on scene, they searched the area. Kip found the spot where the shooter had knelt to take his shots. Matt went back in the restaurant and told everyone the threat was over. He watched as people got up off the floor where they dove to when the shooting began. He checked to make sure no one was injured from the glass or debris.

"How did you escape this time?" Kip shook his head when he saw where they had been sitting.

"Damned if I know. It's a bit of a blur. Jessie bent down when her napkin fell off her lap, and I bent to see why she suddenly bent down, and you see the results."

"Hell, he ruined a good meal." Kip shook his head.

"Yeah, and I was hungry. That steak had my mouth watering one moment, and then all hell broke loose the next." Matt frowned. "I want to get this guy. This is getting downright annoying."

The team got to work processing the scene and questioning customers while the staff tried to clean up some of the mess. One of his officers had picked up sheets of wood to cover the broken windows. What a mess. He was perplexed, and he knew Jessie was too. How did the shooter miss them? It seems they had accumulated more than three strikes and managed to still be alive.

"Matt, sweetheart." Jessie walked up beside him. "I think you're going to have to acknowledge that this isn't luck. We must have some outside help. That's all I'm going to say on the subject." She grabbed his hand and squeezed it.

"You may be right, but I'll deny I ever said it if you tell anyone. All I know is that was way too close for comfort again. How many times can you have a close call and live to talk about it?"

****

"Well played, Basil. That was quick thinking," Elida said. "You saved their lives. What made you think of the idea?"

"By the time I saw the bullet coming I couldn't have stopped it. I did the next best thing and created a diversion." He wiped his forehead with his hand. "I was sweating it."

"You were on top of it. A good reminder to both of us to stay alert. Especially the closer we get to the wedding." She saw Mila on Jessie's shoulder. She mouthed the words to her. "Did you help him?"

"I may have given him the idea. I want him to succeed," Mila said. "We must all work together against the darkness. We need each other too much. Even in our world, we're at odds with each other. I don't think humans understand, and neither do we always that our survival as a species depends upon us standing together and not against each other."

"I know you're right, but it's hard not to want to blame someone else for our trouble. That means we have to own up to our mistakes." Elida frowned.

"That's it in a nutshell. I want Basil to succeed because someday I might need his strength in my life." Mila flew back and forth between Matt and Jessie, waving her wand as she went. They would need extra strength in the next few days.

Chapter 35

Matt nudged Jessie's shoulder. "I'm sorry to wake you, sweetheart. We can go home now. I would feel better if you took the guest room at my place tonight after what we just went through."

Jessie rubbed her eyes and pushed her hair out her face. "What time is it anyway?"

"After midnight. Sorry, I know you have work tomorrow. We can stop by your place to get your clothes."

"I hope you have food. I never did get anything for dinner."

"The kitchen staff made us something and boxed a sandwich for you." He handed her the to-go box. "Let's get going before I get pulled into something else."

He helped her up and supported her with his arm around her waist. "See you at the station tomorrow. Thanks for the help. I need to get her home," he told Dylan as he walked by him.

"Okay, boss. See you tomorrow. We almost have things wrapped up here." Kip saluted Matt as he opened the door for Jessie.

"Let's go. I'm sorry you had to wait so long, but we wanted to work through the scene carefully. I'm hopeful he left a clue or two behind. We are this close to getting this guy." Matt snapped his fingers.

"I'm fine and this should help a lot." Jessie took a

bite of the sandwich the restaurant had made for her. "I've been thinking about the note. I know Buddy was hired by the Harvest Club to scare me. It could be him, or someone hired by Bruce Kingman. I know he's still angry and blames us for Sally leaving him, and thank goodness she did, or she wouldn't be around. I believe he would have beaten her to death eventually. The abuse escalated each year and got harder for her to hide from her family. But—"

"What?" Matt asked.

"I know I'm missing something simple. There has to be someone, a player in the club who was less noticeable. Low key but stood to lose a lot when the club was shut down. I know we'll figure it out."

"Soon, I hope. We are starting to count down the days and hours. I wouldn't want our family members to become a recipient of a night like we just had." Matt glanced at her.

"Oh, heavens, no. My parents would come unglued, and so would yours, I'm sure." Jessie nodded her head. "Yes, indeed, I would like to avoid that if we could."

As soon as they reached the cottage, Matt walked with Jessie into the cottage to get her overnight bag. In no time at all, they were on their way to his place. He pulled the car into the garage, carried her case in for her, and led her to the guest room where he gave her a quick kiss goodnight and nudged her through the door.

****

Jessie was too tired to do much but slip into her night clothes. She climbed beneath the covers and laid her head back on the pillow. As she stretched out her legs, she sighed. She couldn't remember a time when a bed felt as good as this moment. Of course, she had probably thought and said the same words many times in her life, but right now this simply felt the best.

Jessie started going over all the people's faces she had seen in the files for the Harvest Club. Hidden among those many faces was the one, and it would come to her. At least, to her way of thinking, he was one of them. His face was teasing her and lurking at the edges of her mind. Soon he would come into view, and when he did it would be lights out for him.

This had been some night. In her heart she knew the napkin hadn't dropped off her lap, but it was pushed, and that tiny shove saved both hers and Matt's life.

"Thank you, my friend. I know you are here even if I can't see you. We wouldn't be alive now without you and your sister. I hope you can come and meet my family. My wedding wouldn't be the same without you," Jessie whispered into the dark room, closed her eyes, and smiled.

****

"You're welcome, my dear girl. You'll have to meet the character who enacted the plan." Mila sat on the pillow near Jessie's head. "I wouldn't miss your big day for anything. We even have permission to be there. It will be epic. I can't wait to see all the folks you helped who might show up." Mila blew Jessie a misty kiss and flew into the hall to meet with Basil and her sister. She had some good news to share with them both.

"Celeste told me to relay a message to you," Mila said when Basil and Elida arrived. "She couldn't be prouder of you both for a job well done. She encouraged us to stay alert and focused because the countdown to the wedding has begun. She also said we could attend as guests, but we have to be ready to jump into action if and when we are needed." Mila smiled when Basil puffed out his chest with a grin.

"Does she think there'll be trouble?" Elida asked.

"Yes, unless the suspect is apprehended before the wedding." Mila pursed her lips. "The problem is we are dealing with two things at work here." Mila explained what Celeste had told her. "I believe Jessie understands that somewhat but still hasn't figured out who the possible person is. As far as the old and new, she has figured out the possibility of what they are dealing with."

"Did you help her along the way?" Elida asked.

"I may have nudged her dreams and mind in the right direction, but she is quick on her feet and was headed there on her own. She is one human who often surprises me. I'm not easy to surprise either."

"Did our illustrious leader give you any more suggestions?" Basil asked.

"As a matter of fact, she did." Mila smiled. She went on to tell them the points Celeste had made to her. Then the three of them spent the next few minutes exploring all the possible scenarios and making plans in accordance with each one.

"We hope for the best, but plan for the worst. Isn't that what these folks often say? Personally, I want a good fight." Basil fisted his tiny hands and made a few boxing moves.

"What is it with you? You always want to fight. Me, I would rather dance." Elida lifted her skirt and did a rhythmic jig.

The three chatted and plotted who they would they go to the wedding as. The ideas flew between them as fast as they could fly. Finally, they settled on their human disguises and couldn't wait to show them off.

****

Matt glanced at the clock when he opened his eyes. That had to be one of the shortest nights ever. He slipped out of the bed and into the shower, wanting to give Jessie a few more minutes of rest before he had to wake her.

He knocked on her door on his way to the kitchen. Matt smiled when he heard the grumbling behind the closed door. "Sorry to wake you, but you have to get to your shop."

"I know; don't remind me." She mumbled something else which he couldn't hear.

He rushed into the kitchen and made a pot of coffee. He didn't forget the decaf for Jessie. He popped two bagels into the toaster and sat down to wait for her. She didn't disappoint.

"I want to know how after a night like we had you can come out here looking as fresh as a daisy. I'm looking forward to seeing you every morning as long as we both live."

"I make no guarantees." She laughed. "I've been known to have red eyes from crying, and am often cranky. I'm never quite sure what version of me will show up." She took a bite of the bagel he gave her. "Thank you for this, by the way. I'll take it with me if you don't mind. I need to get to the store."

"Sounds good. I'm ready when you are." He filled his to-go cup with coffee.

He opened the door, and she followed him out to

the car. "Don't forget—we are having dinner at the inn with the families tonight. It should be interesting. I'm not sure what my dad will do when he finds out Grams has Ronan Fitzpatrick coming from Ireland to be her plus one at the wedding." She latched her seatbelt when he back the car out of the garage.

"I guess every wedding has some odd things happen. Don't you suppose?" Matt asked.

"With my ability to attract the strange and unusual, I have a sneaking suspicion ours will be on the extreme side of it. Hopefully, our families will be none the wiser. At least, one can hope." Jessie pinched off a piece of her bagel and popped it in her mouth.

"Let's hope so." Matt pulled up to her store. "I think I'll check out your store this morning if you don't mind. I'll feel better about leaving you here if I do."

Matt went about his job checking the back and upstairs. "All clear." He gave a quick kiss as he went out the door. "I'll pick you up after work. I almost forgot you won't have a car."

"I'll try to catch a ride with Peyton if I can. I'll let you know," she told him.

Matt had too many things racing through his mind. Top among them was what, if anything, had the team learned from the crime scene last night?

Chapter 36

Jessie looked around the room at their family members gathered and chatting happily. Katie had made a superb meal as usual. The group appeared like she had described to Matt earlier. Their families were an interesting eclectic group. Matt's brother brought Destiny, and of course, Peyton was there, and she brought Jaxon. They were the sane ones. She never knew what would come out of her dad's mouth next. He tried to argue politics with Matt's dad who seemed less inclined to follow his lead. Her dad would drop the conversation only to start it again later from a different angle. Grams kept telling him to knock it off. His wife ignored him, but her dad was nothing if not persistent. A lot like Jason, Matt's younger brother.

Jason was acting like the resolute flirt tonight and a bit over the top. He meant it all in fun, of course, but he could be annoying. Thankfully, Matt had warned her several times over the past year about his little brother who chased anything in a skirt. She noticed Matt's dad cornered him more than once to talk to him. Jason could be Katie's brother, Liam's, twin in that regard. Poor Destiny was his target tonight but as soon as Madison got here, she would be on his list for sure. Madison was hard not to notice. Jaxon and Peyton would have to help her out. Evan was ready to knock his brother in the head. Matt shook his head and chuckled and gave Evan no help whatever.

She learned one thing tonight—the brothers were competitive, but they all looked up to Matt. And the three of them would be there for each other no matter what. It must have been nice to grow up with siblings, even if at times it was a bit crazy.

"Are you ready to go, sweetheart?" Matt slipped his arm around her waist. "I'll walk you home. I'll grab your overnight bag from the car and meet you at the back door."

"Sounds good. I'm tired." She went to thank Katie and say goodnight to her parents. Jaxon and Peyton had taken Sadie home already. "I'll see you tomorrow, Mom. Love you."

She said goodbye to Matt's parents and shocked Jason when she kissed him on the cheek. "Behave yourself." She chuckled as she patted his cheek.

"Okay, sis. I like the sound of that. I've never had a sister before." Jason gave her a quick hug. "I hope you know I'm goofing around."

"I've got your number." She pinched his arm playfully.

She met Matt at the back door of the inn and walked with him to her cottage. She loved walking through the gardens when they were in full bloom. Tonight was a different story. It was a chilly clear night, and Jessie was feeling a bit nostalgic after the evening.

Matt seemed quiet too. Their lives were about to go through an alteration, and as she had come to realize, change was never easy but seemed to be the one constant in life. How would her relationships with friends and family evolve? She didn't like to think about all the possible adjustments and compromises coming her way, but she needed to. Her life had shifted completely since moving to the cove. At times she hardly recognized herself, and there were probably more changes yet to come that she didn't want to even consider at the moment.

"You're quiet, Jess. What's going on in that pretty little head of yours?" Matt asked.

"After hanging with our families tonight, I guess I realized how much our lives are about to change. I'm wondering if I'm up to the challenge. I like to feel in control." She put her finger to his lip before he could voice what she knew he was about to say. "I know you're never really in control of circumstances, but I like to believe I am. I'm stepping into the unknown with marriage."

"Hey now. You know me. We'll have some challenges, but we'll meet them together." Matt opened his hand for the key.

"I'm sure you're right. I need a plan. That is all. You know how I am in that regard. You've heard me say it often enough." She walked through the door he held open.

"I understand, but you don't have to do it alone unless, of course, you want to. I'll give you the freedom to choose." He smiled at her. "Will you be okay on your own tonight?" Matt asked.

"I'll be fine." She placed her purse on the desk and slipped out of her jacket.

"I'll check your place, and then I'll be on my way. Be sure to set the alarm when I'm gone." He walked around the cottage doing a quick window and door check.

"I will." She followed him to the door. "Call me or

text me when you get home. I care about your safety too, you know." She laid her head against his chest.

"It's been a tough few days for both of us." He lifted her chin and held her face between his hands. "I hope you know how much I love you." He lowered his head and kissed her. "Only a few more days and you'll be hard pressed to get rid of me." He opened the screen door and left.

Jessie locked the door behind him and sighed. He had a way of making everything seem all right. She set the alarm and shut off the lights on her way to the bedroom. Truth was, she would be happy not to spend every night alone. Maybe some of the madness would stop in her life if he were by her side. One could hope.

Her bed had never felt so good. *Hmm, I think or say the same thing often. I'm not sure what that says about me. Maybe I need more rest.* She smiled, stretched out, and rolled over on her side. She glanced several times at her phone, hoping to hear from Matt soon. She was ready to give up and shut off the bedside lamp when he finally called.

"Sorry it took me so long to call you. I stopped to say goodbye to Evan, who was walking Destiny to the car as I was leaving. Our conversation lasted a bit longer than I thought it would."

"I was about ready to turn off my phone and go to sleep. I'm tired," she said. "Still, I wanted to know you're okay. Knowing will make going to sleep easier."

"What's on the agenda for the next couple of days?" Matt asked.

"For one thing, I need to get a run in before the weather gets too cold, which I plan on doing tomorrow. I also need to get my orders done before we leave for our honeymoon. I planned on an evening with Peyton and her sister, Madison, who will be here tomorrow. Then we have our rehearsal dinner and a wedding. Of course, I get a little pampering time with my bridesmaids for manis and pedis, which should be relaxing, on Friday morning."

"I might have to slip by to see you during the day tomorrow to get my fill." He chuckled. "Are you sure you have time to fit in a run, and why do want to when things are this busy?"

"Running always relaxes me, and it clears my mind. I can't tell you how many cases became clearer when I jogged. And an answer to the question plaguing me is what I want most at the moment."

"I hear you. I don't want this guy suddenly popping up and hurting one of our family members."

"Or in my case, alerting my family to this side of my life. I'm not prepared to have that touchy conversation in the next few days."

"You sound tired. I know you're still processing last night. Get some sleep and we'll talk tomorrow. Love you."

"I love you too." She turned off her phone and closed her eyes.

It took a while for her to settle down. She couldn't believe once again they had dodged a bullet, literally. How many close calls could a person have and live to tell about it? *I don't expect anyone to answer me, but I need to think seriously about an answer.*

She went through several rounds of elimination of a possible suspect only to start the process over again. The last problem she addressed in her mind before it finally quit was would Madison also be like them? She didn't know whether to hope she would or secretly wish for the opposite.

Chapter 37

Matt left early for the station. His nervous energy was through the roof. He had a lot to get ready for Dylan, who would be in charge during his absence. Spending a few weeks alone with his girl had him stoked. But before he could get there, he wanted to put a suspect behind bars. They needed to catch a break with this case. Jaxon and Dylan were working around the clock to put a name or face to the guy. Matt had no trouble thinking of the suspect as a man. His brazen attacks were the MO for a male in revenge mode. He could only hope the perpetrator's arrogance would have him making a few stupid mistakes and entrap him.

He stopped to fill his coffee mug and talk to Kip before heading to his office. When he opened the door, Matt stopped in his tracks. Something seemed off. He remained in the hall, called to Kip, and told him to bring Joe, the desk sergeant, with him.

"What's up?" Kip asked when he approached Matt.

"Someone has been in my office. Did you notice anyone hanging around who shouldn't be here?" Matt looked at Joe when he came down the hall.

"Someone came in after you left and said they had a gift delivery for you and Jessie. I told him he could put it in your office. Was that a mistake?"

"Not under normal circumstances, but with all the trouble I've had lately, I think anything is possible."

Matt frowned.

"Strange thing is the guy seemed familiar to me. Of course, we get a lot of deliveries and often have the same men coming and going. That's maybe why I thought I had seen him here before."

"What do you want to do?" Kip stood next to Matt.

"I want the FBI's bomb tech to check out my office, and we need to clear the building." Matt put in a call to the field office in Hanover. "Unless I miss my guess, this bomb can be detonated by phone." He repeated the information to Jaxon when he called.

The unit found enough explosives to have killed Matt wired to his chair. When it was safe to return to the building, he was handed the note that was found nearby. *Boom! Gotcha.*

Matt's hands fisted at his side. He was tired of the whole mess. This was his domain, and the guy had invaded it more times than he wanted to acknowledge. He needed to get his head in the game before both he and Jessie were killed. His gut worked well this time, but "what if" was on the tip of his tongue. There had been way too many close calls, and why? He wanted to talk with whoever it was and see what his problem was. He boiled when he thought of Jessie and how close the bullet came to hitting her last night.

He took his phone out of his pocket. "Hey, sweetheart, I thought I needed to tell you myself." He went on to explain what his morning had entailed already. "I'm not sure you should run by yourself today."

"I'll go to the gym if that makes you feel better."

"I would appreciate it. Neither of us are safe until this guy is caught. Think about who might be a possible suspect and I'll stop by later to talk."

"All right. See you later," she said.

"They might have pulled a partial print on the plastic explosive," Jaxon told Matt as he walked into his office. "You're lucky. What made you hesitate?"

"I knew when I opened the door something didn't seem right. My chair was in a different position, and the box on my desk shouldn't have been there. When Joe told me a guy had delivered a wedding gift, I knew."

"Thank heavens your instinct kicked in. Your chair would have blown when you applied weight to it. Damn, this guy is bold."

"I was thinking the same thing." Matt leaned his hip against the desk.

"Which means he wouldn't think twice about crashing your wedding. You were right to say we needed to have a heavy police presence there. Hidden, of course, but there nonetheless." Jaxon pulled out the plans he and Tom Maxwell had developed. They contained the number of personnel and strategic locations for them to be placed.

"This looks like a thorough plan. You seemed to anticipate every possible scenario." Matt studied the plan in front of him.

"It would be even better if we knew who we were looking for," Jaxon stated. "We are close to eliminating a couple of people, but no closer to identifying the guilty party." Jaxon scowled. "I'd feel a hell of lot better if we had the guy."

"You and me both." Matt nodded. "I'll talk with Jessie later. We both have been a bit preoccupied with family and wedding plans. I'm afraid we are missing something that is staring us right in the face."

"I can't understand why." Jaxon laughed. "I'm amazed you can keep your mind on your work at all."

"A near-death experience brings you back to reality quickly. Would it be okay to make a copy of these plans?" Matt asked.

"These are yours," Jaxon said. "Tom wanted you to have a copy to work with your department on."

"Thanks. I'll make sure Dylan sees them. I put him in charge because I'm too close to the situation, as you know. He'll be in the wedding party, but he knows the guys that won't be. We'll do our part from here."

"Don't worry about it. I'll meet with him myself and give him a copy too." Jaxon turned to leave. "In fact, I'll talk to him before I leave today. No one, and I mean no one, gets into your office when you leave. Lock the door and rig it so you know if someone has. You may have someone in your department that enabled the guy."

****

Jessie couldn't believe Matt's morning. A chair rigged with explosives, which changed the way you had to check a room for issues. Jessie had to stop worrying about what her parents might say, a lecture from her father, or anything else. Their lives were at stake, and she'd better get with it.

After a busy morning and her chat with Matt, Jessie couldn't say she felt any better. She promised him she wouldn't run outside, but her heart rebelled against it. Running in the gym simply wasn't the same as being outside with the cool brisk air as your motivation. Never mind the beautiful view on her running trail of the cove. More than once, she had to alter her life to accommodate the bad guys. She could feel her stubborn streak rising to the surface, and now wasn't the time to press her luck.

"How was your day?" she asked Peyton when she walked in the store.

"Fairly good considering I had a room full of active inquisitive people who can often outsmart me on so many levels." Peyton chuckled as she told her about one of the boys' antics. "Are you ready for dinner with your favorite cousins tonight?"

"If I recall, you're my only cousins. I wonder how it is that the Reynold brothers have no sons between them. Only us lovely girls." She laughed.

"All I can say is as rough as my dad was on me and my sister, a boy probably would have never survived." Peyton frowned.

"Sad but true. Thankfully, they both have changed a smidge. I'm not sure what my dad will do when Grams introduces Ronan to him."

"He'll have a conniption fit right along with my dad." Peyton waved at Molly through the open doors. "Her maternity leave is coming soon, and I bet she'll be happy."

"I'm sure she will." Jessie leaned her elbows on the counter. "Do you want to hear the latest in the saga to stop our wedding?" Jessie asked.

"Of course." Peyton nodded.

Jessie lowered her voice and told her about their evening the night before and Matt's morning. "Each time he gets a little closer to pulling it off. I swear I had some help last night and it saved my life.

"I'm sure you did. And for some reason our guardian ghost isn't going anywhere. I'm guessing he's still needed here."

The afternoon seemed to drag on with a trickle of customers coming and going. The atmosphere in her store seemed strained to her. Their guardian had moved to a new position in front of the open doors to the coffee shop. Tension filled her shoulders while the sensation of tiny spiders walked up and down her spine. She glanced in the coffee shop, where the unease seemed to be coming from. She would have chalked it up to an overactive imagination.

"What's going on? Something isn't right." Peyton stood beside her.

"I don't see anyone, but that doesn't mean anything." That's when Jessie saw their guardian move forward with lightning speed. His shield high and his sword drawn, he began to fight with a dark dragon-like creature soaring around Joe's. This was a different kind of battle and one she couldn't fight. She recalled when she saw the dragon arise in the sky during a thunderstorm and a battle that ensued then. Did such battles take place without anyone knowing? The customers in the coffee shop had no idea what was taking place around them, which gave her pause. The battle went back and forth until the warrior lifted his shield and the light streaked through the center shooting rays of light like a sunburst in every corner of the coffee shop sending the dragon slinking back into the darkness that seemed to open up and swallow him.

What had she seen and what did it mean? Did anyone else see the battle? Something definitely seemed different, but she didn't know what or how. This was a part of the mystery of her life.

Chapter 38

Madison walked into Jessie's store, and Peyton rushed to hug her sister. Jessie didn't have time to ask Peyton if she had witnessed the scene that had just played out. Trying to remember all that she had learned to date about the gift of sight, Jessie knew seeing the unseen world seemed to come part and parcel with what she had inherited. Peyton had similar manifestations along with a few expressions that were unique to her personality. Jessie found it fascinating, and she needed to do further research to understand more about her own distinctive bent.

She would probably spend her lifetime growing in her ability and still not know what she possessed, or did it possess her? She had no idea how it worked. Maybe it didn't belong to her at all but was passed down to be used as long as she didn't abuse it.

"Long time no see, cousin." Madison walked up to Jessie hand in hand with Peyton. "Are you really going to give up your life of freedom for a man? I still find it hard to believe my activist cousin and sister have gotten hooked up with lawmen." Madison laughed.

"There was no greater women's activist than your grandmother Sadie, and she was married happily." Jessie told her about the letter from grandpa Max. "We are following in her great footsteps." Jessie hugged Mady.

"Yeah, but I hope you don't have sons like hers. At least when it comes to my dad, I'm not willing to let him off the hook. He was terrible to us girls. It will take me a long time. I'm not sure I'll ever be able to trust a man."

"You're here with us now, and the cove is a wonderful place. There are plenty of good ones living here. Peyton will show you around. I'm sure you'll love my Matt and your sister's guy too. I can't wait for you to meet him," Jessie told her.

"We are going to have fun, sis. I'm going to do my best to convince you to move here." Peyton smiled at her.

"That's not going to happen. I like working and living where I do. I could never see myself living in a small town, although there have been some strange things happening at the hospital." Madison scrunched her lips tight together.

"You'll have to dish all the juicy details since we're hanging out together tonight." Jessie straightened the basket of bookmarks as they talked.

"Sounds like fun. It's been a while since it's been the three of us. It'll be like old times." Madison squeezed Jessie's hand. "We need to catch up."

"Are you ready for me to take you to my place?" Peyton asked.

"Yes. I feel grungy after the long drive. I'll see you later, Jessie." Madison waved as she followed Peyton out the door.

Jessie settled into her closing routine still thinking about what she had seen earlier in the coffee shop. She would finish her orders in the morning and run at the gym then too. It meant getting up super early, but it was a small price to pay. She needed to make sense of this piece to the puzzle because she knew in her heart that they all fit together.

The whole event was kind of awesome. They fought around the customers in Joe's, and no one had any idea. It made her wonder how many things she had missed over the years. Was this another wakeup call? She imagined the answer would be coming soon in some way. "Hey, my warrior friend. I would like to know what that scene I witnessed was all about," she said softly to him.

****

Matt enjoyed talking to Jessie. He always learned something new each time he did. She was a mystery to him. He loved all the details of her conversations and how her face lit up when she was passionate about a subject. She inspired him, flummoxed him, and at times challenged him to be a better a man. Of course, he didn't let her know all of this because a man couldn't show all the cards in his deck. Sometimes he needed to have a poker face. Those blue eyes looking at him the way she did could make him putty in her hands. There wasn't much he wouldn't do for her. But even with all that, they were no nearer to having an answer than when they began. Hopefully, through the process of elimination, they would soon come nearer to the truth than where they were at the moment.

His girl was a bit distracted today and rightfully so when he stopped by earlier. She had family here, a coming wedding, and a business to get ready to leave for longer than she thought. He wasn't sure what she would think when she found out he had tacked another week onto the end of their honeymoon. He couldn't resist it. He hoped she saw it as a nice surprise and something special that they would always remember.

"Matt, do you have a minute?" Dylan knocked on the door.

"Sure, come in." He motioned at the chair in front of his desk. "Sit. What's up?"

"I wanted you to take a quick look at the men I've assigned for your wedding protection detail. I'm sure about everyone but this guy." He pointed to a name on the paper.

"What's troubling you?" Matt asked.

"He's relatively new to the department, but I'm sure I remember him from somewhere." Dylan frowned. "I need the extra men to work beside the agents."

"Maybe you should put him in a spot where Kenny or Joe can keep an eye on him too. It's always better to be cautious."

"Sounds good. In the meantime, I will try to remember where I saw him before. It might simply be around town."

"You can talk it over with Jaxon too. Dylan, I hope you know I trust your instincts. You'll be in the wedding party, but you'll also be carrying your weapon."

They went over the plans and made a few additional changes which Dylan would run past Jaxon. Matt glanced at the clock. He was having dinner with his dad and brothers. He was looking forward to it. After his awful morning, he needed to hang with his family. They brought a crazy sense of sanity with them. Maybe it was the joking and familiarity. He wasn't sure, but they always lifted his spirits after a tough day.

Matt picked up the files from his desk that he wanted to study later and locked his office like Jaxon had told him to. He rigged the door in such a way that he would know if someone had tried getting in or had tampered with the handle in any way. He was through messing around. He wanted this guy caught and if someone was helping him inside the department, it was time to find out.

He walked with Kenny out to his car. "I bet you're getting excited to meet your new family member."

"To tell you the truth, sir, it's all a bit overwhelming to me. Molly has been amazing, working the whole time she's been pregnant. I think I should be doing more, and I feel a bit useless. She needs the time off, and from what I understand, I'll be happy to have time with her once the baby is born. Everyone says you don't sleep for a while. Molly already gets little enough."

"You know, Kenny, I think you'll do fine." Matt clapped him on the back.

He got into his car, went to start the engine, but hesitated. He got out of the car, looked underneath, and he was glad that he had.

Chapter 39

While the bomb squad defused the explosive attached under Matt's car, he pored over security tapes with Gary. How was it possible someone could place it there right outside the station in broad daylight? After he saw the footage Gary showed Matt, at least he understood. The person arrived in a van with car repair advertised on the side. The figure kept his face shielded from the security cameras on the building. He had to have knowledge of where they were located. Damn, they were no closer to identifying the suspect.

What would he try next before they caught him? Instinct had saved him again, at least that was his explanation, but how many times could he say the same thing and it be believable?

"Matt, your car is being towed to the lab. You'll need to drive one of the patrol cars home." Dylan popped his head in the door. "Did you see anything?" he asked.

"Only this man and his van. Gary has blown-up photos, and we need everyone to take a look and see if they remember seeing either of them. With all the activity around this building, someone had to see something."

"I'll start asking around." Dylan grabbed the photos from Gary. "I want to watch their faces as they answer. You can tell a lot by facial and body language.

Someone had to reposition the cameras. I noticed the angle on them had changed. That can only happen from inside this building."

"You're right about that. I'll leave you to it. You're in charge on the investigative side. That doesn't mean I'll stop searching for answers; it only means I want you in the lead. This is too close to me since I'm one of the targets. I'm also mad as hell."

"I can understand that reaction. I'm angry too." Dylan frowned. "I'll send copies to Jaxon. Maybe the FBI lab can pick up a detail we can't see."

"Do you have any theory on this one?" Dylan asked.

"It's obviously someone who has fed their need for revenge for a while. Reba mentioned revenge, and Jessie said it was someone from the past that was connected to the rising anger of our times. A past case converging, with an ancient spirit rising again in our times, or something like that, according to my girl. Two sides of the same coin." Matt chuckled. "I can't believe I said that. A year ago, I would have balked at even thinking the thought much less speaking the words out loud. A lot of changes have happened this past year. But whatever you do, don't quote me."

"Change is the optimum word. Katie has become Jessie's ardent defender. The lady who used to blow her top at the mention of this side of Jessie's life has suddenly started to research her Irish ancestry." Dylan shook his head. "Go figure."

"That's a head scratcher for sure, but what isn't these days? I'm running to catch up with all that is happening around me."

After Dylan left, Matt placed the call to Jessie that

he wasn't looking forward to. He was damn tired of telling her about another near miss. She would rally around him, but it had to be impacting her concern for her family and wedding guests in two days.

When Matt finished talking with her, she hadn't disappointed him. She came to his defense and talked about needing a plan to take the guy off the street. Still, he could hear the concern in her voice not only for him, but also for anyone who got in this guy's way. Which meant her or anyone at the wedding. She ended the conversation with the idea that they had to acknowledge they definitely had some unseen help. As much as he didn't want to admit it, she was right.

****

She should have been troubled, and in some ways she was. But in her heart of hearts, she knew someone was looking out for them or one of them would be dead already. That didn't mean she didn't want this guy caught. Of course she did, and hopefully before the wedding.

She hashed over what Matt had told her all the way home. There was something familiar about it. The arrogance of the man was something she had seen before. She was sure of it. With Madison here, she would have to put her concern aside until tonight when she was alone. Hopefully, whoever was helping to keep them safe would give her mind a nudge.

He was there slinking around the edges of her mind aided in his anger by the one she saw the warrior battle in the coffee shop. Boy, she was glad that Molly hadn't seen what took place earlier. She'd pack up and move lickety-split. Okay, she exaggerated. Molly had already had two ghosts in her coffee shop, but today was on a different level.

That dark entity had to be a part of what was going on now. With his defeat, it was possible the suspect would be captured. Jessie pulled her car into the parking space behind the inn. Peyton and Madison were waiting for her.

"We want to take you to dinner." Madison held the door open for her to get out of the car. "I need to see some of this town. Peyton is driving. Get in her car."

"Sounds good to me. I need to do a couple of things first. Come with me and you can see my place. All of this could be yours." Jessie gestured with her hands as she held the door open for her cousins.

"Not me. Small towns aren't for me, but I do love your and my sister's pads." She plopped down on the couch.

"I'll be ready in a minute." Jessie went into her room and changed her clothes. She put on her favorite jeans, a cozy sweater, and applied her lip gloss. Before she left the room, she ran a brush through her hair, and she was ready to go. "Let's show her the town," Jessie told Peyton when she joined them once again.

"Nice car, sis." Madison got into the back seat.

"We should change places. I want you to have a better view. I already know what the town looks like." Jessie stepped back to change places with Madison.

Jessie and Peyton described the places around town and took her to one of their favorite spots at the marina. They parked for a few minutes and watched the boats moving in and out of the harbor. To Jessie, this was always a place to calm the tension in her life.

"As long as we are so close, we should eat at Mindy's and then stop by Liam's and Connor's place for a nightcap," Peyton suggested.

"Mindy's sounds good because Liam's place might be like throwing your sister into the wolf's den." Jessie muttered the second part under her breath. Katie's brother, Liam, was known to be a big flirt, and Madison was one pretty girl. Her skin was peaches and cream like Peyton's, but she wore her strawberry blonde hair shorter and let the curls do their thing. All in all, she made an attractive, fetching picture. One thought led to another, and Jessie had no idea how she would keep Matt's brother, Jason, away from her. Oh well, Mady was a big girl, and she could take care of herself. She had enough trouble of her own to keep her busy.

Dinner was awesome, Liam was his usual flirting charming self, and she had laughed enough with her cousins to forget there was any threat still out there. As Jessie got ready for bed, she let her mind wander through the events of the past several days. How many times she had come close to losing the man she loved were adding up. Too many and way too close for comfort for her.

She climbed into bed and texted to tell him she loved him and goodnight. She smiled and fanned her face playfully at his reply. She shut off the light, stretched out on the bed, and closed her eyes. She lay quietly for a few minutes, and then the light went off in her mind. She was off and chasing one lead after another until she went to sleep.

****

"I heard you ask for the nudge, dear girl," Mila whispered in her ear. "You're moving in the right direction." She blew her a kiss and swirled her wand around Jessie's sleeping head. "It's time for you to remember something you buried deep to forget." Mila took her hand and tapped Jessie's head three times.

Mila sat beside her charge on the pillow. She waited, and when she heard her moans and saw Jessie begin to thrash about, she knew her memory was recalling the events of that dreadful day. Mila watched for a few minutes more until she was sure Jessie remembered the detail, and then she touched her head again to bring a sweet memory to overtake the other. Jessie wouldn't forget. Mila was sure of that and sprinkled a sweet mixture of gold dust over her as she slept on.

Chapter 40

When Jessie awakened, she sent Matt a text saying they needed to talk. She remembered the details of her nightmare.

Jessie answered her phone. "Good morning. I take it you got my text."

"Are you all right?" he asked.

"I am. I remembered something important, and I want to talk to you about it in person."

"I'll bring breakfast to your store. How soon can you get there?" he asked.

"I can be there by eight, which should give us almost an hour. Does that work for you?" Jessie glanced at her clock. "I need to get going if you want me to make it on time."

"I'll be there. See you in a few."

Jessie rushed through getting ready and finished with enough time to get to the store before Matt did. She slipped into her jacket, reached for her purse, and punched in the keys on the alarm, locking the door on her way out. Something she couldn't forget without a lecture from the man who loved her. She wouldn't miss having to remember this part of her morning routine.

Jessie shut her car door and turned on the engine. A simple action she had done almost every day without thinking. What if there had been a bomb under her car like Matt's? Something she had never considered before. Another item to put on her list of things to watch out for. At this rate, her list would be pages long.

She arrived at the store and rushed in the back door. Goodness, she had forgotten to even check if she was being followed. At a time when she should be on guard, she wasn't paying attention. Cavalier would be a good word to describe her at the moment.

Placing her purse and belongings behind the counter, she turned on her computer and waited for Matt. She had time to read an email from Jeremy who mentioned he was on his way for the wedding. Jessie couldn't wait to see her friend. They had many great times investigating and doing research together during her days living in New York. She didn't miss the city, but she did miss having coffee or lunch with her friend. He kept her up to date with news in her old stomping ground.

Jessie glanced up when she heard the knock at the door. She held the door open for Matt.

"Hey, sweetheart." He kissed her cheek as he walked in carrying their breakfast. "Did I miss something? I thought you had the day off."

"That's tomorrow. Today is a partial work day for me. I came in to meet with Audrey and pay a few bills." She followed him to the table. "Thank you," she told him when he placed a coffee in front of her. "I'm sure I took care of everything, but I want to make sure."

"I understand, believe me." Matt took a sip of his coffee. "What did you want to talk about?" he asked. "It sounded serious when I talked to you earlier."

"First, let me ask you are you okay after last night?"

"Physically I'm fine, but I'm angry as hell." He

scowled and his fist curled. "Someone moved the security camera from inside the station slightly enough to not capture the suspect's face. There is no way he could have avoided detection if the cameras were in their normal position."

"You must be concerned." She took a deep breath. "That means someone inside is helping the suspect, doesn't it?"

"It sure as hell looks like it." Matt shook his head. "I want this sorted out before I leave. At the moment, I have no idea."

"Well, maybe this will help. I remembered something that happened at the church during our first case. Chief Anderson asked me to help him get something out of the car. Fred was waiting by the trunk, and when I asked him how he was doing, he said something like better than you're going to be. He gave me a hard shove into the chief and jabbed me with a needle. I remember going limp and they fought to shove me in the car saying someone is coming. I recall the sensation of being in a tomb when they closed the trunk." She shuddered. "I buried the details deep inside me not wanting to remember them."

"I understand. That had to be awful." Matt said.

"I still don't want to remember, but it is tied to your suspect." Jessie went on to explain what she experienced in those moments lying on the table while Anderson described in detail what he was going to do to her. "Fred asked to leave because he didn't like the sight of blood. It made him sick. I know you arrested him when he went outside. When we talked a few weeks later, do you remember what you told me about his wife and family being okay?"

"I do, why?" He ate a bite of his breakfast burrito.

"Did you look closely into his family members and Fred? There is something there. I remember when they were carrying me into the house, the two of them talked about all the money they would lose because of me. Anderson was angry and belittled Fred, calling him several names. I could hear even though I couldn't move." She wrote down what she overheard Anderson say to Fred. "You might need to check this out."

"Let me ask you a question. Do you carry your gun at all times? I do remember asking you that then."

"I do, but I try to forget that I have the stupid thing." She rubbed her hand over her the place where the medallion rested on her neck, loving the sense of warmth that came with it. "I could use it if I needed to, especially if I had to save you, but I would rather not have to." Jessie sipped her coffee and pinched off a piece of scone. Jessie went on to tell him about what she saw happen yesterday between her resident ghost and whoever the dark stranger was.

"You never fail to surprise me. You've given me a lot to consider and look into." He took her hand in his and kissed her fingers. "Do you think your friend will remain here while we are gone?"

"Yes, he isn't going anywhere. Because of the artifacts, of course, and us girls as long as we live, he will be watching over us like he told me that day. I'm good with it, and I feel like I'm leaving the store and my cousin in the best of hands. What more could I ask for?" She glanced at him. "Except for someone to continue to watch after you." She softened her voice to a whisper. "I thank you, whoever you are. You've done a good job and I'm grateful."

"Did you say something?" Matt asked.

"No, simply thinking out loud." Jessie walked with Matt to the door.

"I need to get to work, Jess. I want to follow up on some leads including the ones you gave me. I think we may be getting closer to the answers. If you get anything else let me know. Don't work too long; this is supposed to be your day off." He kissed her and left.

Fred was tied into this in some way, but she had no idea how. Was he even out of prison yet? Maybe he wasn't involved at all, but the events of the past week were dredging up memories she tried hard to forget.

Hopefully, Matt would find out soon. It was hard to think of relaxing when your groom might be shot or blown to smithereens at any moment. What if someone tried to snatch her again? *Jessie girl, you have to stop this. You have some help on your side.*

****

Basil sat on the bookshelf between Mila and Elida. "Did you hear what she said? She knows we helped in some way. Is she different than most of these other humans?"

"You could say that. We've worked with her several times, haven't we, Elida?"

"Yes, and with some of her friends." Elida glanced at Basil, who looked ready to twist into the air. The poor boy couldn't sit long enough to think a coherent thought.

"Why?" he asked, zipping around the room.

"Some of it is inherited from her Irish ancestors, and some is because she has seen the thin places and viewed a small portion of what lies beyond the door." Mila grabbed his foot when he flew close enough.

"How can that be?" he asked.

"There are more. They simply become aware because their hearts are open to the plight of others. She is one of our treasures, and this marriage is important. He accepts her as she is, and his love will support her. Together they will be strong." Mila smiled wistfully.

"That's why Celeste sent us here. And I'll be sure to tell her that you've done a good job if we get them through the next few days without any problems." Elida told him. "You'll be a hero at home."

Basil puffed at his chest. "Nope, *we'll* be heroes at home." He took their hands in his. "We need to get a move on it, Elida. We're with him." They rushed to follow their assignment and not let him out of their sights.

****

Some days I wish I could see what is going on around me and other days not so much. I would rather some battles went on without me any the wiser. Jessie unlocked all the doors and got ready for the morning. Audrey would be there soon and then she would leave.

"Hello, dear girl." Reba and her sister came in from the coffee shop with tea and treats.

"Good morning, ladies." Jessie didn't have the heart to mention that Matt had already brought her something. "What brings you at this morning?"

"We wanted to see the bride-to-be before the wedding and to talk a little more seriously before you say 'I do.' " Babs sat down and patted the chair beside her.

Jessie found herself between the two sisters. They were alike and yet uniquely different. "I was sure you had come for a reason. I can tell you have something on

292

that beautiful mind of yours."

"Always, my dear. But I don't always come bearing warnings although most of the time I do. I've heard about all that Matt has been going through, and it's important that you know that you are on the right track. Keep putting the pieces together. I know this case is stirring up some memories that you wanted to keep in the past, but they are important to the here and now. Two sides of the same coin. Keep it in mind," Reba said.

"I will." Jessie glanced back and forth between the two sisters.

"We also have a little something for you to take with you on your honeymoon. My sister and I have adopted you as the daughter we never had but always wanted." Reba dabbed at her eyes.

Babs handed Jessie a card. "You can open it now."

Jessie read the sentiment the sisters wrote in the card and cried. "This is too much," she said looking at the check.

"It's a trifle considering all the joy you've give me and now my sister too. You have to spend it on you and Matt and have a lovely time." Reba smiled wistfully.

"Thank you." Jessie hugged them both.

"We need to get on our way but remember to keep putting the pieces together. The faces on the coin will take shape soon enough."

As soon as Audrey arrived, they talked for a few minutes. Jessie smiled at the warrior standing guard and went to meet her mom and grandma for lunch. Tomorrow was her day to be pampered and then her wedding. Jessie went to start her car but decided to check underneath just to make sure. Thankfully, there was no bomb. The one thing she didn't want to do was become paranoid, and always looking over her shoulder. That was no way to live.

Chapter 41

Matt thought about what Jessie told him. He asked Jeremy and Gary to do some research for him. He filled Jaxon and Dylan in on where his mind was tracking.

"With that piece of knowledge, I'm glad we developed plans for the church the day of the wedding," Dylan said.

"Me too. I wouldn't put anything past this guy if we haven't caught him. I have Gary and Jeremy doing some research for me. Jessie made some suggestions to me this morning. Faces and words she started to recall." Matt explained to them what Jessie shared with him. "I hope we soon have a face to go with our suspect."

Within a few hours Matt had a much clearer picture. Thanks to Jessie, Gary and Jeremy had a place to begin. He had a better idea of who they might be looking for. After he talked with Dylan, he ordered surveillance of the suspect's home.

Matt rubbed his temples and rotated his shoulders trying to work the tension out of his body. The last few days had him second guessing everything he knew about how a criminal mind normally tracked. This guy did things in the open with no fear of being caught. His logical ways of figuring a case had seemed to blow up with each attempt on his life. They were all too close for comfort. The whole experience had left him shaken and concerned for Jessie. He couldn't help but wonder if since he was still alive, their suspect might try to hit a softer target. Hell, she was tougher than most anyone he knew, but their suspect might not understand that yet. If he was right, he had already been lurking around her store.

When all the facts were unraveled, this would end up another sordid part of the tale of his one-time mentor and friend Chief Anderson, who had lost his way. Matt still found it hard to believe at times, but the facts were the facts, and evidence didn't lie.

****

Jessie's lunch with her mom went better than expected. They went to Sadie's favorite place near the marina. Her mom repeated more than once how much she liked Matt and couldn't wait for grandchildren. She tried to put the brakes on her anticipation, but Sadie kept shaking her head. At one point, Grams whispered in her ear, "Let her have her dream. It will happen on your time."

At that point, she could sense the wall between her and her mom start to crumble. Truth be told, she was always put off by how her mom never stood up to her dad's domineering ways. Grams told her once that her silence was how she kept peace in their home and managed to hold her marriage together. And then she reminded Jessie that her mother's actions shaped her for the fight she would have in a man's world. Jessie had her mother to thank, which she found hard to believe. But seeing her mother's freedom in their conversation at lunch, Jessie realized many of her own ideals and thoughts of justice for women were also strong in her mother. In her own quiet way, her mother had expressed those beliefs to Jessie over the years. Why hadn't she seen it before?

Jessie had these two women to thank for her ideals and any progress she had made in living them out. Each generation had to win the battle for themselves in the way that made sense to the times in which they lived. Sometimes she was too gung-ho for her own good. She wanted all changes to happen with the snap of one of her brilliant ideas. But change never comes quickly. Sadie told her more than once, "You gain one step forward only to be pushed back two."

The whole idea frustrated her. Women had been fighting for equality and a place at the table for way too long. At least, she knew she wasn't the first to experience the frustration of minimal results and she wouldn't be the last. Still, Jessie knew she wouldn't stop speaking out whenever she could because women were often under attack. On the job, they were held to a different standard from their male counterparts. They often had to endure comments that no man would put up with to keep a job. She knew it all too well. She had endured them and kept her mouth shut until, unlike her mother, she could keep her mouth shut no longer. Did it get her into trouble? In more ways than one. Did she stop? No way. She wrote articles and joined the voices of other women who were saying the same things.

Jessie had pulled into the gym parking lot when her phone began to ring. "Hi, how's your day going?"

"Hi, back at you. That's why I'm calling you," Matt said.

"Please, don't tell me there's been another attempt on your life." Jessie turned off the engine.

"Thankfully, no. I had Jeremy and Gary do some research on what you told me earlier. They pulled up some interesting information, and I'm following up on it now. At least, we are closer now to a possible suspect than we've been. I thought you might be happy to know. Where are you?"

"I'm at the gym. I promised not to run outside, which as you know, I'd much rather do. Peyton is meeting me, and that should help a bit." She smiled when she heard his grumble.

"I'm sorry, but it is for your safety."

"I know, but it doesn't mean I have to like it. I learned something important today. Do you want to hear it?"

"Sure."

"I'm more like my mom and grandmother than I realized." Jessie went on to tell him about what she learned at lunch.

"I'm sure they helped instill things into you growing up, but you've been able to take their ideas and run with them more than they ever dreamed. They only know a small part of who you've become."

"I think the same could be said by me about them. I'll see you tomorrow night at the rehearsal. Love you."

Jessie waved at Peyton when she pulled in the space beside her. Madison was with her. Jessie grabbed her gym bag. The three of them running together reminded her of the treks they jogged in Central Park together when Madison came for a visit on college break. Today seemed to be filled with happy reminders of a good life.

"Are you ready for this?" Jessie smiled at her cousins.

"I was thinking about the times we used to run together when I came to visit you in New York. Now

I'm living there and you two are gone. It's funny the curves life throws at you." Madison linked her arm through Jessie.

"That's strange because I was thinking about almost the same thing. Leaving off the fact you moved to the city, and we left," Jessie told her.

"Let's do this." Peyton latched on to Madison's other arm.

"Are you excited?" Madison asked. "You only have two days of freedom left."

"Matt and I have an agreement. I told him I would marry him only if he promised me that I could continue to be who I am." Jessie paused with a smile on her face. "And believe me, he knows enough about me to make him scratch his head frequently, and yet he still supports me. He's a keeper."

"I should say so. It looks like you and my sister are doing well in that department. I can only hope there is one left for me somewhere." Madison chuckled.

They laughed their way through the workout, which probably meant they weren't working hard enough in Jessie's opinion. But she didn't care. They were having fun. *Two more days* echoed in her mind every time her shoes hit the track.

Chapter 42

To this point, they had no evidence for his theory or results from the surveillance Jaxon and Dylan ordered, but his gut told him it would come. The problem was, Matt wanted this solved quickly. Dylan suggested, and he agreed, that they had protection staked out for the rehearsal and the dinner to follow as well as the wedding.

While the two men talked, a call came in on Dylan's phone and Matt followed along when Dylan put it on speaker.

"Hey, Dylan. Kenny and I have been watching suspect number two's house. Nothing much has happened until a few minutes ago. Our male suspect number one is approaching the house now. Should we approach them?" Kip asked.

"No, eyes only at this point. Document times; you know the protocol. The fact they're together speaks volumes, but we are still waiting for confirmation on the issue we talked about earlier."

"I'll let you know as the situation warrants," Kip said.

"Sounds good. I'll let you know if the status changes." Dylan leaned forward in his chair. "Matt's listening in on the conversation. At this point, there's a high probability that we're looking at our possible suspects."

"That has to be a load off your mind, hey, Matt?" Kenny said over Kip.

"If the theory holds up, it sure is," Matt said. "I'd be happy to put these guys behind bars without seeing anyone hurt." Matt raked his hand through his hair. "He's been too close to not only me but anyone near me."

"Don't let these guys out of your sight. If they move, you follow, and if you see them heading toward the church, tell me. If they leave in two cars, Joe is your backup waiting for your instructions. Let's get them," Dylan said. "I hope to have the evidence we need to arrest them before they leave the house. Jaxon put a rush on the prints lifted off the bomb."

"We aren't going anywhere unless they do," Kip told them. "You'll have to fill me in on what I'm supposed to do."

"I forgot to mention that you have replacements headed your way in time for you to make the rehearsal. Don't leave until Paul and John get there."

"Sounds good. We'll talk later." Kip signed off.

****

Jessie almost slid out of the chair she felt so relaxed. Who knew a foot massage would be this relaxing? For the first time in days, she was able to breathe a sigh of relief. She had no idea what Matt was doing. They hadn't talked since his morning text. He was working today, even though she had the day off although she would check in on Audrey on her way home.

She loved listening to her bridesmaids' happy chatter. For this moment, she was happier than words could express. Of course, it was hard to hold a coherent thought at the moment. Between her facial, manicure, and pedicure, she was left to feel like a puddle of melted butter. A truly glorious sensation, which she told Katie more than once.

"Jessie, if you could see your face at the moment. I took a picture of you and sent it to Matt. I'm not sure what you're thinking about, but you looked all dreamy eyed."

"That's the extent of it. I'm so relaxed I'm thinking about how relaxed I am and happy you all make me." Jessie straightened in the chair. "You didn't send Matt a photo, did you? You're teasing me."

"I sent it all right. You should hear from him pretty soon." Katie chuckled. "I captioned the picture, you dreaming of him."

"Well, I'll make sure he knows the truth sooner or later." Jessie smiled.

"Let the man have his fantasy," Peyton chimed in. "Every man needs to believe he's a woman's dream man."

Jessie noticed all of her friends nodding their heads like bobble heads, which made her laugh. She reached for her phone and snapped a photo. She wanted to remember this moment. This one would go in her wedding scrapbook. Her lovely friends with their freshly scrubbed and massaged faces, hair pushed off their faces by wide colorful bands, and giggles were more beautiful to her in that moment than she ever recalled. This was a normal in life moment and she never wanted to forget it.

Her cousins, Peyton and Madison, Katie, and Sally, her crazy friends through all her growing up years, and Destiny, a new friend, made this day one to be remembered. Molly definitely would have been one of her bridesmaids, but she didn't want to walk down any aisle almost nine months pregnant and ready to pop. These friends were her special support group who had seen her through the many ups and downs of life, and they were here to celebrate with her this special time. What more could any girl ask for?

Well, she could think of one thing. A peaceful wedding and fun celebration without any menacing interference. One could hope. With a little help, maybe they could stop this guy before he hurt someone. It would be nice not to have a murder for a change. Especially since the intended victim was her future husband if not her. She sighed.

"You okay, Jess?" Peyton sat beside her. Both of them were wearing the toeless flip flops while their toenails dried.

"Yeah. I'm only doing a bit of wishful thinking. I hope that they can catch the suspect before he hurts someone. I mean, the rehearsal is tonight, the wedding is tomorrow, and we're running out of time. And this guy is ready to strike only he knows when. It kind of puts us at a bit of a disadvantage, don't you think?" Jessie leaned back in the chair. "I almost forgot about it all when she massaged my feet."

"According to Jaxon, they are closing in on the suspect as we sit here. Of course, they still have some red tape, but they have a sting operation in place. It'll be okay; you'll see." Peyton glanced at her. "Ooh, I like the polish color you chose. I can't wait for Matt to see you in your dress. I hope the photographer catches the look on his face."

"You know what I find strange?" Jessie asked.

"Have no idea." Peyton shook her head.

"We are sitting here having a normal conversation while all the craziness still goes on in our world. Listen to the fun chatter of our friends." Jessie smiled when she looked around the salon. "It's a reminder that through it all, life goes on and we somehow find a way to survive and find joy in doing it." She blew out her breath and gestured with hands around the room. "This gives me hope, and you do too."

"If you two can quit talking over here, we need to get going. Our lunch reservations are waiting for us." Katie pulled Jessie out of the chair. "Love the color you chose." Katie inspected Jessie's nails. "I don't know about you, but I'm feeling fabulous." She waved her soft green colored nails in front of their faces.

****

Mila followed the ladies out of the salon, listening to their happy chatter. It reminded her of the laughter among the fairies on their special occasions. Lighthearted moments filled with fun, she and her fairy sisters would flitter through their secret gardens. Those times were filled with joy. They also loved to find beautiful dresses and add sparkles on their wings, displaying all the beautiful colors one to another. She sighed. Desire for beautiful things seemed universal. Yes, her charge was right. There was always good to be found even amidst the hardships. Her community was wonderful, the sunsets were beautiful, and she especially loved the peace of a quiet night as the fireflies lit the garden in their merry dance, and she could simply watch.

They weren't all work and no play. But she was on a mission now and needed to keep her eyes peeled.

Jessie was also right—this suspect could move at any time. But something important had changed a few mornings ago, and she would always appreciate the grumpy guy who made it possible.

She hurried ahead and landed safely on Jessie's shoulder. What this situation called for was a bit of sparkle. A celebration simply must have added sparkle. She waved her wand as the translucent sparkles with tiny rainbows of colors settled around the occupants in the car. The celebratory mood in the car grew with each wave of the wand. Oh, how she wished all her sisters could see this now.

Chapter 43

Matt disliked waiting. Every case had an idle period when things were coming together but weren't quite there yet. This one was hitting close to home, or maybe he said that about all of their cases. At least, this one seemed to be simple. He seemed to be the main target, or at least their marriage was. Hell, nothing made much sense right now. Jessie had told him their marriage was important, as if he didn't understand that, but not in the way she saw it. For his simple thoughts, it wasn't about saving the world as much as he was simply in love with her. He wanted to spend his life showing her. Sure, they made a great team, but some major force trying to keep their wedding from happening was beyond his thought process. He would continue to think his way, and his little warrior would think hers. This past year had been quite a ride. He smiled.

"Hey, Chief, we have a problem." Dylan rushed into his office. Matt turned around at the sound of his voice. "When we got the okay to move ahead with the arrest, Kip went to the door. When no one answered, they entered and found the house empty. The two men had escaped on foot out the back of the house undetected. They could be anywhere."

"Ah, hell. Jessie and the ladies are headed for lunch. They need to be on guard until we can get somewhere over there."

"Well, that's a problem. The car Jessie was riding in hasn't arrived yet, and my wife is beyond frantic. Kip and Kenny are searching all over town along with several others from the department. They haven't spotted Peyton's car yet."

"I can't just sit here and do nothing." Matt stood and reached for his jacket. "I need to help search."

"This could be a setup to get at you." Dylan frowned.

"What would you have me do? Better yet, if this were Katie, what would you do?" Matt asked.

"Exactly what you're about to do." Dylan followed him out the door. "No one, not even you, would be able to stop me. That's why I'll be joining you and drive." Dylan grabbed the keys out of Matt's hand. "You're in no condition to at the moment."

Before they got out of the parking lot, Matt got an email message on his phone. It simply read —*Strike three you're out.*—

"Oh, hell." Matt held his phone up for Dylan to read the text.

Dylan answered his phone. After what seemed like forever he told the caller, "We'll meet you there."

"What? Don't leave me hanging." Matt leaned forward in his seat.

"It seems Jessie asked Peyton to take a detour to the store before heading to lunch. She wanted to check in on Audrey." Dylan pulled out of the station and headed toward Jessie's store. "I'll let her tell you what happened."

When they arrived at the store, there were several police cars, lots of people milling around trying to see what happened, and Audrey leaned against the front of the building looking visibly shaken. Inside Matt was met with more chaos. One man was unconscious on floor and Jessie had her gun pointed at the back of the head of another one still begging for his life. He knew he was about to hear an interesting story.

"Sweetheart, give me the gun." He placed his hand over hers. "You don't want to shoot him. He's not worth it."

"You're worried I will shoot him. Don't. I only want to scare him like he did me." She handed the gun to Matt once he cuffed the man's hands behind his back.

"Were you looking for these two?" Dylan asked Kip and he nodded.

"They're all yours," Kip said.

Dylan made a quick call to Katie.

"I can't wait to hear your side, Jess. Lunch may have to wait for a few minutes."

****

"Where is Audrey? Is she okay?" she asked. Jessie's legs wobbled as she walked to one of the chairs.

"She's outside, and I'll let you know once I hear your side." Matt smiled at her. "If she's like I often am, she is probably confused and shaken."

"We were headed to lunch, but I had a sudden urge to stop by here first. I don't know why because Audrey's an old pro at operations." Jessie scrunched up her face.

"You know why," Peyton told her. "We'll need to do some explaining to Madison. She's shaken up."

"What does Peyton mean, Jess?" Matt asked.

"You of all people should know how our minds work by now," Peyton snapped at him.

"Take it easy, Peyton." Jaxon put his hands on her shoulders to calm her. "He's only asking the question on why you ended up here."

"I know, I know, but it was a bit intense in for a while." She glanced at the medics dealing with the guy on the floor.

Jessie saw where their eyes were looking and smiled. "He was her victim. You know that amazing kick of hers. Took him down before he knew what hit him. Now, do you want to hear what happened or not?"

"We're listening." Matt turned his head to keep from grinning at her.

Jessie touched the pendant and instantly felt the warmth move through her. "I wanted to check on our resident ghost and make sure he was behaving himself. I guess I was curious to see if he would leave if I weren't at the store for a few days."

"And has he?" Matt glanced toward the stairs.

"No, he's still there, guarding, as the proud warrior he is." Jessie glanced his way and smiled.

"Could you concentrate, sweetheart, and gives us the details?" Matt reached for her hand.

"I can and will once I can sort all the details out in my mind. It seemed to go down so fast that I don't know what happened when. I'll tell you when I'm ready." She frowned and mumbled under her breath that men could be such pains.

"I heard that." Matt smiled at her. "I'm not telling you what to do. I thought maybe you'd like to get out of here to meet up with your friends is all."

"Yeah, sure." She waved him off. "Whatever." She

took a deep breath.

"If you need help, I saw what happened," Molly told them. "Audrey did too."

"I did too," Madison added.

Matt nodded at Kenny to take their statements. "While they're busy, you can tell me your version of the story."

"When I walked in the store, I saw that dark ugly creature I saw the other morning fly out of the coffee shop and into my store. Our fierce protector—" She pointed at the stairs. "—flew at that dark menace with his shield and sword drawn, and while they battled, I had two hands grab me around the neck. I knew it was him. That slimy weasel, Fred, from my past. There was someone with him, and he had a gun. Thankfully, Peyton made quick work of him. The same smug expression on his face reminded me of the moment when he locked me in the trunk of the car. The look he gave me then still sends shivers down my back. But in one brief moment, I remembered who I am now, and with a strength I didn't know I possessed, I slammed my foot on his and ground my elbows into his ribs. He was shocked long enough for me to lift him and slam him to the ground. The timing was perfect just like in the movies."

"Peyton handed me the other man's gun and that's how you found me. As for the dark creature, my friend there routed him, and I don't think we'll see him again for a while. They are who I told you they were, right?"

"You're right, of course. You have a luncheon to get to and we'll talk later." He lifted her chin and kissed her. "I want to be in on the interview with these two clowns. I know I'm going to learn a whole lot more."

Jessie walked him to the door. She made sure Audrey was okay, and then went to lunch with her friends who had come to Joe's when they heard what had happened. From there at least, she could keep her eyes on what was happening in the store. That way she, Peyton, and Madison would be available if the officers had more questions.

Chapter 44

Matt listened in on the interview with Fred and Tom. Before it ended, he learned the one key piece of information he wanted to hear. The two were angry stepbrothers. They connected when Fred wrote the family from prison, declaring he was Anderson's son. To say the family was shocked was an understatement. Tom was already hurt by the shame his father brought on the family, and Fred's declaration added salt to the wound. Fred was mad for never being a part of the family to begin with. The two stewed in their anger while Fred served time and soon became unlikely partners in crime. Both were ripe to use each other and turn that anger on Jessie and him in the form of revenge. How Jessie figured out, Matt would never know.

Jaxon had given Matt detailed updates on the search of both men's cars and residences right before he walked into the interview. There was enough evidence to keep them both in custody, but at least now Matt understood the why. Jaxon's team recovered weapons, ammo, and some explosive materials. Kip said it looked similar to what had been underneath his car. Key to their investigation was a journal with lots of incriminating evidence. Old Fred hadn't disappointed them. He kept a detailed account of each of his actions including hiring a man that Stuart Adler knew on the outside to abduct Jessie in New York. He met Stuart while on laundry duty in prison. Stuart was still obsessed with Jessie, it seemed. Included in the journal was a detailed diagram that sent the FBI's bomb unit along with a bomb sniffing K-9 to the church to make sure the area was safe.

Matt needed to tell Frank about the dog. He loved all things about the great abilities of his furry friends. Frank had worked alongside them on many cases and his dogs had as good a track record as Jessie did. Matt's logical brain could understand his dogs' ability easier than Jessie's. Frank and his wife would both be at their wedding, and Matt wanted a chance to thank him once again for all the help he had given his department over the past year and a half.

A lot had been answered for him in the events of the afternoon, and once he told Jessie after their rehearsal tonight, they could enter tomorrow with an ability to celebrate a wonderful time with their family and friends.

"Matt, we've arrested Kyle." Dylan walked in his office. "Do you want to sit in on this interview?"

"You bet I do. I can't wait to hear the explanation on this one." Matt followed Dylan to the interview room. He glanced at his watch. There were still a few hours left before he had to be at the church. There had been a lot packed into his day already. Kyle was another family member, one of the cousins who conveniently worked in his department at the station. He was feeding Fred and Tom inside information and also had access to the security cameras.

By the time they had finished questioning Kyle and the others, Matt knew the work to clean up the department was only just beginning. Chief Anderson's corruption ran deep and spread its tentacles into the city government. He had some heavy lifting to do when he got home from his honeymoon. That's when Jaxon let him know they had solved another mystery, and Kingman was involved in an odd sort of way.

****

Jessie watched her hunky cop walk into the church with his brothers. There wasn't a homely one in the bunch. But Matt was by far the best looking to her. This was happening, and at the moment all she wanted to know was what had gone down today. Waiting never came easy to her.

Pastor John gathered the group together and instructed them on the order for tomorrow. They ran through the order and where they would stand a couple of times. Jessie smiled to herself about all the happy chatter happening around her. Matt's brothers were a trip, and so were the officers. They ragged on Matt the whole time. Madison asked her more than once if all the single men in town were this handsome. Jessie assured her that most were, but this group was over the top.

They laughed their way through the practice and the dinner. Jessie figured some of the laughter was pure fun because most people there were clueless as to what was going on, and for those who knew, it was a release from stress.

Jessie was sorry to see the evening end but was anxious to hear what transpired besides what she knew about.

Matt slipped his arm around her waist. "I'm taking you home. I already talked to your parents." He nuzzled her neck.

"You'll get no argument from me." She let him guide her to his car. "Talk about a day filled with differing emotions. One minute I was laughing with friends only to be attacked in my store, then end up celebrating again with friends. A truly monumental last day of being single."

"I hear you." He opened the car door for her. "Dylan said Katie was crazy before their wedding."

"Katie was a bridezilla. And I mean that in the nicest possible way. Every detail had to be perfect, and she ran us all ragged." She laughed.

"Aren't you worried about something not going right?" Matt asked.

"I've planned, and that's all you can do. Seems to me there's always an oops in every wedding. That's what makes them memorable for years to come." Jessie latched her seatbelt. "As long as at the end of the day we're married, everyone has been fed and had fun, and of course, I look beautiful in my gorgeous dress, then I'll call the day a great success." She tapped his arm. "And of course, our surprise goes as planned."

"The first part I agree with, but don't remind me of the surprise. I'm still wondering how you talked me into it." He started the car. "It's those damn blue eyes, but at least we can agree this has been some day."

"It'll be fun; you'll see." Jessie fluttered her lashes at him.

"I'll never live it down." He shook his head. "I want to understand more about the battle you say you saw." He pulled onto the street and headed toward the main road into town.

She retold him the story. "It's all about the ancient

spirit or entity that rises in each generation and tries to gain power. I told you we hadn't seen the last of him, but he would rise again every time he found an opening with someone who wanted to cause harm. Hence, he was one side of the coin, and the one thirsty for revenge was the other. Who knew us getting married would be such an issue? The reason is that you know who I am, have accepted me, and are willing to support me. In laymen's terms, we make a good team."

"We sure do." He squeezed her hand when he stopped at the light. "The best. Because of your amazing insight, we got our suspects and one that was hidden in the department that we had no idea was trouble."

"I can't wait to hear the story on this one." She leaned her head back against the headrest.

"All in good time," he told her. "I thought the evening was fun. My brothers were a hoot. It's been a while since I laughed like that with them. I could feel the tension ease as the evening went on."

"I think I should probably mention that tomorrow is liable to be interesting in more ways than one." She glanced at him.

"How? What should I be prepared for?"

"A surprise guest or two." She chuckled.

"I'm not sure how to take that."

"Me either, but I'm preparing myself for anything."

Jessie took a deep breath and closed her eyes. There would be lots of friends seen and unseen. Would there be any issues because they were in attendance? She had no idea. This was new territory for her. Would anyone else try to stop their wedding? Another question she couldn't answer, but she wasn't about to burden

Matt with her thoughts. It was enough that this day ended well, and they were almost married.

Matt parked the car next to hers, and they strolled through the gardens to her cottage. She would miss the garden in the spring and summer with all its beautiful colors. The best part of it was that she could visit Katie any time she needed to and get her fill. She knew the perfect place to sit and drink the floral scents in.

****

Matt unlocked her door and punched in the alarm code. He placed his suit jacket over the back of the couch. It seemed a bit surreal to him that this would be the last time he brought her home here.

"I could use something cold to drink," Matt said walking into the kitchen. Her fridge was almost empty when he looked, but he could count on her to have a pitcher of iced tea on hand. She didn't disappoint. "Do you want some tea?" he asked.

"Of course." She reached for two glasses and filled them with ice.

"Aren't you taking those?" Matt asked.

"No. We have more than enough between yours and the new ones I got at the shower. Whoever rents this cottage next can use all the dishes or get rid of them. A lot of people like to rent a furnished cottage, especially on vacation." Jessie reached for the glass he had filled.

"Shall we?" He motioned for her to lead. "Let's talk because tomorrow and our honeymoon will be a work-free zone. I have other plans." He waggled his brows at her.

She blushed. "You start. I'll try not interrupt but I won't promise anything."

"You were right about Fred. I have no idea how you figured out he was an unclaimed son from an affair, but you did. Fred came back into Chief Anderson's life during the early days of the Harvest Club. He hooked up with Anderson's son, Tom, in prison. We never knew Fred's last name because the chief never said it. He was simply known as Fred, a troubled kid he was trying to help."

"Yeah, well, that troubled kid is the one who pushed a needle into me and locked me in the trunk. I still can't think of it without holding my breath. Then the little weasel couldn't stick around because he said he didn't like blood. He didn't lift a finger to help me." Jessie's chin lifted and she clinched her fists.

"Down, girl." Matt chuckled. "Where was I?"

"Fred." She blew out her breath and sat close to him on the couch.

"Good old Fred marinated in anger about what he thought his father owed him and the fact you cost him the ability to cash in on it. He plotted revenge for the past year. In the meantime, he hatched a plan with his stepbrother, Tom. Tom was embarrassed by what his father did and looked for someone—anyone—to blame. When Fred was paroled, he made his way to town and plotted with Tom. According to Fred's detailed journal, he did mean to kill us both."

"But why me? I was nice to the guy." Jessie shook her head.

"You're nice to everyone. In case you've forgotten, you're the one that brought attention to Gina's death and kept investigating until you found evidence of the club that was harvesting and selling organs." He reached for her hand. "You were pretty amazing.

Before I forget, in prison, Fred met Stuart Adler who gave him the name of a guy willing to abduct you in New York. You remember Stuart, don't you?"

"How can I forget? I was nice to him too. Thank you. Just doing my job." She laughed and saluted him. "You know—the one you didn't want me sticking my nose into, by the way."

He chuckled. "I did say that, didn't I?"

"Yes, you did." She smiled at him.

"I only thought that way until I realized your talent and quit fighting my attraction to you." He reached for her hand.

"I'm sorry to have interrupted you again." She leaned against his side.

"The other important detail that I don't want to leave out is they sent an explosives team to check out the church. They didn't find anything, but I'm still troubled by something Fred said in his journal. I hope we stopped him before he could act on his maniacal plan." Matt lifted her hand and kissed it.

"What was the plan?" she asked.

"He wrote a ranting note, which was hard to follow and ended with the word kaboom. He said it the other day at the end of the interview. Jaxon is having the station checked with the squad and their trained dogs."

"That's a good idea. I wonder if they should check my store," she muttered.

"Good idea. Fred and Tom did come to your store." He called Jaxon and told him. "I figured out the fact that we are a good team, which made us dangerous to him. That and while he sat in prison, he kept hearing a voice telling him he had to do whatever he could to stop us." Matt went on to tell her about Fred's journal with all the details of what he planned. "He was frustrated that he hadn't been able to kill me with all his attempts or to get you. His last entries showed he was beyond angry."

"Wow. We are a real threat to him." Jessie leaned forward on the couch.

"To whom?" Matt asked.

"That ancient spirit or whatever you want to call him. I'm sure I'll understand more in the days ahead. Is there anything else? I mean besides the joy I had when I took Fred down. I guess Peyton gave Tom what for."

"She sure did." Matt laughed. "In the process we learned that Tom's cousin, Kyle, has been working at the station and was feeding information to them. Thankfully, the family ring has been broken up. Attempted murder several times over will put Fred in prison for a good many years."

"Thankfully. And for now, we are good unless he finds someone else. But that's a worry for another day."

"At least until after our honeymoon. Then I will come back to investigating how far Chief Anderson's corruption reached into our city government." He paused. "There is one more not so small detail. Remember the man who threatened you and some of the business owners and the white car?"

"How could I forget? How does he fit into the story?"

"The man who came into the store also drove the white car. He is Bruce Kingman's partner in orchestrating a part of another revenge story. Bruce, Sally's husband, is still in prison and about to have more time added for embezzling funds from his old boss. He designed a plan with our habitual criminal little friend to try to take down several businesses using fear tactics or make you pay for their protection. They weren't through by any means. They had developed quite a plot but didn't have time to put it all in place before we discovered it. He also wanted to have you abducted."

"Are you kidding me? I told you Bruce was a real jerk." Jessie frowned.

"Yeah. Seems he was mad at you for twisting his arm behind his back. Who knew?" Matt chuckled.

"I think our honeymoon is coming at the perfect time. We can use a break." Jessie rested her head on his shoulder.

"I couldn't agree more," he said.

For the next hour they talked about their dreams, and Matt was happy to simply hold the woman he loved. He didn't want to leave, but they had a busy day coming up tomorrow. He stood. "I should go. Tomorrow will be a long day and you need your rest." He pulled her into his arms. "I love you, sweetheart. I'll see you at the church." He kissed her and pulled himself away before he couldn't.

Chapter 45

Jessie watched him leave until she couldn't see him anymore. She set the alarm and went into her room. Before she shut off the light, she took a peek at the beautiful dress hanging in her closet. A glance at the clock told her it was after midnight and her wedding day. She reached for the envelope with the second part of her grandfather's letter that he told her he wanted her to read on her wedding day.

"Ah, my sweet girl, I see you made it to your special day. Don't be thinking I won't be there to see you as a bride. I'll be sitting among your guests and crying tears as I see you. By now, you have succeeded on your own. I'm sure of it. You have championed the causes of women, continued to fight for their rights, and given a voice to those whose were silenced. I love that about you. You're feisty and determined, like your grandmother. I don't want you to fight when my Sadie gives my gift to you today. I invested for years to take care of Sadie and for my granddaughters to give each of you a special gift on your wedding day. Only a small token of the joy you brought to our lives over the years. Knowing you, my dear girl, you won't need a house or car, but you'll be expanding a business. My gift should cover the cost and give you some for a bit of fun. Love you, my girl. The man you are marrying is getting a gem, a warrior, and a wonderful woman, and don't you

ever let him forget it. Sadie wouldn't let me."

Jessie sighed, wiped the tears from her eyes, and turned off her light. "Thank you, Gramps, and my sweet friends. You mean the world to me. I want to see you all at my wedding."

****

"We wouldn't miss it for the world. I'll be there with my dancing shoes on as will my sister and our new friend you simply must meet."

Mila laid her tiny form on the pillow beside Jessie as she slept. She had spent the last hour with her sister and Basil planning how they would appear. Basil would, out of necessity, go as a young man. She and her sister would go as young women. Sisters of course. The had the perfect dresses and shoes. Celeste gave them permission to interact with the guests and spread a bit of magic and good luck among them.

They would make sure there were no unwanted guests, but there would be plenty of unseen guests. It was sure to be some celebration. At last, she could rest her weary eyes until the first morning light.

****

Jessie blinked, rubbing her eyes when the sunlight found the only crack in the curtains to shine through. She rolled over so it wasn't shining directly in her eyes. Today was the big day, and she couldn't wait. Neither could Matt. He had already texted her a steamy morning message. Jessie chuckled. The man was incorrigible, but she wouldn't change a thing about him. Well, except for his need to lecture her, maybe. She filled the bath with lavender-scented oil and stepped into the tub for a relaxing soak. Next, wrapped in her silky robe, she enjoyed a nice cup of coffee and the scone she purchased especially for the occasion while she texted Matt her own hot message back.

Hair and makeup would be done at the church later by someone Katie had hired and swore by.

She answered her ringing phone. "You aren't having cold feet, are you?" Katie's cheery voice asked.

"No. I'm good."

"I'll see you in at the church in a while. The wedding is at two. Don't be late."

"If I am, you can start without me." Jessie laughed and hung up.

She took another sip of coffee and answered the phone again. "Hi, cousin," Peyton and Madison chorused in unison.

"Hi, to you both." Jessie smiled to herself. She sipped her coffee and listened to their joyful chatter.

"I've almost convinced Madison she should move here. I'll keep working on her. All the handsome guys might convince her," Peyton said.

"Sounds good. I know a cottage that will be for rent soon." Jessie finally finished her scone after three more calls from her mother, Sally, and of course, Sadie. As soon as she thought they were done, the phone rang again, and Reba and her sister sang a rousing chorus of "Happy Wedding day to You," which sounded a lot like "Happy Birthday." How she loved this town and her friends. All these special folks would be there today along with a few that others might not see, but she would know were there.

Before she walked out the door with her dress, Matt called. Her store and the station were bomb free, but she still had an uneasy feeling. Maybe she should have told him, but she had no idea why she was troubled. It could be as simple as her conversation with him about the journal last night or something more. All she knew was if she didn't stop this nonsense, she would be late. She hung her dress in the back seat and the sensation grew stronger. *Kaboom* rang loud in her head, and she knew the warning was real.

"I'd rather be safe than sorry." She texted Dylan. She waited until Dylan came out the back door at the inn. She had no clue if shutting a door could disturb an explosive.

"Let's check this out." Dylan got down on his knees to look under the car and noticed the wires. He stood up and motioned her away from the car.

"My dress," Jessie cried out.

He reached in carefully removing the bag from the car. "Move far away, Jessie." He called Jaxon and told him what he discovered. "What stopped you, Jessie? If you had started the engine there would be no wedding today." He called Matt and told him about the bomb. Jessie could hear his colorful language over the phone. "The FBI explosives team is on its way and so is Katie."

Jessie was happy that Dylan took charge. Jessie placed her dress in Katie's car and went back inside to get her shoes. She grabbed the bag she had packed with gifts for her bridesmaids and Matt's ring. When Katie was driving out of the inn, the team was driving in. Boy, she hoped they could dismantle the bomb without anyone being hurt, including her car.

Jessie once again thanked whoever it was that made her stop. Fred almost won.

Chapter 46

Matt called several times to make sure she was all right, and each time Katie answered the phone and reassured him that she was fine. "No talking to the bride until you say your vows, and that's an order, Mr. Parker." Katie smiled at her.

Jessie sat quietly while Katie's friend worked her magic with hair and makeup. Her curls smoothed to bouncy waves resting softly on her shoulders. The perfect look for the beautiful simple hair piece she had to complete her look rather than a veil.

Her friends, looking simply beautiful in their soft green gowns, gathered around her when her mother and Katie helped her slip into her dress and buttoned all the tiny buttons in the back. When she turned around to see her image, she was once again blown away. Like every bride must feel, she saw herself as beautiful in that moment. She reveled in the praise of her friends, hugged her mother who was in tears, and pulled Sadie into the hug with them. The rest of the moments seemed like a blur. She handed out her gifts, had her first photos taken, and cried when she got a quick peek at the sanctuary where many of her special new friends were waiting, and guests had not yet arrived. Matt was right when he said theirs would be a wedding to remember.

****

Matt could finally breathe. When he heard that the bomb was attached to the ignition, he wanted to beat Fred senseless. But once again logic spoke to him. Jessie hadn't driven her car for a couple of days, and there was time for them to put the bomb in place before he was arrested. He wouldn't always thank his lucky star that she listened to the warning in her head. Dylan had the cottage checked too, and it was clear. More than ever, he was ready to celebrate the day with the love of his life.

Matt arrived at the church in his tux and was greeted by his brothers and groomsmen. To him, it seemed this day would never come. He waited for what seemed like an eternity in Pastor John's office until the time. When he finally went out into the packed church, which still had a few officers positioned just in case, the one he was waiting for was yet to come.

And then the song began. One by one, the girls walked down the aisle until Peyton and Katie walked down together. Then his eyes could only see her. A vision of loveliness in white, holding her father's arm as he beamed with pride. He could hardly breathe as she began her walk toward him. His beautiful warrior, the woman of his heart, was here and he could relax for the first time in days while tears streamed down his face. Evan handed him a tissue before he realized he was actually crying. Her smile lit up the room as she looked at him. From that moment on, he simply moved through the motions. He walked and took her hand as her father placed it in his.

He couldn't remember anything the pastor said, the songs that were sung, only the words in his head that she was finally his. They both got misty eyed as they shared their solemn promise to each other, and he was more than happy to kiss her when he was told to and took his own sweet time as he did. "You're beautiful, Jess, so beautiful."

"Thank you. You're not so bad yourself." She smiled and took his arm leading him up the aisle when the ceremony was done.

All the people greeting them, pictures, and even the trip to the reception were a blur to him, but he could remember his first dance with his wife. Their surprise started out as a slow dance and worked its way to a choreographed fast-paced rendition that had the guests cheering. He hadn't embarrassed himself, and his wife told him he had busted a move. His wife—the idea made him extremely happy. From that point on, he smiled well into the evening.

****

The day was perfect except for a few minor inconveniences. She smiled to herself. Seeing all her friends, both human and those she had helped, made it perfect. Mila and Elida introduced her to Basil. Of course, they were in human form. Mila and Elida came as twin sisters and Basil as a young man who escorted them. They danced the night away and celebrated.

She could sense her grandpa Max there when Sadie handed her the surprisingly large check that would expand her business and then some. Her parents danced, Matt's family were wonderful, and Sadie introduced her to Ronan Fitzpatrick, who came all the way from Ireland to be her plus one. Matt made it through several hours, and Jessie smiled when he shook off his brothers and headed her way.

"Shall we ditch this place?" Matt whispered in a

husky voice.

"Yes, let's." She waved at everybody as they walked out the door.

"Are you happy?" He took a deep breath of the refreshing night air.

"Extremely." She gazed into the night sky. She had plenty of time to tell him about all the folks that come to wish her well.

"Was it everything you wanted the day to be?" He pulled her into his side.

"More than I dreamed of." She sighed. "Have I told you how handsome you look and how much I love you?"

"About as many times as I've told you how beautiful you are and how much I love you." He walked with her to one of her favorite spots and turned to face her and kissed her.

She would always remember it as a kiss for the ages. "I like the way you kiss me."

"If you like that, all I can say is you haven't seen anything yet. Let's go home." He held her hand as they walked to the car.

"Do you suppose you can finally tell me where we are going on our honeymoon tomorrow?" she asked him when he got in the car.

He reached over and kissed her again. "Ever since the moment you let me read your journal, I knew we had to go to Ireland. I have to see the places that you wrote about and the land that produced your ancestors that gave me you. My little warrior and the woman of my dreams."

"Perfect." She couldn't imagine anything better even if she tried.

A word about the author...

I am a multi-published, award winning Amazon bestselling author who writes romantic suspense with a touch of the paranormal. I enjoy writing fiction. The character development, their stories, and the twists and turns in the plot intrigue me. I'm hooked from the first words on the paper, and I have to keep writing to see how the story ends.

I live in Colorado with my husband and family. I am a member of the RMFWPAL (Rocky Mountain Fiction Writers Published Authors League) and have enjoyed becoming involved in my community as one of the many authors living in Colorado. I invite you to read one of my Blue Cove Mysteries and see for yourself why Blue Cove is a special and unusual place. http://www.ionamorrison.com

Thank you for purchasing
this publication of The Wild Rose Press, Inc.

For questions or more information
contact us at
info@thewildrosepress.com.

The Wild Rose Press, Inc.
www.thewildrosepress.com